"THE PRESIDENT WANTS US TO CHASE DOWN A BLOODY FLYING SAUCER?"

McCarter was incensed. "Is he completely mad?"

"This isn't a scam, David," Kurtzman broke in. "We were monitoring the Space Command feed and saw the whole thing as it went down."

"Bloody hell." McCarter spit. "If anyone back there bothered to check our mission profile, Hal, they'll find that we're not quite prepared for that sort of wild-goose chase. We're only packing a three-day load, and we're on foot besides. Plus, I don't have to look at the map to know that he's asking us to go marching into the belly of the beast. There's a bloody war going on in that part of the country."

Brognola had brought up the very same objections with the President and had been overruled on every point. He was counting on McCarter's tried and tested SAS-style professionalism to kick back into action as soon as he was done venting his excess adrenaline. Phoenix Force had to go in.

Frankly, there was no other choice.

DON PENDLETON'S

STONY

AMERICA'S ULTRA-COVERT INTELLIGENCE AGENCY

MAN®

FREEDOM
WATCH

A GOLD EAGLE BOOK FROM
WORLDWIDE®

TORONTO • NEW YORK • LONDON
AMSTERDAM • PARIS • SYDNEY • HAMBURG
STOCKHOLM • ATHENS • TOKYO • MILAN
MADRID • WARSAW • BUDAPEST • AUCKLAND

First edition February 2003

ISBN 0-373-61947-2

FREEDOM WATCH

Special thanks and acknowledgment to
Michael Kasner for his contribution to this work.

FREEDOM
WATCH

CHAPTER ONE

The night-black, bat-wing-shaped B-2 stealth bomber was a long way from home and entering dangerous airspace. Home was Whiteman Air Base in the heartland of Missouri, but the bomber had staged out of the U.S. base at Diego Garcia Island in the Indian Ocean for this mission. And instead of having her belly packed full of air-launched cruise missiles or laser-guided two-thousand-pound high-explosive bombs, this time she was mothering a Pressurized Personnel Pod packed with five men and their equipment.

That didn't, however, make her any less lethal. The men she carried were Phoenix Force, and their lethality was well proved.

"We just got the mission-launch confirmation from the Farm, lads," David McCarter, ex-British SAS commando and leader of Phoenix Force, spoke loudly into the team com link. Though the Triple P was insulated, it was still nestled between the bomber's four F-118-GE-110 turbofan engines and was a bit noisy.

"Echo Tango Alpha in five mikes. Check your gear and get ready to jump."

Thomas Jefferson Hawkins, known to one and all as T.J., opened one eye and flashed a thumbs-up. The ex-Army Ranger was usually the team's jump master, but there was little for him to do on this pod drop. When the countdown began, they would take their places, assume the position and wait for the floor to literally drop out from underneath them. Anyone could fall out of a pod and become a paratrooper. What happened after that, though, was what separated the men from the water balloons on impact.

Rafael Encizo yawned, stretched as best he could in his tight, formfitting seat and settled back down. The little Cuban had been in this business far too long for the ride to work to be anything other than something for him to sleep through. This particular job should be a piece of cake, as well, a snatch and grab in a remote, relatively unguarded location. Just march through the desert to the location, break in, get the target out and carry him to a rendezvous point. He could do it in his sleep.

Ex–Navy SEAL Calvin James wasn't as comfortable as his teammates. Even through the Air Force spec-ops guys who had prepared the Triple P had been given his butt size, the seat they'd installed for him just wasn't cutting it. And the Advanced Low Observable Combat Suit—shortened to the acronym ALOCS—didn't fit as well as he would have liked, either. In combination with the bulky experimental 20 mm/5.56 mm Objective Individual Combat Weapon—OICW—and its ammunition that he was packing on this trip, this wasn't the best commute to work he'd ever had.

"Countdown begins in two mikes," McCarter announced. "Disengage and go to your jump bottles."

The five men unhooked their seat harnesses and fitted their oxygen masks and helmets for the high-altitude, low-opening parachute jump. The HALO jump was one of their favorite insertion techniques. Exiting the stealth bomber at twenty-eight thousand feet insured that no one on the ground could see them coming until the last eight hundred feet. The long freefall also gave them a chance to put their GPS to good use and insure that they hit the right drop zone.

Hawkins ran one more Global Positioning System check to make sure that the navigating device was functioning properly before he stepped out into the night sky over hostile territory.

"GPS running hot," he reported.

"Roger," McCarter replied. "Thirty second countdown starts... Now!"

At the fifteen-second point, the stealth bomber's crew opened the bomb bay doors and dropped the blast shield. That dirtied up the plane's antiradar detection design, but still only gave them the radar return of a small, light plane, not a bat-winged bomber 172 feet wide. The instant the last man was out of the pod, the doors would snap shut and the bomber would bank away to fade from any radar that might have spotted it.

"…three…two…one…drop!"

Since he was guiding the way, Hawkins was the first one out of the pod. He fell feetfirst to clear the aircraft's turbulent air before nosing over into a spread-eagle skydiving position. The others followed behind him at two-second intervals.

As soon as the last man, Manning, had cleared the pod, the bomb bay doors closed and the aircraft banked away in a climbing turn that would take her back to Diego Garcia. Their job done, the pilots turned their thoughts to the cold beer waiting for them back in the Diego Garcia officer's club.

As if they were iron bombs, the guys they'd just dropped off were on their own now.

THE FIVE PHOENIX FORCE warriors were strung out in a vertical file, one behind the other, as they fell through the cold night sky at terminal velocity, roughly 120 miles per hour. A small red navigation light on the back of Hawkins's helmet helped them keep formation with him as they fell toward the earth.

McCarter was the second man in the jump stick and he had his night-vision goggles on, waiting to get low enough to scan the DZ for any signs of an un-welcoming committee. They were dropping into east-ern Afghanistan, never a nice place to visit, but never quite so dangerous as it was right now. The radical fundamentalist Taliban government had been ousted, yet rebel warlords still controlled large areas of the country. And while the Taliban government no longer existed, small pockets of Taliban supporters were everywhere.

As was always the case during that time of year in Afghanistan, there were no clouds over the DZ, so Hawkins had no difficulties staying on target. The moon was down, which favored the jumpers, but didn't affect navigating to any extent. The GPS gear he was using was dual function, which allowed him to get a laser distance and location reading to their drop zone below, as well as their changing position as they fell through the air.

Checking his altimeter against the GPS readout again, Hawkins keyed his com link. "We're coming up on the release point in ten seconds. Prepare to pull."

A chorus of rogers sounded in his ears as he did the countdown "...three...two....one...pull!"

Hawkins pulled his rip cord and got slammed in the crotch with the opening shock for his efforts. Glancing up, he checked to make sure that his night-black canopy was properly deployed. Seeing that it was, he grabbed his chute's steering toggles and made one last GPS check before he prepared for his parachute landing fall.

THE SQUARE, steerable chutes the team was jumping allowed Hawkins to put his feet down within a three-foot circle of the DZ's ground zero. Even as heavily laden as he was with weapons and mission equipment, he landed lightly and stayed on his feet. Before he even collapsed the canopy, he did a slow three-sixty scan, checking with his night-vision goggles to make sure that the team was alone in this barren land.

Before he had completed his security check, the other Phoenix Force commandos were landing close by and, spilling their chutes, joined up with him. For once, they weren't under a split-second timetable on the mission. Their primary goal was to get a man out of a makeshift jail and deliver him to a place of safety.

Their secondary goal was to give their new high-tech combat gear a real-world test. There was a perversity factor that always dogged the development of new military equipment. What worked wonders in the testing phase had a good chance of malfunctioning in the gritty, real world of combat. There was a long list of bright ideas and supergizmos that had performed flawlessly in a lab completely devoid of dirt and grime, or even on the firing range, but failed the hard pragmatism of battle. And every entry on that list of screwups was soaked in the blood of the men who had died trying to make the equipment work.

Before they could head out, the commandos had to dispose of their jump gear. The last thing they needed was for an Afghan goatherd to stumble across it and decide to call in the local militia to have a look. The parachute canopies, harness, helmets and oxygen bottles were gathered up in the smallest possible pile and sprinkled with an incendiary powder. The self-igniting chemical quickly reduced the jump gear to unidentifiable melted rubble. Even the oxygen bottles were made of a resin that burned to ashes.

"Okay," Manning said over the com link, "we need an equipment check. I've got to make sure that the ALOCS are functioning properly before we move out."

The Phoenix Force commandos took up a small star formation around the remains of their jump gear with their weapons at the ready. One at a time, Manning went to each of them and ran a quick diagnostic test on their suit's circuitry, built-in com gear and battery levels.

The ALOCS suits were marvels of digital technology applied to military requirements. The suit reduced the wearer's infrared signature to that of a small animal. Removable, flexible panels could also be fitted to give superior armor protection at a fraction of the weight of an Army-issue flak vest. The best thing about the suit was its ability to camouflage itself against whatever terrain the soldier was moving through. Peizo-electronic circuitry woven into the suit's fabric allowed it to change shades of color depending on the soldier's immediate surroundings.

The accessories that came with the suit were what made the system what it was. The communications system worked off a keypad worn on the right wrist, as well as a throat mike. It controlled both voice and data transmission and gave the commandos a silent way to communicate with one another and, through satellites, with the Farm.

The Kevlar helmet's face shield worked like a fighter pilot's Heads Up Display—HUD—screen. With the OICW's targeting and sighting electronics slaved to the visor, the operator could fire and hit his target without having to even look through his weapon's sight. The GPS unit could also be slaved to the HUD, which could read out range and azimuth to anything the soldier could see.

It took only a few minutes for Manning to complete the checks, and he stowed his diagnostic gear back in his pack. "Okay, gang, we're all up and running."

"Let's get these Buck Rogers suits moving," McCarter growled.

The commandos silently moved out.

Now THAT they were on the ground, in the right place and operational, Hawkins surrendered the point position to Calvin James. The ex-SEAL flipped down his ALOCS helmet visor, cradled his OICW in his arms and set out on a GPS heading to their objective. They had forty klicks total to go, but with an extra hour built into the timetable, they wouldn't have to rush. The intel briefing had indicated that the man they were to rescue was in no immediate danger of being killed. They would save him extra pain if they could get to him quickly, but they wouldn't sacrifice themselves to do it.

Like much of Afghanistan, the terrain they had landed in was broken, a series of ridges and valleys with high mountain plateaus and deserts between them. The sparse vegetation was clustered around the scattered springs in the valleys. Most of the ridges were completely bare of even scrub brush. Centuries of goat-herding nomads living off the land had made sure that almost nothing grew in most of the country.

The ALOCS night-vision system was an improvement over the NVGs they were accustomed to using. The old gear hadn't been bad, but this system had greater range and much better definition. James found that he could pick up basketball-sized rocks against sand of the same color out to a hundred meters and spot something the size of a standing man at five hundred. The built-in nav system gave him constant range and azimuth readings to anything he looked at.

It was almost as good as being in broad daylight, and if they didn't run into too many militia patrols this night, they should be able to stay well within their timetable.

CHAPTER TWO

Stony Man Farm, Virginia

Hal Brognola and Barbara Price were in the Stony Man Farm Annex with the Computer Room crew for Phoenix Force's insertion. The mission should be a comparative walk in the sand when put up against the kind of operations they were usually given. Nonetheless, as the director of the Sensitive Operations Group, Brognola always tried to be on hand when the action teams were deployed to the field. Since he was the man who sent them into harm's way, that was the very least he could do.

As the Farm's mission controller, Barbara Price took a very professional interest in the health and welfare of her guys and personally oversaw every mission they embarked on. In her mind, the Stony Man action teams were hers, not the President's or even Brognola's. Behind her model's face and gorgeous mane of honey-blond hair was a world-class brain. And it told her that the closer she monitored the teams in action, the better she could assist them. The goal was to do the job and bring everyone home intact.

Price turned to Aaron Kurtzman, the head of Stony Man's Computer Room crew. He was deep into the satellite feed he was getting from the mission area.

"I'm going back to my office," she told him. "Buzz me if anything unusual develops."

"Got you covered," he replied without lifting his eyes from his screen.

Kurtzman not only worked the background and intel for mission prep, but he was also a vital factor during the operations themselves. Without the intelligence updates and spy satellite overwatch he and the Computer Room crew provided, the teams would be running blind.

NOW THAT PHOENIX FORCE was on its way to the target, Hal Brognola and Barbara Price returned to the main farmhouse to tend to the realities of running American's most clandestine paramilitary operations group. Things were never all play and no work around the Farm. Like all organizations, the Sensitive Operations Group needed an infrastructure to support it, and they were the core of it.

Part of the well-thought-out system that had kept the Farm off everyone's radar screen for so long was the fact that it was so small and self-contained. Had it been the usual bloated government organization, it wouldn't have lasted even a year. Some low-level, underpaid, paper-pushing blabbermouth would have told someone what was really going on at the little farm in bucolic, rural Virginia. And then it would have been exposed.

With that principle in mind, Brognola and Price took care of the bulk of the administrative details related to service and supply requirements for the Farm and the action teams, while security chief Buck Greene and his blacksuit force looked after the physical details that bolstered their cover as a working farm. So while Phoenix Force worked its way across the barren desert wasteland of eastern Afghanistan, they worked to make sure that the Stony Man commandos would have a secure base to return to when their mission was successfully concluded.

PHOENIX FORCE'S first hour in eastern Afghanistan had passed without incident. At the end of the hour, T. J. Hawkins went up to replace Calvin James on the point position. He paused to double-check their location with the GPS navigation system before moving out again. So far he was impressed with the ALOCS gear they were field-testing. The improved night-vision gear alone was worth any extra weight they were packing.

They were moving into another area of broken terrain with outcroppings rising above the high desert floor. Since holding the high ground had been axiomatic since mankind first learned how to brain its neighbors with big boulders, he stopped to scan the rocks overlooking the path they would be taking.

The outcroppings closest to him were clear, so he snapped on the plus-two magnification on his NVG to check farther in front of them. Out at a little over four hundred meters, he spotted something that shouldn't have been there and clicked in the plus-four magnification.

Going to ground, he clicked in his com link. "Cal," he whispered to James, who was walking his slack thirty yards behind, "I need you up here."

"On the way."

A minute later James slid in beside Hawkins. "What do ya got?" he asked.

"Vector 284." He read the numbers off his HUD. "Range 436. On the top of that outcropping. It looks to me like it might be a guy standing guard."

James focused his enhanced NVGs in on the man. "I can tell you that guy sure as hell ain't looking for his missing sheep," he said, "'cause I know that ain't a shepherd's crook in his hands."

Their new night optics were good enough that the weapon cradled in the sentry's arms could be easily identified as an AK-47 assault rifle, the weapon of choice in most of the Islamic world.

"Shit," Hawkins said, checking out the man again. "It looks like that guy's wearing NVGs, too."

One of the biggest downsides of the collapse of the Soviet Union was that a lot of its military hardware

was now available on the open market to the highest
bidder. While a lot of the old Russian gear was obsolete compared to the latest Western equipment, it
was still a quantum leap for groups who had been
completely unequipped with modern combat aids until the present.

The two commandos went back to cover, and Hawkins tapped out an alert to the rest of the team on his
wristband data keypad.

"What do you have?" McCarter asked over the
com link.

"We've got a militia man with an AK and night-
vision goggles standing guard four hundred meters in
front of us," Hawkins reported.

"Did he spot you?"

"He hasn't moved, so I don't think so."

"Damn," McCarter said. "Wait one. I'm coming
up."

McCarter quickly joined them while Manning and
Encizo held the flanks. "Where is he?"

"Vector 284," Hawkins reported. "A little over
four hundred. Up in the rocks."

"I've got him," McCarter said. "And you're right.
The warlords have finally taken a great leap into the
twenty-first century."

Calling up the map on his helmet visor, McCarter
marked the sentry on the battle array before scrolling
the map to look for a way to get around him. The
problem was that the route they were taking threaded

them through several other areas controlled by the militias of various warlords, which had been spotted from space and inputted into their ALOCS gear.

"Well, lads," he said, "it looks like we have two choices. We can spend an extra day swinging wide to bypass whatever he's guarding. Or we can give these suits a real-world test by going out there and whacking him."

"I vote for taking him down hard," James stated. "In case no one else has noticed, we're a bit thin on the ground to be wandering around out here any more than we absolutely have to."

"That was my thought exactly," McCarter said. "I'll call up the others."

WHEN ALL of Phoenix Force gathered around McCarter, he showed his teammates an infiltration route to the outcropping with the sentry. They would go forward to a lower group of rocks some two hundred yards away from the guard. From there, Hawkins and Encizo would go forward to deal with the man while the others stayed put to provide overwatch and fire support if it was needed.

Even with the advanced camouflage features of their ALOCS suits, the commandos made sure to take advantage of what little cover and concealment they could find on the way up to the rocks. With the opposition wearing night-vision goggles, as well, this was more of a technology contest than they had expected at this early stage of the game.

When the two-man kill team reached the base of the outcropping and was out of the sentry's direct line of sight, Encizo paused and signaled that he was going to go around to the right to get behind the man and try for a silent kill.

Hawkins nodded and signaled that he'd work his way up on his left flank to be Encizo's backup. The Cuban nodded and faded into the night.

Hawkins slung his H&K and drew the silenced Beretta 92 riding in leather in his left armpit. If he did have to shoot, it would have to be a silent kill. After making sure that his gear was secure, he went off to the left and started up into the rocks. Halfway up, he found a good position that gave him a clear shot at the sentry and stopped.

He was in deep, moonless shadow, but for some reason, the sentry turned toward him and looked down. For a frozen second, Hawkins was looking eyeball to eyeball into another set of night-vision goggles. He was made, but the man was a little too slow to react.

Hawkins went into hyperdrive, brought up the silenced Beretta in one smooth move and triggered a single round.

The pistol coughed and the 9 mm hollowpoint round drilled into the sentry's chest above his heart. By the time it penetrated the muscle, it had expanded to more than half an inch in diameter. The guy didn't have a chance.

Encizo appeared behind the sentry just as he slumped and grabbed his AK to keep it from clattering on the rocks. Placing the man on the ground, the Cuban drew his fighting knife, jammed it in the entrance wound in his chest and twisted it savagely, tearing the bullet hole open.

This wasn't the mutilation of a dead enemy, but battlefield insurance. It would now appear that the man had died of a stab wound, not a bullet, and anyone could have killed him that way. In the heat of this part of the world, after a few hours in the sun, it would take an autopsy to determine his true cause of death. They couldn't afford to leave behind signs that they had been through the area.

AFTER ENCIZO silently signaled to McCarter that the way was now clear, he decided to find out what the sentry had been guarding. No one stood on a rock in the middle of the night unless he was guarding something.

With Hawkins watching his six, Encizo carefully took the path to the top of the outcropping and peered down the other side. He didn't need to use his NVGs to see what was going on in the sand below, but they did give him the details that his Mk-1 eyeballs couldn't have seen that far away.

A couple of hundred yards northeast of the rocks,

a large motorized troop convoy had camped for the night. There were half a dozen ex-Russian two-and-a-half-ton trucks escorted by a single ex-Russian BTR-60 APC and a couple of pickup trucks turned into gun carriers. A half-dozen small campfires had been lit, and several dozen men could be seen cooking and talking in the light of the flames. Militia.

"We really don't need to bite into that," Hawkins whispered. "There's too damned many of them, and we can't outrun their vehicles."

That was the element of the mission that had bothered Encizo right from the beginning. It was true that the plan called for them to be on the ground for less than twenty-four hours, even factoring in unforeseen delays. And it was also true that dropping a vehicle with them on their insertion would have marked their DZ to anyone with even a cut-rate radar set running off flashlight batteries. It had been a gamble that had failed.

Nonetheless, the Afghan desert wasn't the greatest place in the world for Phoenix Force to be on foot. Not when its opponents were mounted.

The biggest drawback was that there was almost no concealment for them to use during the movement phase, both into the target and out. Being in the open meant that any guy on a camel could spot them from a great distance and run them down. Throw a couple dozen militiamen mounted on gun jeeps and APCs into the mix, and they would really be behind the power curve. The number zero kept popping into his mind.

Encizo marked the enemy location on his HUD map. "Let's get back," he said.

The two men left their vantage point and started back down to the desert floor and the rest of the team.

MCCARTER HADN'T BEEN idle while Encizo and Hawkins were dealing with the sentry. He had moved the rest of the team well clear of the outcropping before halting again to wait for the two to return.

"What took you so long?" he asked when Encizo joined him.

"I decided to take a look-see at what was so important that it needed guarding by a sentry," Encizo replied, "and I'm glad I did. There's a militia convoy just on the other side of that outcropping."

"Where?"

Encizo produced his map and pointed out the vehicles and campfires.

"Bloody hell!" McCarter muttered. "We could divert again to get past them, but the bastards on the other side of us are already blocking the original alternative route. We've got to try to sneak past them and get back on our original course before sunup."

"I guess this is where we really get to test the ALOCS camouflage features," Gary Manning said.

"And if they don't work as advertised," Hawkins

replied, grinning, "we can always take them back to the manufacturer and demand a refund, right?"

"Take mine back at the same time, will ya?" Calvin James said.

"If I can get it off your body."

"Gary," McCarter said, turning to Manning, "get the Farm on the horn and see if they can find us a way around them."

"Coming up," Manning stated as he keyed their satcom radio and passed on their problem to the Farm.

It took a few minutes for the Stony Man Computer Room crew to get the Keyhole satellite that was in the vicinity online, focused in and sending them its sensor feed. From there, it was child's play for them to read the area and send the information directly to Phoenix Force via the military comsat they had parked directly overhead.

The route Kurtzman transmitted had Phoenix Force detouring to the east through a patch of rugged terrain before joining up with their original route. It would be hard going for a while, but the rough, broken ground would make it almost impossible for enemy vehicles to traverse. It was the "almost" part that McCarter didn't like, but it was all they had to work with.

The commandos reached the new track quickly and made fairly good time through it. At first it wasn't prime vehicle country, but, a little more than an hour farther on, the terrain started to flatten. By the time they were back to their original avenue of approach, most of the broken rocks that had provided their cover were gone. They had just moved out into a diamond formation to cross the open ground when they heard the sound of an engine start up on their flank.

"Take cover!" McCarter yelled over the com links.

The commandos ran back to the first bunch of rocks they could reach, but it was too late. They had been spotted by more militiamen with night-vision goggles.

Headlights snapped on and, engine roaring, a Russian-built BTR-60 armored personnel carrier pulled out of its hull-down position and headed straight for them. Its hatch-mounted 12.7 mm heavy machine gun started hammering, and accompanying it were a dozen muji infantrymen running beside it.

"Oh, shit," Hawkins muttered as he drew a bead on the charging vehicle.

James also saw the armored vehicle and snapped his OICW into position. Since he had the team's heavy firepower, taking out the BTR-60 was going to be his job this time. He would rather have had an RPG, but he had to dance with the girl he'd brought to the party.

CHAPTER THREE

Afghanistan

The original 20 mm ammunition for the OICW Calvin James was armed with had been envisioned as anti-personnel fragmentation warheads that delivered overhead fire on enemies behind covered positions. For special-ops use, though, other projectiles had also been developed, including armor piercing and straight HE. The AP rounds were unique in that they were the smallest shaped-charge warheads that had ever been invented. To keep the round from spinning on its flight path and defeating the shaped-charge effect, the rotating band was a plastic sabot that spun freely in the bore and then dropped off once past the muzzle.

Snapping his single magazine of five AP rounds into the 20 mm magazine well behind the pistol grip, James chambered the first round and switched the ranging sight over to 20 mm mode. Keeping the gun mount on the APC centered in his sight reticle, he touched off the 20 mm round and was rewarded with a hit.

The shaped-charge round made only a quarter-inch hole in the BTR's 12.7 mm gun shield, but that wasn't all. The jet of molten steel from the warhead also drilled through both the breech of the gun and the gunner behind it. The muji screamed and fell back down through the open hatch behind him.

Even with its main armament gone, the BTR wasn't out of business. The APC could carry up to sixteen infantrymen, and it had firing ports in its side armor so they could fire on the move.

The muji driver mashed down on his throttle, and the APC accelerated toward them. The BTR could do fifty miles per hour on pavement, and the desert was packed hard in that area. The men of Phoenix Force were going to be up to their belt buckles in speeding armor in a few seconds.

James took another sight picture and triggered his combination weapon again. This time, though, he got zip for his efforts. He both saw and heard the round detonate on the vehicle's sloped forward armor, but it did no good. The BTR continued toward them as if he hadn't hit it, and he knew what had happened.

The angle of slope of the APC's front armor increased its effectiveness enough that the 20 mm's mini-shaped-charge warhead couldn't penetrate it. If he was going to kill the APC, he needed to shoot at the armor somewhere where it wasn't so sharply sloped.

"I need a side shot!" James called out. "I can't punch through the front plate! Get the bastard to turn to one side for me!"

Hearing his teammate's call, Encizo remembered other tank-killing jobs he'd been on. Hitting any armored vehicle head-on was always the hard way to try to kill it, since the armor was thickest. But since it was usually coming straight at you, that was often the only target you had to shoot at.

Switching off his ALOCS camouflage, Encizo stepped out into the open and blazed a magazine of 5.56 mm tracer at the BTR on full-auto.

Since tracer worked both ways, that got someone's attention and the APC went into a skidding turn in his direction at about forty miles per hour. It also made him a designated target for every AK-packing Afghan in the area. Green 7.62 mm AK tracer fire blazed past his head and chewed up the sand all around him. A blow to the heel of his left boot told him that he had soaked up one of the wild shots.

Now that he had their fullest attention, he ripped off another magazine of tracers in two long bursts and dived back behind cover.

As soon as the BTR turned to focus on Encizo, James aimed his weapon behind the front wheel and fired. The weapon scored on the APC's side armor between the first and second wheels. It didn't make much of an external explosion when it penetrated, so he fired two more into the thin armor in quick succession, emptying his 5-round magazine.

He knew that if that didn't do it, they were screwed.

One of the AP rounds had to have hit something critical because the eight-wheeled vehicle suddenly slammed to a halt. Moments later, a secondary explosion inside the APC blew both hatches on top, and the rear door open. A man completely engulfed in fire fled out the back of the BTR and flopped around until someone dealt him a mercy round.

The death of their armored vehicle made the remaining mujis pause.

With the odds evened a little, the Phoenix Force commandos sent a storm of gunfire into the attackers, cutting them down. A few of the Afghans sought shelter, but there was little in the vicinity to hide behind other than the rock pile Phoenix Force occupied, and they weren't moving. Keeping safe behind their cover, they started to exterminate their opponents one at a time.

When the last two mujis took off on foot at a dead run, James switched the ranging sight on his OICW over to 5.56 mm and started tracking the running targets. Firing 3-round bursts, he took them down one at a time.

When the last shot was fired, the Phoenix Force commandos took the time to replenish their magazines and check over their gear. For all they knew, this could just be the beginning.

Once they'd regrouped, McCarter clicked in his comsat link. "Get us out of here, Bear."

Stony Man Farm, Virginia

AARON KURTZMAN LOOKED over at Hunt Wethers, who shot him a thumbs-up and said, "They're clear for five klicks in all directions."

"David," Kurtzman said over the comsat link, "Hunt says you're clear for five klicks and we'll keep an overwatch on your movement to contact."

"Better do a proper job of it this time, mate," McCarter snapped. He was still on his combat high and wasn't inclined to be nice. Adrenaline was far from a natural tranquilizer. As amped up as he was, he could have made his way through a brick wall with his bare hands.

"We have the Keyhole locked in now," Kurtzman calmly assured him. "Hunt and Akira have instituted a rotating search pattern that should give you enough early warning."

"It'd better. We may not be lucky next time."

"We've got you covered."

"Bear," Hunt Wethers called out from the other side of the Computer Room, "you'd better come over here and take a look at this!"

Kurtzman wheeled his chair out of his workstation

and rolled across the floor to where Wethers and Akira Tokaido were monitoring the U.S. Space Command and NRO satellite feed. The only drawback to the Annex was that it was huge. They had lost the shoulder-to-shoulder intimacy of the old farmhouse Computer Room, but the flip side was that they had more space for new, badly needed equipment.

Every time Stony Man launched a Phoenix Force mission into hostile territory, the Computer Room crew pulled out all the stops to keep track of them. This mission was no exception. Anything that might have an effect on the operational area was being closely watched.

"What have you got?" Kurtzman asked when he was halfway across the floor.

Wethers shook his head. "I'm not sure yet."

When Wethers said that he wasn't sure about something, that meant it was really screwed-up. The one-time academic brought a deeply analytic mind and an equally deep grasp of the mechanics of computer technology to the Stony Man crew. Where Kurtzman was a wizard who could tease his way to his goal using gut instinct, Wethers approached the solution like a loaded freight train on the tracks. He fixed the desired destination in his mind and allowed nothing short of a total meltdown to keep him from reaching it.

Kurtzman rolled his chair in front of the empty workstation next to Wethers and clicked on. The monitor lit up with the logo of the U.S. Space Command streaming across the top. The field showed an image from deep space of Earth slowly turning and the orbits of the various satellites circling it. Center stage was, of course, the joint U.S.-Russian space station *Freedom*. Docked to it was one of the American space shuttles delivering another load of cargo for its ongoing construction.

Long a favorite dream of the would-be space-frontier pioneers, *Freedom* would finally give humankind a permanent foothold among the stars. As far as the vastness of the galaxy went, the space station was hardly even a baby step, but it was a vital one. Every baby had to take a first on the way to adulthood, and so it was with *Freedom*. Unfortunately, the economic and political problems that continued to plague the Russian Federation had delayed its construction by two years. Even more time was being lost by the need to triple-check Russian-delivered components that had been built by men who hadn't been paid well, if even at all, for their work.

But *Freedom* was now a reality in the making, and the Americans were lifting their backlog of long warehoused space-station parts as fast as the shuttle fleet could be refitted, refueled and launched. A small Russian-American crew was living in the completed portions of the space station, working around the clock unloading the shuttles and attaching their cargoes to the rapidly expanding structure.

Beyond that centerpiece of the Space Command display, the low-orbit display was a baffling array of everything larger than six inches long that circled Earth. Lost wrenches, burned-out second stages, long dead communications satellites, discarded garbage and other objects less readily identified joined in a circular ballet. At some point in time, the laws of physics would take over and return the debris from whence it came. Until then, however, it would continue to be plotted so no one ran into it.

"Look!" Wethers said as a lone blip on the monitor started blinking red.

Kurtzman looked, but couldn't find an ID tracking marker on the icon, and that wasn't the way the Space Command conducted business. Space Command guarded the skies not only over America, but also over the rest of the world, as well. Every time someone put another satellite into orbit, Space Command immediately logged it, tagged it and added it to the menagerie. For this item not to be tagged meant that it was a trespasser.

A little-known, and highly classified, mission of Space Command was to keep a sharp eye out for anything that might come too close to Earth no matter from where it came. Along with the man-made debris that had been left behind since the space race of the sixties, it tracked meteors, asteroids and comets, as well. It also kept track of "things" that fit no known category. In Space Command terminology, these were called ''bogeys''. To the tabloids, late-night cable shows and freaks, they were called UFOs.

''Where'd that thing come from?'' Kurtzman asked.

''That's where it gets weird.'' Wethers's fingers punched in a command on the keyboard and the screen flashed to a backward, slow-motion track of the bogey.

''It looks like it might have come out of eastern Russia, but that's no Russian machine. Since they canceled the Buran project, they don't have anything remotely like that. Not even in the project stage.''

When the realities of life had come crashing down on the grand but hollow edifice that had been the old Soviet Union, it swept away their space program along with nearly everything else beyond the bare necessities. There was simply no way that a nation struggling to feed its people could afford to spend money on things like that.

Wethers was right as always; there was simply no way that thing could be Russian. But since it wasn't, what was it?

''Bookmark it,'' Kurtzman said. ''We'll screw around with it as soon as Phoenix recovers.''

As curious as he was, the mission came before anything else.

Unlocking his wheelchair, Kurtzman rolled over to the ever-churning coffeepot that was the centerpiece of the rubbish pile he called his workstation. He filled his less than sanitary cup with an oily load of high test and rolled back into position in front of his keyboard. There was nothing like a nice cup of coffee to keep his mind focused.

A glance at the bank of clocks on the far wall showed him that while it was early afternoon local time, it was coming up on 0200 in eastern Pakistan. A good time of night to do unto others before they did unto you. Biorhythms were the same the world over, and they didn't pay heed to political or religious beliefs.

The militiamen of the various ever-warring factions might be mighty warriors for their God, but they were men like any other and their bodies' internal clocks would betray them, too. In an hour or so, they'd be just like any other men whose brains were telling them to seek the comfort of their beds. Fanaticism didn't override biology. To do that took extensive training in special operations.

EVEN THOUGH Kurtzman had told Wethers to ignore the bogey in space to concentrate on getting Phoenix Force to its objective, he had gone split screen himself to keep half an eye on the mystery spacecraft. Like it or not, anything that was that off-the-wall automatically drew his attention. He couldn't help it any more than a bull could ignore a red flag. His mind fed on the new and different, and this thing, whatever it turned out to be, fit that category to a tee.

"Ah, shit!" Kurtzman muttered when he saw the alert logo flash on the Space Command screen.

"It's maneuvering toward the space station," Wethers said. "They've gone red."

Stony Man's Space Command hookup gave them a ringside seat to the drama as it was playing out. Within seconds of the alert, two previously unseen icons flashed up on the screen. Both were indicated in bright blue, a sign that they were the good guys. The cavalry always wore blue.

"Are those what I think they are?" Kurtzman asked without specifying what he was talking about.

"They have to be," Wethers replied. "When the Guardians go active, they have to go out of the radar-jamming mode that stealths them from detection so they can use their own radars to target the bogey."

A small but powerful series of laser-armed space sentinels, dubbed Guardians, had been launched and was now operational under the control of Space Command. The completely classified robotic battle stations were America's first, and sadly last, line of defense against both ballistic missiles and unknown space-borne threats. This day they would get their first live-fire workout and hopefully would prove worthy of the great expense, in both time and money, that had gone into their creation.

A hush fell over the Annex as they all switched their screens to the drama being played out in the cold vastness of space hundreds of miles above their heads. It wasn't every day they got to watch a real *Star Wars* battle in real time.

CHAPTER FOUR

Cheyenne Mountain, Colorado

The command center of the United States Space Command was buried under two thousand feet of solid granite in Cheyenne Mountain outside of Boulder, Colorado. Once known as NORAD, the North American Air Defense Command, the site, the most secure in the nation, had been built to coordinate the nation's air defense against Russian nuclear bombers and missiles. The end of the cold war had taken NORAD with it, but the command center remained the heart and brains of America's safety umbrella. The new occupants of the Space Command still watched for ground- and sea-launched ICBMs, but its arena had been expanded to include anything that might sneak up on America from the blackness of space.

And it was a bogey appearing suddenly in space that had the command center on the fullest alert possible.

Sixty seconds after the alert sounded, four-star Air

Force General Bernard "Bat" Masterson, Space Command's commander, slid into his command chair in a office that looked as if it were right out of a *Star Trek* movie set. In front of him was a wall-sized screen displaying the totality of near Earth space. A click of a button on his right armrest could sort the seemingly endless jumble of radar tracks on the screen into any of a number of categories. Satellites could be sorted by nation and function, space trash left over from launches going back all the way to the sixties could be blanked out.

And in this case, hostile, unidentified objects could be highlighted.

"He's not veering off, General," the brigadier general duty officer for the current eight-hour shift reported. "We gave him the standard warning message in Russian, Chinese and Japanese, as well as in English. It's either not piloted or it's a real live bogey."

When General Masterson had first come to Space Command, he hadn't been a big UFO fan. Like most fighter pilots, in his younger years, he, too, had seen things in the sky that didn't fall into any convenient category of aerial vehicles. But unlike many of his fellow throttle jockeys, he hadn't jumped on the ever popular "little green men" bandwagon.

Once he had been granted access to the highly classified information that Space Command guarded, though, he'd been forced to reconsider his long-held stance. Too many times, men of sound judgment had reported seeing things that couldn't be explained in any way. Even so, Masterson still needed to put his hands on a machine that hadn't been built by humans before he would be a true believer. But this was looking as if it might be time for him to start reaching for his pen.

If nothing else, if this scenario played out right, it might produce some interesting wreckage for the DARPA people to rifle through. Even with his clearance, the Defense Advanced Research Projects Agency worked with things that he had to fight to get access to.

"Give me his projected trajectory."

The screen flashed, then showed the space station *Freedom* and the space shuttle *Endeavor* docked to it centered in midscreen. Still blinking red, the bogey was off to the left, and a curved dotted orange line of its projected trajectory connected the two. If the bogey continued along its current flight path, it would embed itself in the middle of the space station, which housed a dozen Russian and American astronauts. The impact would destroy both the space station and the shuttle and send the wreckage hurtling back to Earth.

Masterson had pulled the trigger on America's enemies in the skies over both Vietnam and Baghdad more than once. It had been a part of his earning his fighter pilot's pay. He had never started a war in space before, but since that's what the country was paying him to do now, it was time for him to start earning his pay.

"Take him under fire," he said calmly.

At that command, the weapons officer punched his keyboard and two Guardian satellites in that sector of space switched their lasers from the standby to the active mode. Powered by huge solar collectors, these were the most powerful lasers that had ever been built in the United States. And since lasers worked best in the cold, hard vacuum of space, their power was almost unimaginable. Though they had been designed to blast incoming ballistic missiles out of existence, they should work equally well on flying saucers.

As if the bogey had somehow detected the lasers' warm-up, it suddenly changed course to engage them. The Guardian's targeting radars kicked in, blowing their puffers to correct the satellite's attitude and keep their lasers on target as they fired.

Unlike in the science-fiction movies, lasers are almost invisible in space. But the computer simulations that made up the screen's images showed the exchange in glowing purple lines. And the lines showed hits on the bogey.

The bogey didn't sit and take it, though. Orange lines indicating return fire flashed onto the screen, and the lines terminated in the satellite icons. One by one, the icons for the two Guardians blinked out. But their deaths hadn't gone for naught. The bogey broke off its attack and turned away toward Earth.

Masterson waited a few seconds to make sure that the bogey was out of action before taking the red handset from the cradle. He had pulled the trigger, and it was time to let someone else know what he had done.

"Mr. President," he said when the phone was picked up on the other end, "this is Bat Masterson at Space Com. We just had a Golden Trumpet incident.

"Yes, sir, that's correct. A Golden Trumpet and it looks like it's going to crash on Earth," he answered the Man's first question.

"Yes, sir," he answered. "I'll have the information sent immediately."

Without being told, the duty officer was already downloading the tapes of the world's first space battle for the Oval Office. He knew better than to make a copy for his personal video library.

Stony Man Farm, Virginia

THE STONY MAN CREW had also watched the shoot-out in space and cheered when the bogey veered off.

"It looks like we're finally going to have the proof the skeptics need," Aaron Kurtzman said as he watched the radar track of the damaged bogey spiraling down to Earth. "Unless it recovers quickly, it's going to crash."

One of the most popular of the far-ranging, off-duty, bull-session topics around the Computer Room was the existence, or not, of extraterrestrial intelligence.

Kurtzman and Barbara Price were strongly pro on the topic, Wethers and Hal Brognola were con and Akira Tokaido and Buck Greene didn't care as long as the bastards didn't try to jump the fence at the Farm.

Having a chunk of a UFO to put to the test, though, would give them all an answer at least as far as this particular thing went.

"No way, Aaron." Wethers slid right into the long-term argument. "It's going much too fast. It'll break up and burn when it enters the atmosphere. There won't be anything of it left to examine."

Kurtzman shrugged. "Something might survive."

Wethers snorted. "Right, and when it's recovered, it's going have a tag inside saying 'Property of Spielberg Productions. If found please return COD to Industrial Light and Magic, Los Angeles, CA.' I've seen this movie a couple of times already."

Wethers had no doubt that nonhuman aliens were among us. But he felt that they were sitting left of the center aisle in the halls of Congress, not flying UFOs.

Kurtzman laughed. As far as he was concerned, even if this one turned out to have been built on Easter Island and was fueled by the secret magical power source of lost Atlantis, there were still all the others.

They watched the big-screen monitor intently as

the mystery machine entered the atmosphere and started going into breaking maneuvers.

"I'll be damned!" Wethers exclaimed. "There's someone flying that thing."

"The question is, who?" Kurtzman replied.

The craft was halfway through its breaking maneuvers when it seemed to go out of control again and plunge deeper into the atmosphere. Apparently, the satellite lasers had scored a big hit before they had been blasted out of existence.

The mysterious craft slowly recovered into a more shallow flight path and saved itself from breaking up as Wethers had predicted.

"I can't believe it," he said softly. "It's going to make it."

When the radar readout showed that the bogey had descended to 120,000 feet, it started into a wide spiraling turn.

"He's bleeding off his speed like a space shuttle," Wethers pointed out.

"Looks like it," Kurtzman agreed.

The bogey continued its course until it had dropped down to fifty thousand feet. There it straightened and headed northeast. It was down to some twenty thousand feet when it suddenly seemed to go out of control again. This time, it didn't recover, but made a rapid descent over the barren highlands of central Asia. It made what might have been a controlled landing, skidding on its belly for a quarter mile before coming to an abrupt halt.

It was night in that part of the world, but the image Kurtzman was watching saw through the dark. He waited for the dust to clear and was surprised to see that the machine was seemingly still intact.

"Give me a blowup of that area with the geopolitical boundaries," he snapped.

The map image instantly enlarged, showing the crash site in greater detail. Dotted black lines crossed the terrain indicated the accepted national boundaries of Afghanistan, China and Pakistan.

"Ah, shit!" Kurtzman exclaimed.

The bogey had landed in one of the most disputed areas on Earth.

The three nations came together in this area, and they all had staked a claim to this desolate high desert. The Afghans and Pakistanis based their claim on cultural and national history, but the Chinese wanted the territory because it was suspected to hold some of the world's largest untapped oil reserves. While both the Afghans and the Pakistanis would fight to the death for it, oil or not, the smart money was on the Chinese winning that fight when it came. And as soon as they had the equipment ready to start drilling holes in the desert, there was little doubt that they would. They would also send an army in to take and hold the region regardless of what anyone thought.

"Zoom in on the machine."

The image changed again to a view that was equal to what would have been seen from an aircraft flying in daylight two thousand feet over the mysterious machine.

"Holy shit!" Kurtzman almost came out of his chair. "Will you take a look at that!"

The machine was now seen to be a classic UFO shape. It was round, apparently lensatic in cross section, with a prominent bulge on a third of the upper surface. This was the shape of a thousand disputed, grainy, amateur photos and an equal number of officially discounted pilot reports and dozens of movies, as well as TV programs about Roswell, New Mexico, and Area 51.

The United States Space Command had just shot down a flying saucer.

"What do we do now?" Wethers asked.

"Nothing." Kurtzman shrugged. "We'll let Barbara, Hal and Katz know, of course. But my bet is that the space cadets in Cheyenne Mountain will be calling all the shots on this one and we won't get called in. We're busy dealing with something more in accordance with our reason for existence. We're busy rescuing a human from terrorists. We can handle that."

"Bear! Look!" Akira Tokaido almost shouted from the other side of the room. "It disappeared."

Kurtzman looked back at the screen and saw a blank spot in the desert where the machine had been.

It was as if the space satellites had a speck of dirt on their sensor lenses. Everything, both the bogey and the terrain it sat on inside a circle a hundred yards in diameter, wasn't being picked up and showed as a dead black circle on the screen.

"Now what?" Wethers asked.

"Beats the hell out of me." Kurtzman's fingers flew over his keyboard, trying to tease out a solution to the black spot on his screen.

"Damn!"

Kurtzman reached out and hit the intercom button to both Price's and Brognola's offices. "Hal... Barbara. I think you need to get over here ASAP. We have a situation in Afghanistan. We just had a battle in space, and a UFO crash-landed close to Phoenix's AO."

"On the way," Price responded.

Brognola rogered a second later.

Even with the high-speed electric tram connecting the farmhouse to the Annex, it took a couple of minutes for the pair to make the trip. That was the only drawback of the new facility, the distance from the farmhouse. But balanced against the pluses the Annex offered, it was a small price to pay for what they were getting.

"What happened?" Brognola said abruptly as he entered the room a step ahead of Price.

"Space Command just shot down a bogey that attacked the space station, and it crashed in Afghani-

stan,'' Kurtzman said. ''It's not in Phoenix's immediate operational area, but I think we've got a hot one
here.''

''Damn,'' Brognola said.

''We caught it on tape,'' Wethers added as he
keyed in the command to run the sequence.

Brognola stood, transfixed, as Wethers showed the
contact from the first sighting to the spiraling reentry
and the final crash.

''What's Space Command saying?'' he asked as
soon as he saw the Guardian satellite icons blink off
and the bogey head for Earth.

''Nada...zip,'' Kurtzman said. ''The minute this
got started, they locked down tighter than a nun's
knickers, as Mac says. The only reason we still have
the feed we do is that we're hardwired to their data
links.''

''Jesus!'' Brognola's hand snaked into his jacket
pocket for the roll of antacid tablets he was never
without. He thumbed a pair off the half-depleted roll
and popped them in his mouth.

''How far is that impact site from Phoenix's position?'' he asked.

Kurtzman keyed up Phoenix Force's approach
route and withdrawal route and overlaid it. ''Much
too far,'' he said. ''And remember, they're on foot
this time.''

''Damn.''

Price spun on him like a striking cobra. "Hal, you're not thinking of diverting them, are you?"

"I know the Man's going to want a presence there, and I don't see him sending in a Marine landing force. Not in a region crawling with the troops of various warlords."

Price was about to launch into a protective tirade when the red phone warbled. It was a noise that could cut glass, but it let everyone within hearing distance know that the President of the United States wanted to talk to the leader of his number-one clandestine-operations group.

Brognola crossed to it in three strides and snatched the handset from the cradle. "Yes, Mr. President."

"WE NEED Katz in here ASAP. We have to work up an operations plan," the big Fed stated as he replaced the handset.

"Jack can have him here in an hour," Price replied.

As a matter of routine, the Stony Man operatives checked in with her whenever they weren't on mission but were away from the Farm. The men of Stony Man were all volunteers, but the realities of their jobs required that they be able to be contacted, and recalled, at any hour.

"Do it," Brognola said.

Price reached for the cell phone she was never without. "Katz," she said into the phone moments

later, "we need you back here ASAP. I'm sending Jack to pick you up."

She looked up as she switched off. "Do you want me to contact David?"

"Not yet."

Once more the flying fickle finger of fate had ended up in Stony Man's nose. He was afraid that wouldn't be the only place it got stuck.

CHAPTER FIVE

Afghanistan

After dispatching the BTR armored vehicle and its infantry accompaniment, the Phoenix Force warriors hadn't encountered any more surprises until they got within a mile of their objective. The sprawling stony structure holding the captive they were after was too big to be a house and too small to be called a proper fortress. Perched on a rugged hilltop, it was a perfect storybook bandit hideout. The problem was that it was full of real bandits.

Phoenix Force's objective wasn't the fort itself, though, but the person of one Alef bin Afghani being held captive inside. This part of the country was still pro-Taliban, and bin Afghani, the nom de guerre for a West-leaning moderate anti-Taliban resistance leader, had been betrayed while on the way to meet U.S. representatives. He was captured by pro-Taliban forces who, rather than killing him outright, decided to keep him alive in hopes of sucking in some of his followers in rescue attempts and killing them, as well. When the Phoenix Force commandos freed him, they would escort him to a rendezvous point to be returned to his group to continue the fight.

This wasn't a usual Stony Man mission, but bin Afghani was holding the anti-Taliban resistance movement in this part of the country together with his bare hands, and he was the best hope the U.S. had of keeping it alive. But rather than risk the poorly armed resistance forces in a rescue attempt, the President had been convinced to send in his number one counter-terrorist team to get him out.

With the muji hideout situated on the high ground, the Phoenix Force commandos were headed for a nearby rocky hill that was the only piece of terrain that provided a good vantage point. David McCarter and the team had detailed, high-resolution satellite photos of the area courtesy of Stony Man, but nothing beat a personal recon.

The problem was that they had to cross several hundred yards of open ground and a road leading to the fort before getting to their observation point. Again, their ALOCS suits would get a real-world workout doing that.

Rather than try the crossing in one group, McCarter sent T. J. Hawkins and Rafael Encizo first while the others took positions in the rocks to provide covering fire if they were discovered.

Once more Hawkins and Encizo headed out into

the sand. The former Ranger took the lead, his NVGs dialed up to Plus Four to watch their planned destination point. Encizo hung back a couple of yards using his NVGs on the Plus Two setting to scan their more immediate surroundings. They moved quickly, but not so quickly that they didn't check each and every rock and scrub for signs of muji habitation.

The two were approaching the road when McCarter cut in on their com links. "Freeze, guys. There's a jeep coming."

McCarter had put James on his right flank and Manning on his left for early warning, and James had picked up a flash of headlights.

In the open, Encizo looked for a nearby rock for them to hide behind, but the area was almost all bare sand. He then spotted a slight depression in the desert to their left. "T.J.," he radioed, "on your left and right behind you, a dip in the ground. Go for it."

The two commandos slid into the dip just as the headlights appeared in the distance. The depression was only twenty feet off the road and wasn't deep enough to completely hide them. Their backs remained exposed. It would be up to the ALOCS system to hide them now.

McCarter and his men kept their weapons trained on the speeding vehicle as it approached. Firing on it would blow the mission, but he wouldn't risk Hawkins and Encizo for any Afghan.

Encizo and Hawkins also had their weapons aimed

toward the road, but kept their heads down. It was a short wait, though, before they heard the vehicle pass without slowing. A few minutes later, McCarter was back on the com link. "You're clear now."

Stony Man Farm, Virginia

THE MEETING WAS CONVENED in the Annex rather than the War Room in the farmhouse. While any of the Computer Room screens could be slaved over to the farmhouse, seeing the bad news larger than life all around them added a touch of reality to the unreal situation they had met to discuss. It also allowed them to keep a close eye on Phoenix Force's progress at the same time.

The players were waiting when Yakov Katzenelenbogen breezed in and took his place at the table.

"This had better be good," Katz said in way of greeting. "I was finally beating that bastard Yevchenko. He's not half as good online as he is in person."

"It's good," Hal Brognola promised him before turning to Kurtzman and Wethers.

"Aaron, Hunt, how about bringing Katz up to date."

"Well," Kurtzman said, smiling, "it looks like you're going to have to pay off on our bet about UFOs."

"How's that?"

"We had what looks like a close encounter of the third kind."

"I'll be damned." Katz wasn't a dyed-in-the-wool UFO fan, but the thought of actual proof of an alien intelligence was intriguing to him.

Wethers brought the Space Command tape of the attack onto the big screen and narrated the action as it played out. His show-and-tell ended with the unidentified machine stealthing itself at the crash site in the Afghan desert.

"What's the mission?" Katz asked as he turned to Brognola.

"The Man wants us to cancel the Phoenix snatch job over there and send them after it. We'll try and pull bin Afghani out later."

"If he's still alive by then," Katz commented. The Israeli fighter knew the man Phoenix Force had been going to set free. In a land locked in seemingly endless chaotic violence, he could truly be said to be a rational man.

"He's one of the few friends we have left in that whole godforsaken country, and we can't afford to lose him."

"It can't be helped." Brognola cut off that line of thought abruptly. "The President wants them to disengage and go into a recovery mission at the crash site. He says that it's of ultimate national importance and takes precedence over everything else."

"Mind if I ask why?" Price asked. She was used

to the President's usual thinking processes, but wanted to hear it laid out.

"For all of the obvious reasons," Brognola replied. "The fact alone that this unknown vehicle apparently attempted to destroy the space station is not the least of them. Beyond that, we get into some issues I'm not free to discuss right now. But for overwhelming reasons of national security, we've been instructed to find out what that damned thing is as quickly as we can."

"Has Space Command come up with anything yet on its probable origin?" Katz asked.

Brognola paused before answering. That, of course, had been one of the first questions he had put to the President, as well. But, instead of getting an answer, the Man had deftly sidestepped the issue. Brognola had a gut feeling that he'd been holding back critical information, but that wasn't something one could ask him without losing his job.

"Not yet," he answered.

"Before we get too carried away here," Price interjected, "has anyone talked to David about this yet? Phoenix didn't go in there prepared or equipped for a salvage operation like you're talking about. President or not, I'm not sure that they'll be able to carry it out."

Brognola glanced up at the clock showing mission local time. "Can you hook up with him?" he asked.

"We have comsat coverage for the entire duration," Wethers replied.

"Get him on the line."

THE PHOENIX FORCE commandos had cleared the plain with no further problems and were moving up to their observation point overlooking the sprawling stone structure holding bin Afghani when the comsat radio in McCarter's command helmet clicked in. He signaled a halt and replied. "McCarter."

"David," Brognola said, "something has come up. The Man wants you to abort."

"This had better be bloody important." McCarter sounded disgusted. "We're only fifteen minutes away from our observation point, and the objective itself is only thirty minutes farther on."

"It's important, all right," Brognola said as he proceeded to brief the Briton on the shoot-out on the edge of space and the crash of the unidentified machine.

"The President wants us to chase down a bloody crashed flying saucer?" McCarter almost shouted. "Is he completely mad?"

"This isn't a scam, David," Kurtzman broke in. "We were monitoring the Space Command feed and saw the whole thing as it went down. As they used to say, 'This is not a drill.' It really happened."

"Bloody hell," McCarter spit. "If anyone back there has bothered to check our mission profile, Hal, they'll find that we're not quite prepared for that sort of wild-goose chase. We're packing only a three-day load and we're on foot on top of it. Plus, I don't have to look at the map to know that he's asking us to go marching into the belly of the beast. In case you missed it on CNN, there's a bloody war going on in that part of this bloody country, and it isn't too bloody nice this time of year.''

Brognola let McCarter rave on as long as he needed so he would listen when he was done.

He had brought up the very same objections to the President himself and had been overruled on every point. He was counting on the Briton's tried and tested SAS-style professionalism to kick back into action as soon as he was done venting his excess adrenaline. McCarter loved a challenge, and this was one of the better ones that had popped up lately.

When McCarter paused to take a breath, Brognola cut in. "I have a resupply being laid on that will bring you up to speed on the equipment you'll need, including a vehicle and heavy weapons.''

"How about including a small army on that list while you're at it?" McCarter said. "You know, some extra bodies to provide the mujis with targets to keep them busy while we try to tiptoe past them.''

"It may come to that," Brognola admitted. "But with the Chinese close by in force, the President wants to avoid that if there's any way he can.''

"The five of us are really looking forward to going

head-to-head with the world's largest land army when it comes steaming across the border to grind up the Afghans. We've never done that before—it'll be a novel experience."

"It's going to take at least a full day to get everything to Pakistan," Brognola went on. "We're sending Able Team over to make sure that nothing falls through the cracks on that end. But, for now, I'd like you to disengage, pull back as far as you can tonight and find a safe place to hole up during the day. We'll find a good drop zone with concealment somewhere nearby and you can move in on it tomorrow night."

"We'll do it," McCarter conceded.

"Check back in when you reach your RON site," Brognola requested. "By that time, we should have your resupply on the way."

"Will do."

"This had better work," Price said as soon as the line went dead. "Or the President is going to have to go shopping for another clandestine strike force."

Brognola had his game face on when he turned to her. "That's exactly what I told him."

"I hope he heard you."

"I do, too."

Pakistan

CARL LYONS SQUINTED against the high desert glare as he stepped off the C-141B Starlifter at the Pakistani air force base at Quetta, Pakistan. Damn, that sun was bright! His first deep breath brought him the familiar smells of the Middle East. One could argue that geographically Pakistan was part of the Indian subcontinent rather than the Middle East, but the smell was the same. And, he thought, it didn't smell like roses.

Gadgets Schwarz, Rosario Blancanales and Jack Grimaldi followed Lyons off the jet transport while the man from the DARPA space development lab who'd flown with them stayed behind to talk to the pilot. Lyons didn't know quite what to make of this guy he'd been saddled with. But at least the bastard was closemouthed and, as soon as they delivered him to Phoenix Force, he'd become McCarter's problem. If he proved to be too much of a problem, it'd be easy enough to leave him under a pile of rocks in the desert and blame the mujis for it.

The hangar the C-141 had taxied up to was part of the facilities the Pakistani air force leased to the Americans. Back in the phase of the cold war that had been played out between the Afghans and the Russians, the base had been used to clandestinely support the U.S.-backed mujahideen forces battling the Soviets. Today, it didn't have that much business, but it was still in operation to support the more mundane American interests in the region. Today's exercise, though, would be a throwback to the bad old days.

When Able Team walked into the hangar, an American Air Force senior master sergeant wearing a crew chief patch on his faded flight suit stormed up to them. "Which one of you jokers is Williams, John J.?"

"That's me," Jack Grimaldi replied with a grin, knowing full well what was coming next.

The crew chief looked him up and down. "Mind if I see your ID?"

"Not at all." Grimaldi reached into a pocket and pulled out his cover ID passport and handed it over.

The sergeant flipped it open, studied the photo, looked back at Grimaldi and shook his head. "It's a sorry-assed day in this man's Air Force when any asshole can walk in here off the street and take off in one of my birds."

"I've flown Herkys before, Chief," Grimaldi said, trying to calm the man. "I've got several hundred hours in them, including the AC versions."

The sergeant eyeballed him severely. "You one of those flying mercenaries for the Company?"

"Something like that, Chief. You know how it is, I can't tell you anything."

"Right." The man shook his head. "And I can't say anything when my bird comes back all shot full of holes. If it comes back at all."

He leaned forward, his nose only inches from Grimaldi's. "But I'll tell you what, Mr. Hotshot CIA pilot. If you mess up my plane, I'm going to chase your sorry ass down if it takes me the rest of my life."

"Why don't you come with us, then, Sarge?" Grimaldi grinned. "That way you won't have to chase me so far. I have to make a LAPES delivery on this run, and I could use an expert to give me a hand."

That stunned the crew chief. Usually the Company operatives were so tight assed that they wouldn't tell you which whorehouse they were going to across the street, much less anything about one of their missions. He didn't think things had changed that much, so he decided to call this joker's hand.

"You know, mister," he said, smiling thinly, "I just might take you up on that."

"I'm dead-assed serious," Grimaldi said. "I'm gonna need a loadmaster anyway, and it might as well be you instead of one of my guys."

He paused, and it was his turn to give the sergeant an eyeballing. "If you've got the balls for it."

"You're on," the crew chief said as he extended his hand. "I'm Bill Keyton. Most of my friends call me Buster."

Grimaldi took his hand. "My friends call me Jack."

"Okay—" the sergeant was all business now "—let's get this goat screw on the road."

"Why is it that we always have to go through a version of that routine every time we have to talk to these guys?" Lyons asked Grimaldi as the sergeant walked off to get a loading crew together. "It really gets old."

"It's just the cost of doing business with guys who don't like us very much," the pilot replied.

"Why not, dammit?" Lyons asked. "We're both on the same side, aren't we?"

"Not from the way they look at it."

CHAPTER SIX

Afghanistan

After reluctantly leaving the fortress and the captive bin Afghani behind, the Phoenix Force commandos marched until just before dawn, when they stopped to hole up for the day. They rotated guard duties and slept while their resupply was being put together in Pakistan. Late that afternoon, Yakov Katzenelenbogen called to give them their resupply drop zone location.

"It'd better be more accommodating than this place," David McCarter said. "The sand fleas here are as big as tanks and just about as well armored."

"I didn't have Aaron check for fleas." Katz chuckled. "But we found a good drop zone. It's well off the more traveled routes, so you shouldn't get too many visitors and it's big enough for the Hercules to get in. It's also got a large outcropping nearby for you to RON in while you wait for the plane. As a plus, it also has a spring at the base of the rocks."

"We can use the water," McCarter admitted. "The damned fleas have been drinking all of ours."

"Jack's scheduled to take off at first light tomorrow," Katz said, "and he'll call in when he gets close enough for you to pop smoke."

"We'll be there," McCarter promised. "And tell him to add a case of cool ones to that load."

"Will do."

When dark fell again, Phoenix Force set off for the RON—Remaining Over Night—site, reaching it in just a few hours. Katz had promised that it was a quiet area, but even so, they kept watch. With so many warring factions, it was the prudent thing to do.

MOST OF THE RESUPPLY equipment Phoenix force would need for its new mission had come in from the States with Able Team on the C-141. A Hummer light utility vehicle and a quarter-ton trailer had been appropriated from the Air Force base to finish off the want list.

While Buster Keyton's crew was palletizing the load for the drop, Able Team and Craig Waters, the DARPA lab man, went to the base rigger's room to be issued parachutes. Waters was the only one of the plane's crew who would be jumping, but the chutes were wise insurance for anyone who had to venture into the skies over Afghanistan.

After Rosario Blancanales helped Waters get fitted with his rig, he took him aside to try to at least give him a run-through of the drop procedure. There was no way that he could make an experienced jumper out of the man in an hour or two, but telling him what he could expect would be a start and might keep him from breaking his legs. It was well into the night when all preparations were completed, so they went to get as much sleep as they could.

Dawn was breaking when the team assembled again in the hangar. While Blancanales went through his parachuting drill with Waters again, Grimaldi was on the horn to Phoenix Force, telling McCarter that they were about to depart. Schwarz and Lyons were getting final instruction in the fine art of the LAPES delivery technique from Sergeant Buster Keyton. They were on the clock now and it was ticking.

An hour later the sun was up, and Grimaldi had the C-130 Hercules headed down the runway at Quetta. It would be a short flight to the Afghanistan border, where the fun would really begin.

AS HAD BEEN EXPECTED, the bogey's crash landing hadn't escaped the notice of many who had a keen interest in both Afghanistan and space. The Russians and Chinese, to name just two, also had their own versions of America's Space Command. To be sure, neither of their command centers was buried under millions of tons of solid granite, but they had radars, satellites and kept a close watch on the skies. They, too, had seen the shoot-out in space and had tracked the bogey back to Earth.

Then there were the locals.

Afghanistan was a fairly large place, and the population density was sparse. The war that had raged almost unabated since 1979 had further thinned out the population. Nonetheless, the UFO had had the bad luck to fall in an area that was still hotly contested by various tribal warlords who wanted total control.

No war was as brutal as a civil war, and this one was no exception.

The same rugged terrain the mujis had used to such good advantage against the Russian invaders for ten years was once again being used as a weapon, but against one another. And the center of this terrain was close to where the bogey had landed.

A mobile patrol of one of the warlords had actually witnessed the crash and had immediately gone to investigate. Since they didn't have a radio on their vehicle, no one knew where they were going or when they were overdue. Because of that, no one knew that as soon as their Toyota pickup had come within line of sight of the machine, it had been destroyed by the same weapon that had killed the two Guardian satellites in space.

One second the truck was bouncing along the desert at a good clip and the men were excitedly talking about the shape of the strange plane. Then without warning, the pickup was instantly turned into twisted, flaming wreckage with the men part of the fire.

The next vehicle that approached the crash site saw the still smoldering wreckage of the first truck and stopped to see what had happened to it. They dismounted with half of the men going to the wreck while the others excitedly looked at the strange bubble that appeared in the desert. Their vehicle, an aging Russian GAZ jeep, was also quickly incinerated, but since they hadn't been in it at the time, most of the mujahideen had survived.

And one of them had a radio.

AFTER AN UNEVENTFUL night at their RON site, Phoenix Force stood-to early the next morning and prepared to receive the drop. While his four comrades watched the approaches to the DZ, T. J. Hawkins climbed high up into the rocks as air guard. From his vantage point, he was the first to spot the inbound C-130.

"It's incoming," he sent over the com link. "Vector 196 at six thousand."

"Roger," David McCarter sent back.

On the desert floor, Calvin James stood in the center of the DZ and readied a mini-smoke grenade. Its signal would give Jack Grimaldi both their location and the wind direction at ground level.

"Phoenix, this is Flyboy," Jack Grimaldi radioed from several miles out. "I'm inbound, pop smoke."

James pulled the pin on the grenade and dropped it at his feet. "Smoke out."

Grimaldi easily spotted the smoke plume against the monochromatic expanse of sand and rocks. "I have white smoke," he radioed back.

"Roger, white," James replied as he quickly cleared the DZ. "Bring it on."

Even though Phoenix Force had seen no signs of the opposition, this was still was potentially a hot DZ and Grimaldi brought the transport plane straight in on a shallow dive. He dropped his landing gear, flaps and rear ramp as he lined up with the far end of the DZ. For a LAPES delivery, he had to be right on the money to keep from mashing the goodies. There was no point in bringing them this far if he wasn't going to make a clean drop.

LAPES was short for Low Altitude Parachute Extraction System, and it was the fastest way to get something on the ground in one piece that anyone had ever come up with. The "low" part of the designation meant having the plane's wheels less than three feet off the ground. The "parachute" part meant that drag chutes would be deployed to snatch the loaded pallets out of the end of the aircraft as if they had been shot from a catapult. That was the "extraction" part.

No one who had ever witnessed a LAPES delivery ever forgot it.

INSIDE THE AIRCRAFT, Carl Lyons and Gadgets Schwarz were standing by to assist the crew chief deploy the LAPES chutes. With the three pallets to be delivered in a single pass over a short space, the timing was critical. So was staying out of the way of the pallets when the blast of the turboprops caught the drag chutes. No human had ever survived going down with a LAPES delivery in one piece.

"Stand by," Buster Keyton shouted over the roar of the engines.

Each of the men stood at the open ramp with a bundled-up pilot chute in his hands. When the time came, they would throw the little chute out through the open rear ramp to catch the prop blast. The pilot chute would snap open, pulling the larger drag chutes out of their pack and, in turn, they would snatch the pallet out of the plane.

Looking out the open rear ramp, Able Team could see that Grimaldi was bringing the Hercules closer and closer to the ground. It looked as if he were trying to land it, but he was going much too fast. A loud rumble told them that the plane's main gear had contacted the desert floor and Keyton shouted, "Throw one!"

The crew chief threw his pilot chute out the open ramp. It instantly popped open, jerking the drag chutes out of their pack and into the roiling slipstream behind the plane. The risers snapped tight and the pallet, Hummer and all, left the ramp as if it had a rocket strapped to it.

"Throw two!"

Lyons threw his pilot chute, and the second pallet was on its way in a flash.

"Throw three!"

Schwarz tossed his and, suddenly, the aircraft's interior was cavernously empty. "Jesus!"

As soon as the last pallet had cleared the ramp, Grimaldi jammed his four throttles up against the stops, and the four 4,500 HP Allison turboprops screamed. With her props beating against thin, high mountain air, it look a little longer for the transport to gain altitude, but the pilot needed two thousand feet under him to make sure that the second part of his delivery arrived intact, as well.

This was an all-or-nothing deal.

"HOT DAMN," Hawkins exclaimed as the dust raised by the skidding pallets settled. "All three of them made it through intact."

Usually on a LAPES drop, particularly one when the plane's landing gear wasn't in contact with the ground, a pallet or two bounced on impact and ended up crushed or tipped over. That was why Grimaldi had risked hitting a rock and touched down his wheels.

"Just as long as the Hummer came through," McCarter replied.

"He's inbound again to drop off the mystery package,'' Encizo said as he watched Grimaldi go into a sharply banked turn at the end of his climb.

"I'll go down there to pick up the pieces," Hawkins volunteered.

"If he doesn't make it, just bury him there," McCarter said.

Brognola had held off until the last minute before mentioning to McCarter that the President had saddled Phoenix Force with a tourist for their new mission. No professional liked to have to keep track of an FNG, particularly one who had absolutely no idea what was going on. That would certainly be the case with this guy.

What in the hell was a darpa anyway? He had forgotten to ask Katz.

INSIDE THE PLANE, Buster Keyton and Rosario Blancanales hovered on either side of Craig Waters as he stood in front of the open door at the rear of the aircraft's cabin. Carl Lyons stood behind him with a slight smile on his face. He always got to do the fun part.

"Like I said—" Keyton leaned close to be heard over the roar of the turboprops as he snapped Waters's static line to the cable running the length of the cabin "—all you have to do is step out and the parachute will do the rest of the work. There's nothing to it."

Waters fought to keep his eyes open under his jump

goggles, but looking through the open door at the desert rushing past him two thousand feet below was wreaking havoc on what little breakfast he had been able to get down. He swayed a little, and Lyons grabbed his parachute harness from behind to keep him on his feet.

"Coming up on the DZ in zero five," Grimaldi called back on the intercom. "...four...three...two... do it!"

Keyton nodded at Lyons, who threw Waters out the door. The government man had time for only a short yelp of surprise before his static line snapped tight and popped the chute out of his back pack.

"Not too bad for a cherry," Keyton commented as he watched the canopy float to the ground.

"We'll see what happens when he hits," Lyons said.

"Yep." Keyton grinned. "That's always the final test. I got a twenty that says he'll bounce like a rubber ball."

"If he breaks a leg on impact," Lyons said, "they'll shoot him like a horse."

Keyton had been thrown a few curves by these guys, but this one was completely unexpected. "You're kidding, right?"

Lyons didn't break a smile. "I never joke about shooting people."

Keyton gulped.

"THE RESUPPLY WENT off without a hitch," Yakov Katzenelenbogen reported to Hal Brognola, "and the government man is on the ground safely, too. They'll be ready to go as soon as they get the gear unpacked.''

"Good," Brognola replied. "At least something's going right. I'll pass that on to the Man."

Having to report to the Oval Office every time someone burped during this operation was wearing a bit thin on Katz. A job like this was difficult enough without having the President of the United States breathing down their necks. Having that Waters guy on hand was bothersome to him, as well. Phoenix Force wasn't in a good place to be shackled with dragging around extra weight.

On the odd occasion when the team had hooked up with an outsider, he had been either CIA, DEA or from one of the armed forces. This Waters guy was a scientist, a researcher apparently, and Katz wasn't sure whether he'd be a serious detriment or any kind of asset. But the President had personally added him to the mission lineup, and McCarter was stuck with him. For now, at least.

If he proved to be too much of a pain, as soon as they had a contact that developed into a firefight, he could easily become a casualty.

That was cold, but the Phoenix Force warriors lived by a reality few had to endure.

"What's their ETA to the crash site?" Brognola asked Katzenelenbogen.

"David and I haven't worked out the route plan yet," Katz replied. "I just sent him the latest enemy locations they're going to have to work their way around, and I'm waiting for his input."

Phoenix Force wasn't targeted against the warlords now, but considering the situation they were in, it was still proper to call them the enemy.

"I need to pass that on to the White House as soon as you have it."

"You'll know it as soon as I do," Katz said without smiling.

Brognola took that as a hint to leave and decided to go back to the farmhouse and give the operations crew a break. He knew that the intense scrutiny from the Oval Office wasn't making anyone's life easier, his own included. But he also knew that the President had more on his plate than the peace of mind of the Stony Man crew.

What the Man couldn't seem to get down, however, was the fact that these people worked best when left alone to do their jobs. This was not a political campaign, and micromanaging from the Oval Office just wasn't cutting it this time.

CHAPTER SEVEN

Afghanistan

T. J. Hawkins was glad to see that the man who came down in the parachute had made a reasonable landing, considering. He hadn't broken anything vital and was still breathing when Hawkins got to him. He was, however, lying flat on his back with a horrified expression on his face.

"How ya doing, partner?" Hawkins asked as he reached down to punch the releases on the man's harness to free his canopy before the wind caught it and dragged him halfway across the desert back to Pakistan.

Still flat on his back, the man looked around, wild-eyed, took a deep breath and said, "I'm not sure."

Hawkins laughed. "At least you're honest. Your first jump?"

"And I won't be making number two." The man sat up. "Not in this lifetime."

Hawkins laughed. "I say that myself every time I

jump out of a perfectly good airplane. You'll get used to it, though. Take my word for it.''

He extended his hand to help the man get up. "By the way, I'm T. J. Hawkins.''

The man pulled himself to his feet. "Craig Waters,'' he said. "DARPA space development lab.''

"So, you're a rocket scientist.'' Hawkins grinned. "How about that? I've never met a rocket scientist before. Say, maybe you can help me with something. See, we guys were kind of wondering who you'd pissed off to get stuck with this assignment.''

Waters shook his head as he looked around the desolation he had just arrived in. "I can't fucking believe that I volunteered for this.''

"So did we.'' Hawkins laughed. "You're in good company.''

Hawkins quickly divested Waters of the rest of his harness and grabbed the risers for his chute to roll up the canopy. "Come on, I'll you take to meet the rest of the guys.''

The first several steps Waters took were tentative as if he was making sure he hadn't broken anything. Hawkins grinned knowingly.

ON THE OTHER END of the desert drop zone, the Phoenix Force commandos were busy unstrapping their gear from the LAPES pallets. Just because their gear had arrived with no trouble didn't mean that no one had seen it coming down. From here on out, to stay out of trouble, they would have to keep on the move and be ready to shoot first.

To that end, the Hummer was freed first. While Gary Manning fueled it from the gas cans, Calvin James attached the .50-caliber machine gun ring mount behind the front seats. Where they were going, they would need the long-distance, heavy firepower that only a Ma Deuce could provide. The others were quickly loading their supplies into the trailer the vehicle would tow.

When Hawkins walked up with their mystery guest, the men paused to see what this unknown joker was going to bring to the game.

"Gentlemen," Hawkins announced, "may I present Mr. Craig Waters, one of those rocket-scientist guys we keep hearing about all the time."

Everyone sounded off in turn with their name and a welcome to sunny Afghanistan.

At the end of the introductions, Waters looked around with a puzzled expression on his face.

"What's the problem?" Encizo asked.

"Where's the rest of your men?"

"What you see is what you get, pal." James smiled.

"But," Waters sputtered, "who do you work for?"

James smiled. "Mostly for my paycheck."

Waters paled. "I was told that there would be adequate security in place to cover me while I made my inspection of the crash site. That was part of the deal.''

McCarter grinned wickedly. ''That's what you get for volunteering, boyo. The first rule of living a long life is never to volunteer.''

''Oh, Jesus!'' Waters muttered.

''Him, too.''

''What is it that you're going to be doing here?'' Encizo asked casually. ''We usually don't get drop-ins when we're on the job.''

''I'm supposed to examine this aircraft, spacecraft, whatever it is,'' Waters explained. ''Find out what makes it work and make a report when I return.''

Encizo let his eyes sweep the barren horizon. ''If we return.''

Being a rocket scientist, Waters was quick to pick up on what he had gotten himself in for. Back at the comfort and security of the DARPA lab at Edwards Air Force Base, this gig had seemed a reasonable venture when it had been presented to him. He'd had no trouble signing on after watching the Space Command video back in the briefing room. Now he was beginning to wish that he were a used-car salesman or something and had never heard of this operation.

Nonetheless, in for a penny, in for a pound. He had to do what he could to make this thing work and stay alive at the same time. He had no military experience, but he knew that the first thing he had to do was to make sure these five men didn't see him as too much of a liability.

"Is there anything I can do to help you guys?"

"Thanks," McCarter said, "but we have it pretty well covered. Just have a seat on the nearest rock. We'll be ready to roll before too much longer."

Waters found a convenient rock and did exactly as he had been told.

ONCE JACK GRIMALDI had ten thousand feet of air under him and was well out of range of shoulder-launched antiaircraft missiles, he relaxed. Strellas were known to ruin a perfectly good day and, so far, this had been a pretty fair morning. He knew, however, that circumstance could change in a flash. The second part of this mission had the potential to be a world-class rat screw.

He keyed the intercom. "Buster," he called back, "can you come up here for a minute?"

"What's up?" the crew chief asked when he entered the flight deck.

"Well," Grimaldi said, "we've got a secondary mission I kind of forgot to mention to you before we took off. We need to slide over close to the Chinese border and take a couple of pictures of a crash site."

"You're going to what?" The crew chief almost exploded. "You didn't tell me anything about that when you talked me into this. Those mujis are flat-assed crazy, but those Chinese don't screw around, either. We show up on the radars of one of their combat air patrols, and they'll splash our butts without thinking about it twice.''

"It just slipped my mind." Grimaldi shrugged. "The primary mission was to get those loads on the ground, and this was a secondary concern.''

"You bastard."

"Guilty as charged," Grimaldi replied cheerfully. "At least that's what my dear old mother has always said. But we still have to do it, chief.''

Keyton had been in the military long enough to know how this particular game was played. He didn't have to like it, but it had to be done. He'd volunteered for the trip, and he wasn't about to parachute out and walk back to Pakistan.

"Son of a bitch!" He shook his head slowly. "What are we supposed to take a look at?"

"A crashed flying saucer," Grimaldi replied as casually as he could.

"Give me a fuckin' break, Jack," the old sergeant snorted. "If I'd wanted a hand job, I'd have stayed in Quetta and driven down to Sin City."

"I'm not kidding, Chief," Grimaldi said. "There was some kind of UFO that attacked space station *Freedom,* and it got shot down before it could do any damage. It crashed over by the Chinese border, and we're going to try to take a couple of pictures of it."

Buster peered at him in disbelief. "You're not kidding, are you?"

"Nope."

"I'll be damned."

"My guys will run the cameras, and you're welcome to sit up here if you want."

"Why not?" the crew chief said as he slid into the empty copilot's seat. "If I'm gonna get shot down, I might as well get a good look at it coming."

"Better buckle yourself in," Grimaldi told him. "I don't expect any trouble, but this is Afghanistan and these guys have a bunch of leftover missiles we sold them. I might have to do a little fancy flying if they shoot at us."

"You get me killed, mister," Keyton growled as he reached for the shoulder harness, "and I swear to God I'll come back and haunt your sorry ass."

Grimaldi laughed. "Get in line, chief, there's a bunch of guys ahead of you."

Stony Man Farm, Virginia

NOW THAT Phoenix Force's resupply was on the ground, the Stony Man Computer Room crew went back to watching the crash site. But there was still nothing to see. The dead black circular area around the site looked like a sensor or screen malfunction, but they knew it wasn't. Somehow the mystery craft was hiding itself from close observation.

The area outside the blanked-out spot, however, showed a desert littered with recently burned-out vehicles and a crashed chopper left over from an earlier battle. It remained to be seen how soon it would be before more junk would be added to the collection.

"It's still stealthed," Aaron Kurtzman announced when Hal Brognola walked up to his workstation.

"How about visual light?" Brognola asked.

Kurtzman switched screens, and the blank spot became what looked like a mottled, multicolored bubble that still obscured the details of whatever lay under it.

"As you can see," he said, "it's no-go that way, either."

Brognola shook his head. "Maybe the cameras on the Herky will be able to pick up something."

"If the Keyhole cameras can't break through that, I've got a brand-new thousand-dollar bill that says the plane won't be able to get a clear picture of it, either. If anything will work, a man on the ground might be able to see through it if he gets close enough. But there's no way for us to know if that will work from here."

Brognola shook his head. "The Man's not going to like that."

"Well, if he doesn't like it, I guess he can always hike his butt over there and take a look at it himself, can't he?"

Brognola chose to ignore Kurtzman's smart remark and walked away. This was no time to get in an argument with the one man who was vital to unraveling this mess. Phoenix Force was doing the footwork, but Kurtzman was helping Katz choreograph the dance, and the floor was far too crowded for any slipups.

The only change for Phoenix Force was the satellite overwatch that should be able to find gaps in the muji lines for them to slide through unchallenged. If that didn't work, the whole plan was out the window and it would be time for the President to risk going to war when he sent in the 101st Airborne or whoever he had standing ready in the wings.

And Brognola knew that he would do it, too. This incident had his hackles up, and he was breathing fire.

Brognola would have preferred taking a more measured approach to investigating this problem, but that hadn't been offered him. He had to ride the bull he'd been given or get out of the arena.

Worse than that, Phoenix Force also had no choice.

YAKOV KATZENELENBOGEN was in the communications room in the Annex talking to David McCarter on the comsat radio. A table full of the latest satellite photos, maps and hand-scribbled notepads cluttered the table in front of him.

"It looks like you'll be okay for the seventy-five kilometers as long as you swing out south the way we discussed. But you'll still have to keep a sharp eye out. That area's been an active battle zone recently, and there's likely to be scattered units from several warring factions. They'll shoot first if they see you before you see them.''

"We're about to move out," McCarter sent back, "and we're counting on you guys to watch our six, our three and our nine for us."

"I have the Bear, Hunt and Akira working on it and we're doing our best."

"You'd better."

Near the Chinese Border

GRIMALDI HAD CLIMBED to twenty thousand feet as he approached the area of the crash site. He wasn't going to fly straight to the target area right away, but wanted to get a good look at the surrounding area before he committed himself to anything.

"I'm seeing signs of a recent battle around here," he said to Keyton.

"Seems that way."

Grimaldi was putting the C-130 into a wide turn when Keyton called out, "I've got an inbound fast mover. Ten o'clock high at thirty thousand."

Grimaldi looked to his left front and saw the plane coming in from the east. "From the contrails, it looks like he's out of China."

"It's multiengine, so it's not MiGs on a CAP." The sergeant relaxed a bit. Going head-to-head against a MiG fighter Combat Air Patrol in a lumbering old Herky Bird wasn't his idea of having a nice day.

"He's moving fast, too," Grimaldi said. "Probably a recon Badger."

"Just as long as he ain't packin' air-to-air."

"As far as I know," Grimaldi replied, "they don't have that capability."

"They'd better not." Keyton watched the high-flying jet. "I had a missile shot up my ass one time, and I didn't like it very much."

At some other time, Grimaldi would have liked to hear the Air Force veteran's war story about air-to-air rockets, but that was going to have to wait until he could have a cold one to go with the BS factor that accompanied all such tales. Right now, he was busy.

The twin-engined, Russian-designed Tu-16 Badger bomber was old, the basic design dating back to the fifties, but the Chinese state factories had ground out hundreds of them and they were still the mainstay of their bomber fleet. In modern times, many of them had been converted to carry recon cameras instead of nukes, and Grimaldi hoped that was the case this time. If the Chinese had decided to up the ante on the first hand, his old Herky wasn't fast enough to escape the blast of a nuclear weapon.

With the Badger coming in so much faster than he was, Grimaldi decided to sit back and see how the Chinese fared before he went bulling his way in. If the speedy bomber made it through its run unscathed, he'd get in line and give it a try himself. He went into an orbit several miles away from ground zero and tried not to be too obvious as the Badger banked around for a west-to-east run. That was smart because the plane would be almost back inside Chinese airspace at the end of the run.

The Badger was about a mile away from ground zero when it blew apart in midair. A flash of light raced up from the center of the UFO's protective screen and hit the center of the high-flying jet. For an instant, nothing seemed to happen, and then it just simply exploded. From the boiling fireball in the air, it looked as if the plane's entire fuel load had detonated all at once.

"Jesus!" Keyton breathed as he watched the burning pieces of the Badger flutter to Earth. "What in the hell hit that thing?"

That was Grimaldi's question, as well, but he was busy trying to get his aircraft turned so he could get out of the area. He had seen the highlight clips of the space battle tape and had wondered at the time how the machine had waxed those two defense satellites. Now he knew.

Whatever kind of weapon was mounted on that flying saucer, it was obvious that he didn't want any part of it. And since discretion was the greater part of valor, he slammed his throttles up past the stops as the Hercules went into a steep bank and pointed the nose back the way he'd come. Maybe if it looked as if he was running away, the damned thing wouldn't shoot at him.

He sure as hell hoped so.

Stony Man Farm, Virginia

THE COMPUTER ROOM CREW had watched the Chinese recon plane get zapped. In fact, they'd had a clear shot of the burning wreckage showering onto the sand to join the other debris that was piling up.

Hal Brognola didn't even wait for the last chunk to hit the ground before he reached for the red phone.

"Brognola here, Mr. President," he said into the handset. "We've had a problem arise."

Brognola quickly recounted the abortive Chinese recon run and what it had meant for Grimaldi and the Hercules—a quick escape back to Pakistan.

"Yes, sir," he answered after receiving his instructions.

"What'd he say?" Aaron Kurtzman couldn't keep himself from asking.

Brognola looked up at the big screen for a while before answering. "He said he hopes that Phoenix can get through."

Kurtzman doubted that was the extent of the President's message. But he, too, hoped that the gods of war would lighten up on McCarter's people.

CHAPTER EIGHT

Afghanistan

When Phoenix Force moved out of the drop zone, Gary Manning took the wheel of the Hummer. David McCarter was in the front passenger seat navigating, and Calvin James stood behind them on the .50-caliber machine gun. With the bulk of their supplies stowed in the quarter-ton trailer, there was enough room in the topless vehicle for the six men. It was nothing in excess, to be sure, but at least they didn't have to sit on one another's laps this time.

Manning drove quickly and aggressively, trying to pick the smoothest route through the boulder-strewn desert. The press of time was on them. The faster they could take care of this, the less chance they would have of ending up in someone's gun sights. Even so, he knew that he also had to keep the speed down to keep from throwing a dust plume too high in the clear blue sky.

The route to the crash site Katzenelenbogen had

sent from the Farm wasn't very linear, but zigzagged back and forth, taking full advantage of the irregularities in the terrain to provide them with maximum cover and concealment. Backed up with Aaron Kurtzman's Computer Room crew keeping an eye on them from on high, it should work if they kept down their dust plume.

Even so, everyone was keeping a sharp eye out in a three-sixty.

"Got a dust sign," James reported. "Three o'clock, out about two miles."

Since he was standing behind the .50-caliber machine gun, he had a better view than Manning did from the driver's seat of the low-slung vehicle.

"Bear left a little." McCarter looked up from his GPS screen. "There's a ridgeline about two thousand meters ahead we can put between us and him."

As Manning made the course correction, Craig Waters looked over his shoulder nervously to see if he could spot the dust plume. He was still processing the facts of his new surroundings and the cold, hard fact that he had put his life in the hands of whoever these guys were. The terrain looked almost familiar, and he had to keep telling himself that this wasn't like the deserts of California, Arizona and New Mexico. The people who lived here would be more than glad to kill him the first chance they got.

T. J. Hawkins saw the look on concern on Waters's

face. "Don't sweat it, Craig. That's just the ten-o'clock shuttle to the next oasis."

If these hardcases didn't stop joking around when he was ready to have a panic attack, Waters was going to scream.

Manning skidded to a halt when he reached the cover of the ridgeline and turned to McCarter. "That bastard snuck up on us," the Canadian said tensely. "How 'bout asking the Bear where he came from?"

McCarter clicked in his satcom link and spoke briefly. "He says that it was a civilian vehicle, with no weapons showing, so he didn't want to bother us with it."

Manning felt too exposed to have someone else making his combat decisions for him. "How 'bout asking him to alert us to everything right down to the camels so we know they're coming?"

"Will do."

When the all-clear came from the Farm, Manning pulled out of cover and continued on their way.

Stony Man Farm, Virginia

NOW THAT Phoenix Force was well en route to the bogey's crash site, the Stony Man Computer Room gang was full-time, up-close, watching over them with everything at their command.

Fortunately, Afghanistan was known for clear skies so they could use the satellite's optical gear instead of having to go to the nonvisual sensors and translating the IR and MAD readings to images before they could see where everyone was. With the streaming video feed from space, the view was as if they were sitting a thousand feet above them. It was like the Greek Gods on Mount Olympus watching the Trojan War unfold below them. Zooming out from the speeding Hummer allowed them to monitor an area roughly four miles around it and should be enough to give Phoenix Force adequate warning of approaching enemy forces.

Hunt Wethers was monitoring a different screen that covered a fifty-mile radius with the spacecraft at ground zero. There was no lack of enemy gunners in the immediate vicinity of the target to keep track of, but his main interest was in the buildup of military muscle taking place right inside the Chinese border.

As with anything else that occurred within its self-declared "sphere of interest," the Chinese leadership wasn't allowing something as trivial as a national border keep it away from what it thought was a major prize. Fortunately, though, that remote end of the Red Chinese empire wasn't heavily garrisoned. No more than a division was spread out to guard several hundred miles of border, and it would take time for them to mass their armor and infantry. Regardless, they were already on the move.

"It looks like the Chinese are going to go for it," he told Yakov Katzenelenbogen. "They're driving their tank transporters and fuel tankers right up to the border. I'd give them a kickoff time of a couple of hours at the most.''

Katz studied the screen for a long moment, calling up the markers for all the enemy forces.

''If they make a heavy push,'' he replied, ''that might keep the warlord busy long enough for our guys to get in fairly easy. Keep a watch on this while I talk to David.''

Reaching for the comsat radio, he sent his call to the NRO satellite in geosync orbit over the Middle East. Thank God for the digital age; it made reaching out to touch someone so much easier.

Afghanistan

THE PHOENIX FORCE commandos were halted again in a well-covered position to allow a muji patrol Kurtzman had spotted to move on. They were taking their time, so James had dismounted to keep watch from behind a rock. McCarter was studying his map and checking his GPS when he got the call on the satellite radio.

''Phoenix,'' he answered.

''David,'' Katz's voice came in loud and clear over his earphone, ''we have a situation developing to the east of the target area that might give you guys a good window to move in close to the site.''

''Send it.''

Katz quickly briefed him on the buildup of Chinese forces along the border and suggested that they use the coming clash for a diversion.

"When do you see this taking place?" McCarter asked.

"Hunt says that he thinks their lead elements are going to jump off in an hour or so, two at the most. The mujis have spotted them and are moving armored reinforcements into that area, as well."

McCarter went back to his map and located the area of the Chinese troop movement. "Send me a downlink of all the muji units you're tracking," he said.

A moment later, he had an update and marked the plots. "That must be what's been keeping them on the move around us," he commented. "We're having to hole up every half hour or so to let someone get out of our way."

"Aaron says you're clear right now," Katz said. "That patrol you've been watching has cleared your vicinity and shows no sign of slowing down."

"Stay on us," McCarter said.

"We're right here," Katz replied cheerfully. "Air-conditioning, hot coffee and all."

"Bastard."

Stony Man Farm, Virginia

WITH PHOENIX FORCE in the clear for the moment, Barbara Price took the time to go to Hal Brognola's office for a little chat. She was onboard for this mission, as she always was, but she knew that Brognola was withholding something from her. She respected the fact that the President told him things that weren't to be repeated, even to her and Katz. But that didn't mean that she wouldn't try to get information out of him. In the deadly game Stony Man played, information was power, and she wanted to top off her tank.

She found Brognola in his office eating a ham-and-cheese sandwich while he kept half an eye on the monitor showing the now familiar scene of the crash site. She knocked on the open door and walked in.

Brognola was in midbite and nodded toward his guest chair. She slid into it.

"What do you think it is?" she asked.

He swallowed and said, "Honestly, I don't have the slightest. But what I think isn't what's important."

"What does the Man think it is, then?"

Brognola pondered that for a moment. "I don't think he's given its origins much thought, if that's what you mean. He's looking at it as a threat, pure and simple, and he doesn't really care where it came from. Now that it's on the ground, though, he wants information, of course. But if that isn't easily forthcoming, he's going to obliterate it to remove the threat."

"Cruise missile?" she ventured.

"At least."

While probably effective, that kind of solution didn't bode well for Phoenix Force if it was anywhere in the neighborhood. "What's his launch criteria?" she asked.

"That's where it starts to get a little sticky. I pressed him for clear criteria and he wouldn't give me any. He's going with his gut on this one."

"Not his guts." Price tried to keep the bitterness out of her voice. "The guts of our people."

"He says that he's keeping them in mind…" He paused. "But he also says that if the machine looks like it's preparing to take off again, he'll have no choice."

Price leaned her head back and closed her eyes. "How did we ever get to a place like this, Hal?"

Brognola glanced at the monitor. "I'll be damned if I know."

Just then, the intercom on Brognola's desk sounded. "Hal," Katz said, "the Chinese just jumped the fence. A company-sized armored column is probing the muji positions, and the Afghans aren't running."

Brognola wrapped up the last of his sandwich, stuffed it in his pocket and stood.

"Time to go back to work."

WHEN BROGNOLA and Price walked into the Annex, half the screens were showing the deep-space view of a tank battle in the desert. This wasn't some one-sided battle, either; the Afghans were giving as well as they were taking. Columns of greasy black smoke rose in the clear sky from more than a dozen burning vehicles on each side, and it was difficult to tell who was getting the upper hand.

The winner of this battle would be the first side that didn't pull back. And the smart money, as always, was on the Chinese. The Afghans were fighting for their homeland, but they also knew when to retreat to the mountains, where tanks couldn't follow them. It had always worked against the Soviets, and if things went bad, it would work against the Chinese, as well.

Price watched the raging battle. Men were dying down there by the tank full, but she didn't care. This bloody distraction gave her men a better chance of completing their mission. She sent a quick prayer to the gods of war to stiffen the Afghan forces so they wouldn't collapse too quickly and pull back.

"Katz," she said, "get this to David and tell him that this is his chance."

"I already did."

Afghanistan

WITH KATZ and Kurtzman guiding them, Manning was able to drive the Hummer to within a mile or so of the crash site by early afternoon. They couldn't see the crashed machine itself yet, but had it spotted on the map.

"Find a place to hide," Katz warned over McCarter's earphone. "You've got a muji truck approaching on your left front. Range about three kilometers."

Once more, Manning found a hiding place behind an outcropping, and McCarter and Rafael Encizo piled out to try to get a better look from higher in the rocks. Depending on electronic eyes in the sky was all fine and good, but nothing beat using a bare eyeball to get an accurate estimate of the situation when it was coming at you.

When the truck appeared, it was an old Russian two-and-one-half tonner with at least a dozen mujis riding in the back and a couple more in the cab. There were no heavy weapons on board that they could see, but every man had his AK in his hand. That was the second thing that no Afghan male left home without; the first one was his hat. The truck passed by Phoenix Force's hiding place without as much as a single head turning.

"Doesn't look like they saw us." Encizo brought his field glasses down from his eyes.

"This time," McCarter replied.

The truck continued straight toward the downed craft and out of their direct line of sight. Katz came back on the satcom link and reported that it had pulled to within a quarter mile of the site and stopped. A second later he reported that it was being fired upon.

WITH THE CRAFT'S weaponry concentrating on the mujahideen, McCarter saw this as their best chance to close the rest of the way in. Katz had also spotted a likely hiding place for them within a fairly short distance from the crash.

"Go for it," he told Manning as he and Encizo jumped back in the vehicle.

Manning dropped the clutch, and with all four tires spinning, the Hummer shot forward. At their rate of acceleration, the loaded trailer was bouncing from one wheel to the other, but he was counting on the weight to keep it from tipping over. He was leaving a towering dust plume behind them, but with all the tumult going on around them at the moment, it might not be noticed.

"There it is!" McCarter shouted, and pointed to another cluster of bare rocks between them and the mystery craft. "Pull in behind it!"

Manning headed for the rocks and found that they had the leeward side. The winds had scoured out a depression in the sand behind the rocks that was big enough to completely hide the Hummer, and he drove down into it.

"According to the tac screen," McCarter said as soon as they were stopped, "it should be about four hundred meters on the other side."

Quickly throwing desert-camouflage netting over both the Hummer and the trailer, the commandos climbed up in the rocks to see what was causing all the fuss. James stayed behind with the vehicle, but had his ALOCS uniform dialed to blend in with the background rocks and had thrown a corner of the camo net over his Fifty so it wouldn't be too obvious.

Craig Waters joined the men on the climb, trying to keep low as they were doing. His heart was pounding as if it were trying to beat its way out of his chest, and his breath was coming in gasps. He didn't know if it was fear or anticipation, but it was making him dizzy.

When he stopped to catch his breath, Hawkins reached down, took his hand and pulled him the last couple of feet. He slid in beside him.

As Kurtzman had told them, the shield around the machine looked like half of a shimmering soap bubble about a hundred feet in diameter, and a shadow of the craft could be dimly seen behind it. They couldn't see clearly enough to pick up many details beyond that the machine was shaped like a flying saucer and had some kind of cupola on top.

Whatever it was, it was like nothing any of them had seen before. Outside of a science fiction movie, that was.

When Waters poked up his head, he looked as if he were about to wet his pants with excitement. His earlier fear evaporated like spit on a hot plate. The fact that he was actually seeing what for all intents and purposes appeared to be an extraterrestrial spacecraft with his own eyes had him amped up big-time.

Like most of the men involved in the exploration of space, he had always wanted to have the age-old question "Are we alone?" answered once and for all. Unlike many of his comrades, however, he hadn't been shy about expressing his beliefs that UFOs were a fact. To hang on to his job, he had kept it low-key, of course, but he hadn't suppressed his true feelings on the subject.

Now, only a quarter-mile away from proving it once and for all, he was beside himself with excitement and started to stand up.

"Keep your fuckin' head down," Hawkins grated. "You wanna get it shot off? Those bastards're good shots."

Waters took cover again. "Sorry," he muttered.

"Sorry ain't gonna keep you alive, buddy."

Hawkins wasn't pleased at being saddled with keeping track of this complete FNG. He had to admit, though, that the DARPA guy wasn't as bad as he had expected him to be. In fact, he figured that on his home turf, Waters would be okay to kick back with and have a beer. At least he would have some interesting rocket scientist stories to tell. Just as long as he didn't start writing mathematical formulae on the cocktail napkins and waving them around. Hawkins never got the punch lines to those jokes.

Right now, though, he was just a pain in the ass because he had to be kept alive.

CHAPTER NINE

In the rocks

"We've got a vehicle approaching again," Calvin James called out over the com link as he swung around the Fifty to cover their rear. "Another damned BTR coming up fast on the left."

At James's call, the men in the rocks crouched as low as possible in the natural crevices and depressions and trained their weapons in that direction. This was no time to have an armored vehicle catch them in the open trying to climb down. Plus, if it went south, they had better fields of fire from on high.

Again the mujis didn't spot them, and the APC rolled past in a cloud of dust, continuing toward the downed craft. It stopped short of the burning truck, and a handful of men piled out of the rear door while a couple more joined the machine gunner on top with loaded RPG launchers in their hands.

From their rock pile, Phoenix Force watched the proceedings intently. If the mystery machine could deal with an armored vehicle, their thin-skinned Hummer would suffer the same fate, only faster. It was nice of the mujis to provide a trip-wire force for them.

The mujahideen gunners were excitedly examining the wreckage of the truck and the charred bodies, and a pair of them headed for the shimmering bubble. Suddenly the bubble changed to the color of lead and a burst of light shot out of it, cutting down the men before striking the APC square on the sloped front plate.

The armored steel glowed red for an instant before the vehicle exploded.

The Afghans who had been checking out the wrecked truck took off as fast as they could run, but it did them no good. The bright beam swept the desert from left to right, incinerating them as they ran. When the last man burst into flames, the light winked out and the dome went back to shimmering like a soap bubble.

"Damn," Hawkins said as he watched the blazing wreckage send yet another smoke plume into the desert air. "That thing's downright unfriendly. And it doesn't seem to care if you've decided that you've made a mistake and want to go home. If it catches you, you're fried."

Waters had never smelled burning human flesh before, but he didn't need to ask one of the commandos what the smell was. And he also didn't want to poke his head over the top of the rock to gawk any more. In fact, he really wished that he were somewhere else.

LEAVING ENCIZO in the rocks to keep watch on the bubble, the Phoenix Force warriors went back down to the Hummer for a conference before they talked to the Farm again. Now that the nature of the mystery machine had been so graphically demonstrated, they had to take a hard look at their options, which weren't many.

A mission was a mission, but they hadn't signed on to commit suicide. Even so, since they were on the spot, they might as well try to do something.

"We can't even try to get the Hummer any closer than this," Manning stated flatly as he looked at the readouts on McCarter's tac screen. "If you look at the plots on the wrecks out there, we're probably right on the edge of some kind of detection zone as it is. Any closer than this, and sure as hell it's going to zap us like it did the BTR."

McCarter had eyes and could read a map, so he had no arguments with Manning's assessment. Since they had absolutely no experience factor to go on this time, they were going to have to make it up as they went along. And he hated it when that happened.

"We're close enough, though," Manning said, "that I think it's worth a try to see if we can do the old low crawl up to it for a bare-eyeball look. The damned thing fired on the running men, but it left them alone once they hit the ground. Maybe that works going toward it, as well."

"Or maybe it was because they were dead?" James suggested.

"Some of them were still moving," Manning pointed out. "At least for a while. But it left them alone."

"I don't know about that." James shook his head. "That thing's bad news."

"I'll go with you," Hawkins spoke up. "I've been a flying-saucer freak all my life. Too many nights spent reading comic books as a kid, I guess."

"Maybe you were just born a space cadet." James snickered.

Hawkins stiffened to attention and saluted. "Commander Buzz Corry of the space patrol at your service."

Craig Waters watched this lighthearted horsing around in complete amazement. His earlier eagerness to see the craft had evaporated as quickly as it had come. Whatever the machine was, it was deadly and these guys had to be nuts! They had just watched it burn an Afghan patrol to crisps, and they didn't seem to be concerned in the least about moving right in and taking a closer look.

Worse than that, since he was the reason that they'd made this trip, he had to go with them. He should have done what his mother wanted and gone into medicine.

"Before we do anything," McCarter said, "I want to talk to Katz again. Maybe they have some new information."

"My bet is that they don't know any more about that damned thing than we do," James said. "Maybe less."

"Then we're screwed."

"Tell me about it."

HAL BROGNOLA, Barbara Price and Yakov Katzenelenbogen were all crowded around the big-screen monitor when McCarter's voice came in over the satcom radio link.

"I guess you saw our latest little dustup here?" McCarter asked.

"We did," Katz replied. "You're going to have to be very cautious."

The satellite's optics had been focused in on the crash site to give them a view of the destruction of the muji BTR and crew in living color. Had it been a late-night rerun of a fifties movie, they would have thought it an overly dramatic special-effects extravaganza. But the satellite's space eyes gave the scene a hard edge no director could ever achieve.

"Did the Afghans do anything to provoke it?" Brognola asked.

"They were in the vicinity." McCarter laughed harshly. "Apparently, that's more than provocation enough with that thing."

Brognola had seen that himself, but he'd had to ask. The President would have done it, and he was acting for him in his absence.

"Gary and T.J. want to try a low-crawl approach," McCarter continued. "They think the machine won't fire on them if they keep low to the ground."

"Wait one while I check something," Katz said as he walked over to a smaller monitor and replayed the tape of the craft's latest attack on the Afghans.

"Hal," he said, "they might have something there. It looks like the machine didn't shoot at anyone who hit the ground. If they tried to run, though, it got them."

"David," Brognola said, trying to stay neutral while making his point, "you know we need any information you can get. The President is concerned."

"Bugger him and *Air Force One* at the same time," McCarter said. "We want to know what the bloody thing is, as well."

Brognola made the only decision he could. "Do anything you think might work."

"Right."

"OKAY," Hawkins said. With the decision made, he went into full tactical mode. "Since we don't have any idea how that damned thing works, or at least how its weapons sensors work, I have an idea. Obviously, our weapons aren't going to be of much use against it, so I suggest that we go in clean in case it zeros in on metal. No guns, no knives, just us.''

"Okay by me," Manning said. There was a good chance that the machine fired on any large mass of metal, so that made sense.

''I'd like to take my camera," Waters spoke up. "I need to have photos."

Hawkins looked over at Manning. "What'd you think?"

The Canadian shrugged. "I guess."

"You guys are nuts," James said.

Waters knew that assessment included him, and he wholeheartedly agreed. If he somehow survived this, he was never leaving California again.

THE THREE MEN STOOD behind the cover of a large boulder at the end of the outcropping. They had settled on wearing their com links and little else besides their ALOCS suits. Along with Waters's camera, they had also brought along Manning's multitool in case they actually got up to the machine. But beyond that, they might as well have been in their skivvies.

Hawkins took a deep breath and keyed his com link. "We're moving out."

"Roger." McCarter's curt reply sounded loud in his ear phone. "Good luck."

Keeping his belt buckle biting into the dust, Hawkins low crawled around the rock and into the shallow dip in the earth to his right. He'd had his belly to the ground many times before, but he sure wished that he were a bit smaller today, maybe the size of a fourteen-year-old girl with anorexia. This was one time where a Ranger-developed chest and biceps weren't working to his advantage.

He heard quick breathing behind him and knew that the government man was hot on his heels. Waters had been grilled on how to do a proper military-style low crawl, but Hawkins knew that if he was left to his own devices, he'd probably get to his feet and race for the craft or turn and run. It was hard to tell with him if the fear or the curiosity was the stronger driving force.

"Keep lower, dammit!" Hawkins heard Manning whisper over the com link, but knew it hadn't been meant for him. His buckle was digging a furrow deep enough to plant a winter crop. He'd be digging sand out of his crack for a week to come if he survived this.

The depression Hawkins was following led them straight up to the bubble. The problem was that with his head down, it was difficult to judge how far he had come. He slowly raised his head for a peek and saw that the shimmering shield was less than a hundred yards in front of him.

"Another hundred yards to go, Gary."

"Don't stop," Manning replied.

When Hawkins raised his head the second time, the

bubble was a little more than a yard in front of him, and he stopped short.

"David," he sent back to McCarter, "I'm right in front of it. Gary, I'm going to go for it, but I'll only go halfway through first. Since we don't know if the com links will work inside, if it doesn't zap me, I'll move my boots. If I don't move, get the hell away from this thing. Move fast, but for Christ's sake, keep down."

"Good luck, pal."

"Right." Hawkins took a deep breath. "Here goes."

In his career both as an Army Ranger and with Phoenix Force, Hawkins had been up against the very best that men who were trying to kill him could throw at him. The pucker factor was something he was intimately familiar with. Pulse pounding in his ears, pupils pinpointed, tight chest and almost numb fingers that adrenaline racing through his veins gave him was his drug of choice.

This time, though, he was about to OD on it and it didn't feel good.

Taking a deep breath, he reached out with one finger and tried to touch the shimmering shield, but could feel nothing. He pushed his entire hand through and again felt nothing.

He'd thought at least he'd get a shock or a buzz, but it was as if the bubble weren't there.

Emboldened, he took another deep breath, held it

and wiggled halfway through. The light inside was bizarre, like being inside a constantly turning kaleidoscope as it shifted and changed colors. But he now could clearly see the mystery machine.

Reaching up, he keyed his com link. "Gary, I'm inside and you've got to see this thing."

When he heard nothing in return, he wiggled his boots in the prearranged signal. Someone tapped him on the foot in return, so he crawled on through and slowly stood.

Now he knew what the guys at Roswell had felt on that day back in 1947. The spacecraft in front of him had made a fairly good landing. Looking beyond it, he saw the gouge it had cut through the sand on the way in. The craft had hit something, more than likely a rock, that had dented the forward curve of its saucerlike main body. But otherwise it looked to be intact.

He heard a noise behind him, turned and saw Waters emerge through the shimmer like a man stepping through a curtain of falling water. The scientist stopped right inside, stunned as he looked at the UFO.

"Move it, Craig," Manning growled as he crawled through behind him. "Christ on a crutch," the Canadian said as he stood. "Will you look at that thing?"

Waters was doing exactly that, his breath coming quick and shallow. The guys back at the lab would hand over their SUVs, titles and all, to see what he was seeing. Remembering that he had his camera, he raised it, but couldn't take the shot because his hands were shaking so badly.

DAVID MCCARTER had watched through his binoculars as the three men crawled into the otherworldly shimmer of the shield. As soon as Manning disappeared, he keyed his com link. "T.J.?...Gary?... Talk to me."

When there was no answer, he acutely felt their loss and switched over to the satcom link to talk to the Farm.

Stony Man Farm, Virginia

BROGNOLA WAS SITTING by the comsat radio when McCarter's call came in. "They're inside," the Briton reported, "but the bloody com links don't work."

Katzenelenbogen had expected something like that to happen. But since Hawkins had signaled that he had gotten through alive, that should mean that all of them were still alive. It was the "should" part of that, though, that worried him. If that damned thing actually was extraterrestrial, the Earth's rules of "should" might not apply.

It also worried Barbara Price. She was hardened to sending the Stony Man action teams into danger. It was her job. But before, she had always sent them against men, not an unknown spacecraft. If praying would have helped, she would have assumed the position right on the spot, but her experience had taught her that the gods of war were immune to petty piety. They responded best to audacity. Since audacity was Phoenix Force's stock-in-trade, there was nothing for her to do.

She grabbed a bottle of orange juice from the fridge and sat down to wait. Patience was also a primary military virtue, and she was well practiced in that part of the art.

Afghanistan

CRAIG WATERS WALKED toward the machine as if he were in a trance, never taking his eyes off it.

"Hold on, partner," Hawkins called out to him. "Let Gary lead from here on. You're our pet rocket scientist, but he's the booby-trap expert."

Waters stopped but didn't change the focus of his gaze. Whatever this craft had come from, it looked exactly like the fanciful designs that had adorned the science-fiction pulp magazines of the fifties. He could hardly believe what he was looking at.

Manning walked past Waters and stopped within arm's length of the craft to study it. It looked to be made of steel, and he couldn't see much in panel lines, so it had to have been welded together. There was a big hatch on the side of the cupola and several small darker circles that might be sensor or video pickups, but that was about it for identifiable features.

"I'm going to climb up there and see if I can get the hatch open," he told Hawkins. "If it zaps me, you guys get the hell out of here."

"Go for it."

"Do you mind if I take a few pictures?" Waters asked.

"Sure," Hawkins said. "They'll make great Christmas cards. Your friends will think you stopped by Roswell."

CHAPTER TEN

Afghanistan

Not being able to communicate with the men inside the shield wasn't sitting well with McCarter. With them gone, he was committed to holding his position in the rocks until they returned. Phoenix Force simply didn't leave anyone behind, which meant that he, James and Encizo were committed to dying in place if they were attacked before they returned.

All in all, this was shaping up to be a classic lose-lose situation.

"David," Aaron Kurtzman's voice came in over the comsat channel, "there's a small group of bandits moving up on your left, range about six hundred yards. It looks like a dozen men in two vehicles. They might be looking to find cover at your position."

"Damn!" McCarter muttered before he clicked in. "Roger, we'll take care of them."

"Calvin," he called over the com link, "the Bear

says that we have bandits coming up on our left. Two vehicles and a dozen troops.''

"I'm on them," James called down from the rocks.

Since their Hummer was their only hope of getting away alive, they had left it well out of sight in the depression behind the rocks. James had pulled the Fifty off the vehicle mount and had taken it and a tripod up in the rocks, where he could cover the approaches with its heavy fire. Since Hawkins had left his OICW behind, its 20 mm fire was also available. Even so, they were too thin on the ground to get into a prolonged conflict.

The first vehicle to appear was a battered old Russian GAZ jeep, but the other was a fairly new Toyota pickup with an improvised machine gun mount, packing a 7.62 mm RPD machine gun, above the open cab.

Since the pickup with the machine gun was the greatest threat, both James and McCarter decided to team up on it, leaving Encizo to deal with the GAZ. This had to go down quickly, and they couldn't afford to give the enemy a break.

CALVIN JAMES CRANKED back twice on the Fifty's charging handle and heard the satisfying double metallic thunk of the first .50-caliber round being stripped off the disintegrating link ammo belt and fed into the chamber. Next to the crisp snick, snick of a pump gun loading 12-gauge double-aught buckshot, this was the greatest sound in the world of military mayhem.

The Fifty's belts were loaded with a three-to-one mix of ball and armor-piercing rounds. Since they might have to shoot at night, the tracers had been left out so as not to give away their position. People tended to forget that tracers worked in both directions.

Rather than make this a "fair" fight, James opened up on the Toyota as soon as it closed to within five hundred yards. The Ma Deuce started speaking, and everyone in the vicinity listened.

His first burst was aimed at the gun crew, and the heavy .50-caliber slugs did their grim butchery. The mujahideen fighter behind the Russian machine-gun mount disappeared in a bloody spray and fell over the side.

McCarter triggered a 20 mm antipersonnel round from the OICW at the same time and was rewarded with an airburst of the frag warhead right over the bed of the pickup. When he reacquired the target in the ranging sight, they were short at least two men.

With the machine gun out of action, James concentrated on taking out the vehicle itself. His second long burst went into the engine compartment. The Fifty's AP slugs zipped through the body work as if it were made of tissue paper and continued on to punch holes through the engine block. The engine seized so fast that the truck almost upended itself as it came to a sudden halt.

Encizo had had similar results with his GAZ jeep and its four riders. With his M-249 5.56 mm SAW switched over to full-auto, he dumped half of a hundred-round assault pack magazine into the occupants. The range was far for the normal 5.56 mm round to be effective, but he was loaded with the more powerful NATO SS-109 ammunition with its heavier bullet, and it worked fine.

With a dead driver at the wheel, the GAZ careened out of control, hit a rock and overturned.

Seeing the GAZ go end over end, James shifted targets and put a sustained insurance burst into it from radiator to taillights. When the chunks stopped falling, there was only a riddled hulk left in the sand. And that included the mujis who had been riding in it.

Swinging his smoking weapon back to the Toyota, James looked again for signs of movement in that wreckage. When he was sure there were no survivors, he decided to save the ammunition. They might be stuck where they were for a long time and he would need it.

"Looks like we're in the clear again, David," he spoke into his com link.

Two more plumes of smoke rose into the clear desert air to join that of the BTR. If they had a few more visitors end up like that, they'd have an effective smoke screen to hide behind. The downside was that it let everyone within several miles know something was going on here, and they didn't need that.

NOW THAT THEIR minibattle was over, David McCarter clicked back into his comsat channel. "Katz," he said, "clear the area around us."

"You're looking good right now for at least a couple of klicks in all directions," Katzenelenbogen replied. "It doesn't look like anyone noticed you wasting that bunch. The Chinese and Afghans are going at it hammer and tong a little farther to the east, but it doesn't look like it'll bleed over on you unless the mujis fold."

"Damn," McCarter replied. "I always wanted to be caught up in the middle of a bloody great tank battle. You know, man against steel beast."

"You still might get a chance," Katz cautioned. "They're really butting heads hot and heavy, and it might reach your neighborhood."

"Can you see anything from the ship?" Kurtzman cut in and changed the subject.

"No," McCarter replied. "The shield's still blocking our vision."

"I was afraid of that."

"Me, too."

GARY MANNING TOOK his time as he examined what had to be the controls for the hatch on the outside of the cupola. Surprisingly enough, they were relatively simple and didn't seem to be alien at all. When the hatch popped open, he pulled it back the rest of the way and peered inside. Again, he found no surprises, only what looked like an air lock for any old human spacecraft.

"I'm going inside now, guys," he yelled down to Hawkins and Waters.

Manning left the hatch open wide as he entered the air lock. He emerged a moment later and waved. "I've got the inner hatch open."

"Let us get up there before you go inside," Hawkins said as he hoisted himself up onto the disk part of the craft. Turning, he extended a hand to Waters and pulled him up beside him.

The DARPA man was almost vibrating with excitement as he walked through the inner hatch after Hawkins. The interior of the craft was dimly lit, and it took a second for his eyes to adjust to the light. As soon as he could see clearly, he looked to his left, toward what should be the front of the craft. Two helmeted figures hung motionless against shoulder harnesses in their seats.

Hawkins spotted them at the same time and automatically reached for a piece, before remembering that they were completely unarmed. The two figures were slumped forward and hadn't moved.

"Are they dead?" Waters asked.

Even though it sounded like a line from a bad movie, he hadn't been able to keep himself from asking. Everything else on this trip so far had been like something out of a movie, so why not this?

"Check them out," Hawkins said. "But they look dead to me." He took a deep breath. "And they're starting to smell a little that way, too."

"Aw, shit!" Waters said when he pulled the body back upright and saw the face under the helmet. "They're fucking Russians."

"What do you mean?" Manning asked.

"Their flight suits and helmets." Waters sounded disgusted. "They're standard Russian-cosmonaut issue. We've been had, guys."

"But where'd they get this flying saucer? We don't have anything this advanced."

"I'll be damned if I know," the DARPA man said seriously. This had ruined what should have been the crowning moment of his life, a real honest-to-God close encounter, and he was angry. "But I'm sure as hell gonna find out."

"While you guys are doing your thing—" Hawkins pulled the dead Russian copilot out of his seat "—I'm going to play with the controls."

"Be careful," Manning cautioned. "We don't have Grimaldi here to fly it for us."

"I'm cool," Hawkins said as he slipped into the seat.

The controls were all marked in Cyrillic lettering, which went with the Russian pilots. But some of the instruments had the tags of the American companies that had made them. What looked a lot like a standard video screen positioned in front of the left-hand pilot's seat showed a scene of the desert in full color without the interference of the shimmering bubble. The screen in front of his seat, though, was dead, showing flat black.

Something very interesting was going on here, but Hawkins didn't have the background to figure it out. That's what the DARPA guy was on hand for. Rocket scientists were supposed to know stuff like that, and he was just a grunt.

He could, however, figure out for himself the function of the swivel handgrip with the trigger that sat on the right handrest of his seat. It looked exactly like the control stick for an arcade video game where the player shot at cyber robots with cyber blasters.

Reaching out, he wrapped his right hand around the grip, being careful to keep his finger off of the trigger. To his surprise, a screen in front of him lit up.

"Gary," he called out, "I think I just activated some kind of weapons system here."

Manning and Waters both jumped.

"Dammit, T.J.," Manning growled, "keep your hands in your pockets, will you?"

"Sure."

Hawkins had no such intention, however. Not when it came to new toys. Particularly when the new toys might be able to shoot at things.

CALVIN JAMES CAUGHT a series of dust plumes at the same time that McCarter's earphone clicked in.

"Someone must have gotten a radio message off before you waxed that last convoy," Katz said. "You have an armored column closing in on the crash site. A dozen odd T-72 tanks and APCs, and they're moving fast."

"Thank you, O Lord," Encizo intoned, "for what we are about to receive. Please remind us to be grateful."

"We see them," McCarter sent back.

There was no way that they could take on main battle tanks and do anything but die. And they couldn't abandon their teammates, so it was time for them to do a Houdini number. They readied their weapons and sunk into the irregularities in the rocks and tried to pull them down on top of them. Hopefully, the ALOCS suits would hide anything that stuck up.

HAWKINS DIDN'T LISTEN to instructions very well and had continued to explore his discovery. Guns of any kind were his favorite toys. He soon learned that by rolling his hand he could change the view on the ship's screen and was using it to check out all the approaches.

When he caught the dust plumes of the fast-moving tanks, he muttered, "Oh, shit!"

Waters glanced over and saw a group of armored vehicles rushing toward them on the screen. "Is that what I think it is?" he asked.

"It is," Hawkins answered curtly.

The tanks and armored vehicles weren't marked with national insignia on their tan camouflage paint, but he figured them to be Afghan rather than Chinese. And when they got close enough, they couldn't miss seeing McCarter and the other guys in the rocks.

Acting on impulse, he tightened his finger around the trigger and was rewarded with a red sighting ring suddenly appearing on the screen.

"Gary," he said over his shoulder, "do you think this thing's weapon is still powered up?"

"Damned if I know." Manning looked up from the panel he was examining. "Why?"

"I think I'm targeting the bandits," Hawkins replied. "At least I've got a sighting ring on my screen. I'm gonna try to fire."

"No!" Waters almost jumped out of his skin. "We don't know what—"

"I do know," Hawkins cut him off abruptly. "What's going to happen when those tanks get much closer is that our guys're gonna be in a world of hurt. I'm not going to sit here and watch that happen. Not while I have what might be a gun in my hand."

That was a soldier's answer, and there was nothing Waters could say to that.

"Do it," Manning said as he joined his teammate.

Rolling the sight over to lay the crosshairs on the

base of the turret ring of the lead tank, Hawkins squeezed the trigger all the way back against the stop. A piercing whine sounded from a bank of equipment behind his seat, and the targeting screen suddenly went blank.

It cleared just as suddenly, and he saw that the lead tank had been stopped dead in its tracks. Its turret had been blown off and was lying upside down on the sand on fire, sending greasy black smoke up into the sky.

"Whooee!" Hawkins shouted as he rolled the sight over on the next vehicle and fired again.

One of the tanks immediately replied with a 125 mm main gun round, but all he heard was a muffled explosion as the HEAT projectile detonated against the bubble. If the tank gun couldn't get through to them, this battle was as good as in the bag.

He laid the sight on the tank that had shot at them and blew it to oblivion, as well. It took three more shots from the craft's "death ray" for the mujis to decide to evacuate the area. Even so, it took a lot longer for them to turn their tanks around than it did for him to shift his sights and fire repeatedly.

By the time Hawkins was done, there were close to a dozen burning hulks littering the sand.

"Man," he breathed, "I ain't had so much fun since the hogs ate my little brother."

Waters had such a puzzled expression on his face

that Manning had to explain. "Don't mind him—he's a Southerner and he talks funny."

Hawkins turned around in his chair. "What the hell is that thing I was shooting, Waters, a laser?"

"I think it might be," Waters said. "I need to get a closer look at it and see what they've done here. We have lasers that could have done that, but we've never mounted them on atmospheric vehicles."

"If you want to check it out," Hawkins said, "from all the noise that was going on while I was shooting, I think its power pack is in that panel right behind me."

Waters and Manning moved in to take a look.

FROM SPACE, the spy satellites had captured Hawkins's turkey shoot in the desert and had relayed the carnage to Stony Man Farm in living color. If they'd had a sound connection to go with it, it would have been better than watching the CNN coverage of the close of the Gulf War.

"Unbelievable," Yakov Katzenelenbogen said as he shook his head. "We need a dozen of those things, whatever they are. Talk about rendering armor as obsolete as horse cavalry."

"As well as aircraft carriers, large buildings and a dozen other things I can think of," Aaron Kurtzman said dryly, "including cities."

"Which is why the President is so fired up about us investigating that crash," Hal Brognola pointed out. "If you own something like that, you're pretty much going to own the world."

"The only question I have," Kurtzman asked, "is was it operating on autofire or did our guys take it over and use its weapons themselves?"

"Either way—" Katz ran the tape back to watch the tanks again "—it was damned fine work. It saved our guys."

Brognola had to agree with that as he reached for the red phone. He knew that the Man was getting the same feed they were and he knew that the President would want to confer after watching it.

CHAPTER ELEVEN

Inside the Machine

Hawkins kept watch at the weapons screen console while Waters and Manning cautiously continued their probe into the machine's innards. Occasionally, he shifted his screen over to look over at Phoenix Force's position and wished that he could communicate with them. He knew McCarter was tearing his hair out wondering what the bloody hell was going on with them. The Briton had no way of knowing if they were still alive, but Hawkins knew that the guys would hold their position to the end as long as there was any chance that they would return or their bodies could be recovered.

Phoenix Force wouldn't leave a man behind, dead or alive. Never had and never would.

"Gary," he called out, "why don't I go back outside the shield and let the guys know what's happening."

"I don't know about that," Manning replied cautiously. "We don't know enough about how this thing works yet. It might not let you back in or something like that."

Hawkins had to admit that Manning had a point. He'd seen what it had done to the mujis in its automatic-defense mode, and he didn't want to join the charred corpses sprawled in the sand outside the bubble. Maybe the machine had only opened up for them because it knew that its previous crew was dead. No assumptions could be made about this machine. Even though the crew had been Russian, he still wasn't convinced that the Russians had built it.

After all the stories he'd heard about captured UFOs being tested by the Air Force at Dreamland back in Nevada, this could be a UFO the Russians had captured and learned how to fly. Now he understood why Brognola had been so insistent about their investigating it.

If it was a real alien UFO, that would be a big deal for sure. But if it was truly Russian built, the U.S. had a real problem.

NOT WANTING to get too involved with the craft's propulsion system at this point, Manning and Waters had decided to concentrate on the vehicle's weapons systems first. Since Waters knew about a couple of projects in the test-flight stage that Manning didn't know of, he had pushed the decision. Powering spacecraft by chemical rockets wasn't the only thing American engineers were working on. From what they had seen, though, the weapons system might be something entirely new.

The two men were removing what Waters felt had to be the brain of the automatic-fire-control system when they uncovered a dull black module that had what looked like a digital counter attached. When Waters cut one of the wires holding the module to the harness, the counter flashed alive and started counting down.

"Oh, shit!" Manning yelled. "It's a bomb!"

Hawkins was out of his chair in a flash and headed for the air lock. "Get out of here!"

Waters looked puzzled for a moment before Manning grabbed his arm and pushed him toward the exit. He managed to snatch up his camera before he was shoved through the air lock. He caught himself on the slope of the disk just in time to have Manning push him to the ground. He landed face first and had to collect himself before he could follow the other two.

"Get a move on!" Hawkins yelled.

Waters took off as fast as he could.

McCARTER WAS STARTLED to see the shimmering shield around the flying saucer suddenly vanish. An instant later, the hatch in the side of the cupola flew open and three men bailed out and started running away from it as fast as they could. Apparently, the weapons system had been disabled, because the craft didn't fire at them.

An instant later, a muffled explosion sounded, followed by a big gout of flame shooting out of the hatch. The three men went face first in the sand and vainly burrowed for cover.

"Run!" McCarter shouted to them over the com link.

When another, larger explosion shook the craft, the three men got back to their feet and sprinted for the rocks. Behind them, the mystery spacecraft was explosively disassembling itself.

BY THE TIME Hawkins, Manning and the DARPA man reached the rocks, the flying saucer had been dissected by the demo charges and was now burning with bright flames that had to be from thermite charges. When fire burned itself out, there would be little left for anyone to examine, except for globs of molten metal and scattered small bits ripped by explosives.

"What in the hell happened down there?" McCarter asked.

"The damned thing was booby-trapped." Manning fought to catch his breath after his sprint to safety. "Craig and I were trying to remove a module from the fire-control system when it started a countdown."

The Canadian shook his head. "Damn, it was just like in a movie."

"We're drawing attention," Encizo announced. "We need to get the hell out of here."

McCarter glanced over and saw the dust plumes speeding toward them. He couldn't tell if they were from Afghan vehicles or Chinese this time, but it didn't really matter. They had worn out their welcome, and with the craft destroyed, there was no reason for them to stick around.

"Get the camo net off the Hummer and get ready to roll," he ordered. "We'll sort the rest of this shit out on the way out of here."

James grabbed his Fifty, Encizo got the ammo cans and the commandos scrambled down out of the rocks.

Hawkins slid into the driver's seat, and James quickly mounted his gun again.

"Help me drop the trailer," McCarter said as he turned to Encizo.

During the time they had been there, in between incidents, the Hummer had been refueled from the gas cans in the trailer and the extra ammo had been already transferred, so the trailer was deadweight they didn't need.

Pulling the locking pin on the hitch, they dropped the trailer. Encizo paused long enough to wedge a frag with the pin pulled under some of the trash in the bed. Anything to delay pursuit even a little.

"Let's go," McCarter said as he took his seat and activated the tac screen.

Hawkins selected first gear and four wheel drive

before dropping the clutch and powering away from the outcropping. Running without the trailer, there was no way any muji was ever going to catch him.

As HAWKINS RACED across the desert, Waters looked back at the column of smoke rising from the burning wreck into the China-blue sky. This had been the chance of a lifetime, and he'd blown it big-time. He tried to console himself with the thought that they'd been working under pressure and not in the controlled circumstances of a lab. If the machine had been back in the secure hangar at the Edwards DARPA facility, they could have taken however long they needed for the technicians to go over it for explosive devices before messing with it.

This had been a rushed battlefield recovery, and all he had to show for it was a couple of rolls of film.

If he was lucky, his boss would just transfer him to the sanitary engineering department for this screwup.

"Bandit coming up on our right!" James called out just as he triggered the Fifty.

Manning was on the OICW and switched over to the 20 mm ammo feed as he swung the weapon on target, a speeding pickup with half a dozen mujis in it.

James's Fifty was on target first, though, and he walked the heavy .50-caliber slugs, a mix of ball and AP, into the cab. A second long burst went into the bed of the truck and a third into the engine compartment. When he was done, the truck was stopped dead and on fire.

Manning refrained from adding a 20 mm antipersonnel round to the mix. They might need the ammunition later.

"Where to now?" Hawkins asked McCarter, who was concentrating on the navigating.

"Just head southwest, away from here."

"Gotcha covered." Hawkins snap-shifted into fourth and put the pedal to the metal. This was one time that they weren't worried about leaving a dust plume.

Stony Man Farm, Virginia

BACK AT THE FARM, the Annex was buzzing. Katzenelenbogen was on the comsat link to McCarter, guiding the Hummer away from the crash site. Now that the mystery machine had gone up in smoke, the Chinese were pulling their armor back, as well. But the Afghans were still rushing reinforcements to the border in case they tried again and the area was still crowded.

"How long do you think it'll take them to get in the clear?" Hal Brognola asked.

"We're racing against the sun this time," Katz replied. "I think I can get them clear of the majority of enemy forces by nightfall, but I don't want Jack to try to make the pickup in the dark. I think it'll be better for them just to hole up somewhere and wait for daylight before we try to get that plane in there.''

"Do that," Brognola said. "We don't need any more screwups on this. And when you talk to Jack, tell him that I want him to evacuate them to Diego Garcia, not Pakistan. I don't want to have to try to explain to the Air Force where he picked the guys up from.''

"Makes sense.''

"Also, pack your bags for Diego, as well." Brognola announced. "We'll be leaving as soon as Barbara can whistle up our transport.''

Katz grinned. "I didn't think this was going to be the end of it.''

Brognola didn't smile. "If the President has his way, we've hardly even started.''

CONTINUED AFGHAN traffic in the region meant that the Phoenix Force commandos couldn't relax as they tried to make their way to their pickup zone. Katz hadn't designated the exact PZ yet, but it had to be somewhere to their southwest. With the sinking sun in their faces, the deep shadows on the desert made it difficult for the commandos to spot the enemy. Even Katz watching for them from on high didn't help all that much. Every shadow on their side of a rock outcropping could be hiding a muji gun jeep.

Katzenelenbogen wasn't unaware of what Phoenix

Force was dealing with. He'd had his boots in the sand of more than one desert in his days. When he saw the shadows lengthen, he placed a call to them.

"David," he radioed, "Hal wants you to find a RON site and wait it out. He doesn't want to risk sending Jack in to pick you up tonight."

McCarter knew that remaining overnight in that part of Afghanistan was going to be sticky, but it beat running the risk of stumbling into a muji camp in the dark. Even with their advanced NVGs, the desert was dangerous at night. And trying a night pickup could be suicidal.

McCarter checked his map against the terrain. "We're coming up on a likely RON site in a few minutes. We'll check it out and give you a call."

The site McCarter had spotted was a bluff facing east against the prevailing west wind. As he had expected, the leeward side offered a depression to help hide the Hummer. The cliff was tall enough that a guard at the top would have a good view of anyone approaching.

The team pulled in and got ready to spend the night. It would be a cold camp and no one would get much sleep, but it was better than getting ambushed in the dark.

SIBERIA WASN'T the legendary barren, frozen wasteland. True, it could get very cold for all but a few months out of the year, and it was also true that it wasn't a densely populated region. But it wasn't the North Pole, either. Although the polar regions were well-known and had been very well mapped, for a number of reasons, the biggest having to do with the fact that no one really cared, even today much of Siberia could be rightly labeled as being *terra incognita.*

That was why every Russian ruler from Peter the Great to Mikhail Gorbachev had used the uncharted vastness to stash things that they didn't want anyone to see.

Siberia was dotted with tens of thousands of nameless graves, along with other things not so easily explained. There was a complete squadron of brand-new Korean War-era MiG-15 fighters sunk up to their bellies in the tundra. The secret mission they had been sent there for had been canceled, and no had bothered to retrieve the planes. The crews had walked out.

One branch line of the famed Siberian railroad, running through southeastern Siberia, was as straight as a die when the land was flat before snaking up into the mountains, where it disappeared into the dense forests. Never did it even come close to an inhabited area. Since no Russian in his right mind would have dared ask where that rail line went, it was all but invisible. Even when the occasional small train switched off onto it, no one asked where it was going. The Russians had been well trained not to ask questions.

Anyone who had the nerve to actually follow the line would have found that it terminated in a tunnel. Again, that was nothing any Russian would ever want to question or investigate. They knew better.

In the valley on the other side of the tunnel was a facility known as the Redevok Forestry Station 105. Siberia had vast forest lands, so having a forestry center there made sense to anyone who might have dared to ask. At least to someone like a NATO intelligence analyst studying the region during the cold war. So it was that this complex went down on the books as a forestry center. Problem solved, move onto the next one.

Even when Forestry Station 105 grew a huge antenna farm in the eighties, no one questioned it. After all, the poor bastards stuck out there couldn't get cable. No sweat, it was just a forestry center. The action that was worth watching was all taking place at Star City and the Ramenskoye test flight center, where the Russians were playing with their real interesting stuff.

Who wanted to watch trees grow from space?

It was obvious that Forestry Station 105 had fallen on hard times since the Russian Federation had been formed. Several buildings looked semiderelict, abandoned vehicles spotted the area, the grounds were overgrown and few men could be seen. The runways were clean, however, and the hangars looked as if they were being kept up. So, too, were the main buildings and what had to be a line of troop barracks. Running a satellite IR scan of the area, though, would have shown more active heat sources than the casual visitor would have expected. And many of these IR sources were in what looked to be open ground.

Something was going on at Forestry Station 105. But since no logging was taking place within several hundred miles, the question was what? The problem was that no one, Russian or not, had bothered to ask that question. And since the question hadn't been asked, no one was keeping an eye on the place.

CHAPTER TWELVE

Forestry Station 105, Siberia

"That is the end of it," Artyom Chazov said as he watched a monitor displaying the video feed from a Russian spy bird in high orbit over Afghanistan. Forestry Station 105 did more than look after a seemingly endless sea of trees. In fact, Chazov had never cared in the least for trees or any other growing thing for that matter. He was the director of the secret research facility that was the real reason for the forestry station's existence.

Chazov's second in command looked to be close to tears. "Once more, Comrade Director," he said, "the Americans have stymied us."

Even though the machine he had labored on for so long had been destroyed, Artyom Chazov wasn't defeated. He had known adversity before.

Chazov had been born the son of a pig farmer who, for a few brief shining years, had been a hero of the Soviet Union as a tank commander during the Great

Patriotic War. As a child, Artyom had watched in fascination as fleets of sleek jet aircraft had taken off from the base near his family's farm by day and he had watched the stars by night. He had dreamed that he would someday become a part of his country's space program he learned about in his Soviet school.

He was an excellent student, and his father's war record was enough to get his son transported from the stinking pigpens to the polished halls of TsAGI, the Central Aerodynamics and Hydrodynamics Institute, to try to fulfill his dreams of space.

Once there, though, he ran into the unspoken but very real rigid caste system that dominated the Soviet educational system. He was the son of a pig farmer, not the son of one of the Moscow elite.

He quickly joined the Communist Party and became a dedicated Marxist to try to fit in, but even that made little difference. It also made no difference that he turned out to be one of the brightest students who had ever studied at the institute. He truly believed in the Marxist ideals that those who could, should be allowed to do. But Marx was just a mummy in a gaudy Moscow mausoleum and the Soviet system had turned into what every dictatorship did, an old boy's club. And he wasn't part of the club.

Upon graduation at the top of his class, he expected to be assigned to work at one of the major aerospace design bureaus. Instead, he was stuffed away in an obscure agency that evaluated foreign technology.

This agency's title, the Copper Research Organization, said nothing at all of its mission, but that was the Soviet style of hiding things from spying eyes.

Being a true Marxist, Chazov accepted the assignment, thinking that he would soon be able to work his way out of it. With the layers of secrecy and the cover-your-ass mentality that dominated the Soviet system, he learned early on not to ask questions. That trait, combined with the fact that he was several degrees smarter than the average Russian scientist, allowed him to quickly rise to the second in command of his agency. He soon learned, though, that he wouldn't be transferred out of it and decided to make his own fate with what had been given him.

Since the agency's director was a time-serving drunk, once Chazov was in the second seat, he used the secrecy of the agency to expand its scope. In the university, he had been introduced to Western thinking and had overlaid it on his Marxist idealism. He still believed in the proletariat, but he wasn't above using Western methods to achieve its victory. He also wasn't above using foreign technology, as well as just examining it, and that had led him and his team to Forestry Station 105 in Siberia.

STRIDING TO A SECURE computer console, Director Artyom Chazov typed in the code that would give him a scrambled microwave link to the only man in the federation he truly trusted, General Fedor Komarov of the old Soviet Strategic Rocket Forces. The general held a high position in the new government, but it gave him a valuable cover for his real work, engineering the new revolution.

"Comrade General," Chazov said when Komarov's face appeared on the screen. "The downed craft in Afghanistan was completely destroyed. It looked as if its self-destruct mechanisms were activated."

"That is good to hear, Comrade Director," the general replied. "I was concerned when you couldn't remotely activate them."

"So was I. But that leaves us only the second machine, and it has not yet completed its test program."

"You must hurry that up so we can keep to the timetable," the general said. "The plan requires that the space station be destroyed before the Yankees can install its offensive missile weaponry."

"Is there any sign that the Americans know of my site?" Chazov asked. The launch of Aerial Vehicle 1 on its ill-fated mission had been done under the cover of an elaborate deception plan. The general had arranged for the use of a giant An-22 cargo plane to fly over the station just as the aerial vehicle had taken off. The craft had hidden itself under the giant plane until far away from the station and, had it not crashed in Afghanistan, it would have returned the same way.

"Not as far as we know," the general said. "But I'm sending you a security unit from my old command. I'm concerned about your remoteness. It would be too easy for a strike team to get in without being detected.''

"Our remote location has served me well so far,'' Chazov replied. ''Foreign intelligence thinks that this is a forestry station.''

"Trust me on this one, Chazov,'' the general said, reprimanding him. ''I am old to the ways of the Yankees. There is still a chance that they will tie you to the craft.''

Chazov hated allowing outsiders into his facility, but with the second prototype spacecraft in final testing now, it couldn't be risked in any way however remote.

"As you command, Comrade General. I will leave the matter of our security to your discretion.''

"I will have them in the air within the hour,'' Komarov said.

"We will be waiting.''

That done, Chazov turned his back on the scene of burning wreckage in Afghanistan. That was the past and he had the future to look forward to. And that future was waiting for him in Hangar 3.

That the vehicle he had pinned all his hopes for his nation on had originated somewhere else didn't bother him at all. It had come to him and he had developed it, and that was all that mattered.

THE RUSSIANS HAD a long history of buying and borrowing, or stealing when they couldn't do either, from more technologically advanced nations. For example, the Russians had experimented with jet engines even before the Germans and British had gotten started, but little useful had come of it. After World War II, they used captured German jet aircraft, German aircraft engineers and British jet engines bought on the open pre-cold war market to jump-start their jet air force. The MiG-15 fighter of Korean War fame had been powered by a copy of that British engine.

This process continued in full swing during the cold war era. Spies and Communist sympathizers worked full-time to keep the Soviet Union informed of Western technology. The great secret of nuclear weapons was handed over to the Soviets by American Marxist traitors. Battlefield recoveries from the many surrogate wars fought during the cold war era also provided much-needed tech intelligence to be copied and put to use.

The first Russian air-to-air missile was an exact copy of an American Sidewinder that failed to detonate but pierced the wing of a Chinese MiG jet fighter over the Straits of Taiwan. The Red Chinese, then Russian allies, gave the intact missile to the Soviets, who immediately put it into production.

Chazov still didn't know where Aerial Vehicle 1 had originally come from, but he didn't need to know and really didn't care. All he cared was that it was his project, and it had more potential to put Marxism in space than all the rockets that had ever been built.

When the history of manned space flight was written, his name would play large as the man who made it practical.

He would also be known to the future as a hero of the new revolution.

Boris Yeltsin's hijacking of the Soviet Union hadn't caught Chazov unaware. He had seen it coming once Gorbachev had started that glasnost nonsense. While the economic and social collapse that followed Yeltsin's takeover devastated the Russian space program, it hadn't affected his project. He took steps to insure that he wouldn't suffer no matter what happened in Moscow.

Most of his rivals, the scientists working at Star City, were openly pro-Western. They thought that the end of the Soviet era would bring them even greater glory and bigger budgets. But they had bet on the wrong horse. What the Russian Federation brought them was lower pay and slashed funding. The fact that their misguided decision to join with the capitalists on the construction of space station *Freedom* was over two years behind schedule showed their folly. It would be more than just a folly when the space station became a rain of burning debris falling from the skies.

General Komarov and a strong cadre of socialists were dedicated to doing just that as the opening shot of the new revolution.

Chazov wasn't the only Russian who hadn't welcomed the new order of the so-called democratic Russian Federation. They were legion and while they had to keep a low profile, they took a page from Lenin's book and organized themselves into cells. Guided by Komarov, they could only win and his Aerial Vehicle 2 would play a large part in bringing about the final victory.

This time, the revolution would be final because the traitors who had betrayed the Soviet Union would be dead. So would be anyone who stood in their way.

Afghanistan

THE PHOENIX FORCE warriors were up well before the sun rose over their desert RON site. Kurtzman's Computer Room crew had kept watch over them throughout the night, but they still kept two men on guard at all times just in case. None of them had had very much sleep in the past several days, and it was starting to catch up with them.

Rosario Encizo was crankier than usual before he had his coffee. "Flying Jack had better not hump the pooch today," he grumbled as he lit off the heat tabs under his canteen cup to make his brew. "I've enjoyed just about all of this place that I can stand."

Calvin James smiled as he bit into a MRE fruit bar. "Anyone hearing you'd think that you're not a happy warrior."

"Get stuffed, Cal."

"David," Katzenelenbogen radioed David Mc-

Carter at first light, "your Primary PZ is only seven klicks from where you are right now. There's a valley that looks clear enough for Jack to get in and out of. You'll need to make an on-the-ground recon and give him the final clearance. But it looks pretty good from here."

"Let it get a little lighter," McCarter suggested, huddled over his own heat-tab fire brewing water, "and we'll check it out then. A man needs his cuppa in the morning."

"No problem." Katz knew better to get between McCarter and his tea.

JACK GRIMALDI HAD spent most of the night preparing for the extraction. He and Katzenelenbogen had communed via cyberspace to find a suitable PZ for him to get into. When they located both a primary and a backup site, they plotted his exit route to Diego Garcia. Only then did the pilot have a chance to bag a brief nap.

Buster Keyton had worked all night servicing the Hercules Grimaldi would fly and was waiting for the pilot on the tarmac at first light.

When Grimaldi saw the sergeant in his flight gear, he knew that Keyton wanted to go along this time, as well. Grimaldi had risked him on the first flight, but the stakes had just gone up. Plus, since he wouldn't be returning to Quetta this time, he didn't want Keyton to be AWOL.

"Buster," Grimaldi said, holding out his hand, "I'm sorry, but I can't take you with me this time. I'm afraid that your days of strap hanging as a Yankee air pirate are over."

"Damn—" Keyton grinned as he shook Grimaldi's hand "—it was worth a try. I had so much fun, I was thinking of transferring to the CIA."

"Forget it. We're not CIA. They're a buncha weenies."

Keyton laughed. "Good luck anyway."

"Thanks, I'm going to need it."

Grimaldi strapped himself into the bird, ran through his preflight checks and then waited for the call from Phoenix Force that the PZ was suitable. He was airborne five minutes after he received it.

With clearance through Pakistani airspace secured, the Stony Man pilot waited until he crossed over into Afghanistan before getting his belly down in the dirt. A Herky wasn't an agile craft, but it didn't handle badly at low levels.

Approaching the PZ, he keyed his mike. "Mark it," he radioed.

"Roger," McCarter called back. "Smoke out."

"I have vanilla," the pilot acknowledged the white smoke. "I'm turning on final now."

"We're ready."

The Hercules came in fast and low again; Grimaldi had her flaps dumped full and her gear down. Phoenix Force had cleared the immediate vicinity of the crash site by forty miles, but there was still the question of roving muji patrols so this pickup would have to be made on the quick.

The instant the C-130's wheels touched down, Grimaldi snapped the props to full reverse and locked both brakes. A billowing dust cloud shot up into the air behind him, but it couldn't be helped. He had to get slowed before he ran out of flat ground.

At the end of the braking rollout, Grimaldi snapped his port-side prop controls into full forward without cutting his RPM and stomped down on the right rudder pedal to activate the brakes. The plane pivoted to the right and was pointing back the way it had come, the rear ramp coming down as it groaned to a halt.

"Go! Go! Go!" he shouted into the radio.

HAWKINS WAS BEHIND the wheel of the Hummer, and before Grimaldi even called, he was off the brakes, popped the clutch and was on the throttle full bore. The heavily laden vehicle shot forward with McCarter clutching the grab bar in front of the passenger seat. James had a death grip on the spade handles of his Fifty, and the others held on as best they could.

"What the bloody hell is wrong with you?" McCarter shouted at Hawkins.

"I want to get out of here!" Hawkins yelled back.

The Hummer was doing forty-five miles per hour when he lined up on the gaping rear opening under the tall tail of the Herky.

"On approach," he radioed to Grimaldi. "Start your takeoff now!"

In the cockpit, Grimaldi came off his brakes and brought all four props out of the feathered position into full forward. The turboprops screamed as they clawed the air, and the Hercules started its takeoff roll just as the Hummer hit the bottom of the ramp.

"Christ on a cross," McCarter muttered as the Hummer shot up the ramp into the dim interior of the plane. Like most race car drivers, he never felt comfortable when someone else was driving. Particularly someone like Hawkins. Every Southerner styled himself a moonshine runner, and Hawkins had watched *Thunder Road* one too many times as a kid.

As soon as the Hummer cleared the ramp, Hawkins slammed on the brakes, locking them down. When the vehicle skidded to a stop mere inches from the end of the cargo floor, the aircraft was thundering along the desert at almost liftoff speed.

"Whooee, Mama!" Hawkins hammered the steering wheel. "What a fuckin' ride!"

James reached down and grabbed Hawkins by the collar. "You ever do anything like that again, Bubba, I'm going to squeeze your head off. You leave that *Cannonball Run* shit at home. Got that?"

Hawkins turned with a big grin on his face. "Cal! How can you say something like that? You've never seen such a masterful exhibition of Southern driving in your life, and you were there to witness it firsthand, my man, up close and personal. That's a whole lot better than seeing it on *Real TV*."

"Your ass, T.J."

Grimaldi nursed the aircraft off the ground and tucked up his landing gear. "How about tying down that thing back there," he called over the intercom. "I don't want it rolling around if I have to go evasive."

"We're on it," McCarter called back.

"When you're done back there," Grimaldi added, "you guys might as well get settled in for a long flight. We're going to Diego Garcia instead of back to Pakistan. Hal doesn't want to have to explain to the Pakistanis how and why you guys got on the plane."

"Just as long as it takes us as far from here as it can," Encizo muttered when James told him of the change in plans. "I've had it with this place."

CHAPTER THIRTEEN

Stony Man Farm, Virginia

"Okay," Aaron Kurtzman said as he turned in his wheelchair to report to Barbara Price. "Jack picked them up without a hitch. They'll be clearing Afghan airspace real soon."

"Good," she replied.

The past several hours had been a mad scramble with her trying to get Hal Brognola, Yakov Katzenelenbogen and a planeload of supplies to Diego Garcia for the second phase of this so-called mission. The Afghan operation had been tough enough, but this next phase would really be pushing the envelope in ways she didn't like.

But, as Brognola had reminded her right before he'd left, this was what the President wanted, so he was going to have it one way or the other. And the other way he was ready to use meant sending American military forces, which risked going to war with Russia.

Stony Man had been instituted as a dirty-little-jobs outfit, an organization devoted to taking care of business on their level so America's major muscle didn't have to get involved. In the nuclear age, all-out war was to be avoided at all costs, and the concept of a surgical strike force had been invented. It looked good on paper and, so far, it had worked just as well in practice. It was that "so far" bit that worried Price when it came to sending the teams to invade Russia.

The Stony Man warriors had operated inside Russia a number of times before, but almost always the mission had been planned in conjunction with Russian Federation officials. This time, they would be going it alone without anyone in Moscow knowing that they were on the ground inside Mother Russia, and that concerned her.

The federation's defense apparatus wasn't what it had been in the glory days of the cold war, but it was still not to be mistaken for a stroll in the park. The Russian bear still had all her claws.

Diego Garcia Island

DIEGO GARCIA WAS a remote island in the Indian Ocean that served as a staging area for U.S. forces keeping track of the Middle East situation. During the Gulf War, it had proved invaluable as the home base for the B-52 bomber fleet that had hammered the life out of Saddam's vaunted Republican Guard units.

Things weren't quite so busy now, but the facilities were being maintained just in case some other lunatic in the region with delusions of grandeur needed a high-explosive lesson in B-52 diplomacy.

Several miles out, Jack Grimaldi checked in with DG air-traffic control and gave them his mission code word. Since it had been generated in the Oval Office, it got him instant VIP status instead of a bunch of asinine questions about who he was and a severe buzzing by the flight of air-to-air-missile-armed F-15 Eagles. He was tired and didn't want to play "mine's-bigger-than-yours" macho games with overly eager fighter jocks.

When the details of his landing had been worked out with the tower, Grimaldi clicked in his intercom. "Wakey, wakey, guys," he called back to the commandos. "We got clearance and we're going in."

The transport runway was clear as Grimaldi banked the C-130 for the downwind leg of the landing pattern. Dropping his flaps and gear, he touched down on the first fifty yards of the runway and put his props into reverse pitch to kill his speed.

As soon as he had slowed to taxiing speed, a Hummer with a yellow-and-black Follow Me sign on the back led him to a huge hangar. The door was open, so he drove the Hercules inside and switched off the fuel feeds.

"End of the line," he called out as he scrambled to undo his shoulder harness buckle. The next time he had to fly one of these damned things all by himself, he was going to have a relief tube installed. His bladder was about to burst, and peeing his pants just didn't go with his image.

McCARTER WAS unpleasantly surprised to see Yakov Katzenelenbogen waiting for them in the hangar. The way the mission had gone, it didn't bode well that Stony Man's tactical adviser was on hand for the debrief. It could only mean further complications.

"Now what?" he asked bluntly.

"Come on in," Katz greeted him. "Have a cold one and something to eat first. Hal's still setting up the briefing room for us."

"He's here, too?"

Katz nodded.

"Bloody hell."

Along with a welcome cooler of American beer, a substantial buffet lunch had been provided by the Air Force mess hall, and Phoenix Force needed no urging to dig in. MREs could keep a person going, but no one had ever mistaken the field rations for real food. It was amazing what they could do with plastics and gene splicing nowadays. They could almost make it look and taste like food.

"Not bad for a tube steak," Hawkins said as he speared his second Polish sausage from the steamer.

"That's what your girlfriend said about me." James grinned.

Manning almost choked at the expression on Hawkins's face. Those two needed to find a stand-up-comic gig to work during their off-duty time.

WHEN LUNCH WAS OVER, Katzenelenbogen returned with an armed Air Police escort to take Phoenix Force to the briefing facility in the base headquarters building. More armed guards were posted outside the doors.

"A bloody dog-and-pony show," McCarter muttered when he saw them.

"They're just on hand to keep us from being mobbed by our adoring fans," Hawkins said.

They were escorted through the building into a soundproof multimedia room and found Hal Brognola waiting for them. As soon as they took their seats, he stepped up to the podium.

"The President wanted me to extend his congratulations on the mission so far," he said. "He understands that the loss of the craft was through no fault of yours. So you're off the hook for that."

"Glory be," Hawkins muttered.

"I don't know if I like the sound of the 'so far' part of that," McCarter spoke up.

"The next part should be a walk-on," Katzenelenbogen cut in. "A cleanup job as it were. And you'll have the Ironman's guys to help you with it."

"Oh, I like that part even better," McCarter said.

"We won't be able to handle it on our own and will need reinforcements. Jolly good, Katz."

As the original Phoenix Force leader, Katzenelenbogen had worked with McCarter long enough to know how to handle the Briton when he had his knickers in a twist. And from the masterful sarcasm, they were well bunched up today.

"Their part of the mission will primarily be in the data collection end of it," he explained. "Your team will handle the entry and security chores."

"What's this mystery target?" McCarter asked.

Brognola snapped on a three-foot-by-three-foot video screen showing a satellite aerial view. "The next target," he said, "is a remote experimental station in Siberia. We think it's that flying saucer's home base."

"So, that damned thing really was Russian?" Manning asked.

"That seems to be what it looks like now," Katz replied. "But that's a tentative ID. We'll know a little more about it after you guys go in and clean that place out down to the bare concrete."

"If it was Russian," Manning asked, "why didn't we know anything about it until now? I thought the NRO satellites kept track of anything that even remotely looked military in that place?"

"The Keyhole birds do a good job, but Russia's a big country. Actually, the site you'll be hitting has been on the books for a long time, but it's been listed as a forestry experimentation center.''

"Right. They've been seeding burned-out forests with flying saucers.''

"The runways and hangars we've seen were supposedly used for the flying water tankers they use to fight the forest fires.''

"How'd we find out that this was the place?'' McCarter asked. The source of information was often more important than the information itself, and that had to be the case this time. Something wasn't right with this, and he wanted the bad news up front.

"Actually, by accident,'' Katz replied. "Space Command was running a backtrack on the flight path of that UFO attack on the space station and the radar plot showed that if it had come from Earth, it would have originated in that part of the world. Examining that possibility, they saw that it apparently had been launched in a narrow window when our spy birds were below the horizon.''

"Bloody convenient, what?''

"That being the case,'' Katz continued, "they went looking for another satellite that might have been in the sky when it took off. To make a long story short, they found a Chinese bird that had been on the scene during that time frame and it was running a download, instead of a real-time, imaging system. They hacked into it, downloaded its imagery and spotted this place.

Since then, every U.S. and NATO source has been running through the archived data on it.''

"Any conclusions?'' McCarter asked. "Beyond that it's not a bloody sawmill?''

"Our preliminary findings,'' Katz said, "indicate that the site is some kind of a rogue research operation. Just another one of a hundred things that fell through the cracks when the Soviets bowed off of the world stage.''

"Right.'' McCarter laughed. "They were building a flying saucer and someone just conveniently forgot about it? Not bloody likely, mate. The Russians have always kept close track of their better ideas like that.''

Brognola stepped into the conversation again. "There may be a connection with that site and what Moscow is calling 'reactionary elements,' who are trying to return to the bad old days. They have admitted that several advanced-technology projects kind of disappeared during the political unrest of the early Yeltsin coup days. They suspect that they were hijacked and hidden by hard-liners.''

"Here we go again.'' Encizo shook his head. "Why can't those bastards just lie down and die like good little Communists. Every time we turn around, there's another nest of them that didn't hear the news.''

"Are we working with the Russians on this one at all?'' James asked.

Brognola paused. "Not this time.''

McCarter took a deep breath. "Isn't this going to be a little bit like inviting a war with the Russian Federation, Hal?" he asked. "The last time I heard, they were still an active part of the nuclear club and a wee bit touchy about insults to their national sovereignty and all that bumwadding. And if I remember correctly, the Russians have never liked invaders very much."

"That's true enough," Brognola said smoothly. "But our plan is to have you guys in and out before anyone in Moscow notices or has time to react. From there, the Oval Office will smooth things over."

"And their air-defense troops will all be on bloody holiday, right?" McCarter snorted. "Or maybe knitting sweaters for their grannies?"

Brognola hated it when McCarter got sarcastic. He did it so damned well.

"We're going to send you in by stealth bomber again, so you're not noticed."

"Right."

CRAIG WATERS HAD KEPT his mouth shut so far and had just sat and listened to this verbal free-for-all. He still didn't know who these guys really were, but his appreciation of them had just gone up several notches in the past couple of minutes. In Afghanistan they had seemed to be just a deep-cover commando unit, the classified military muscle of a hundred movies and paperback thrillers. Now it looked as if they had some kind of direct line into the White House. Taking an operation inside Russian territory had to have been approved at the highest level.

Even so, they weren't discussing the biggest, and to him, the most important part of this mystery. How had the Russians been able to develop such an advanced spacecraft without anyone knowing anything about it?

His job at DARPA was to stay informed of foreign space-flight research, and he was good at his job. He even knew which moron at NASA had innocently handed over a complete set of space-shuttle blueprints to the Russians, who had quickly put them to use to build their short-lived Buran space vehicle. He knew of a dozen other Russian hypersonic, near space designs that had been in the metal-cutting, prototype stage when everything had fallen apart.

He hadn't, however, heard or seen a single thing that would have led to the vehicle he had been inside. And he had a hard time believing that it had been designed in a vacuum without any of the other Russian design teams knowing anything about it. The Soviets simply didn't work that way. That was the real mystery in this whole affair, and everyone was completely sidestepping it.

He also wanted to know what was going to happen to him and stuck up his hand.

"Mr. Waters." Brognola nodded at him. Anything to get McCarter to shut up.

"Ah…" Waters began. "I know that I'm not part of your organization, sir, but I've got a couple of questions if that's okay."

"Certainly."

"Number one, I have to make a report to DARPA about what I saw in Afghanistan—" he shrugged "—but I don't know what to tell them."

"As long as you don't tell them who you were with or any details about how you got to the crash site, you can tell them anything you like about the wreck."

"I mean," Waters stated, "I know that the pilots were Russians, but I also know that the machine wasn't. I'm a specialist in Russian space technology, and I know what they make."

Brognola's eyes narrowed. This was the one area he hadn't wanted to get into. "If the pilots were Russian and it took off from a Russian base, why wasn't it Russian?"

Waters knew these guys had to have high clearances, but a lifetime of watching his mouth around anyone he didn't work with was a hard habit to break.

"Let me just say that I know almost as much about Russian space technology as the guy who's in charge of it. I have thick dossiers on all the scientists, suppliers and fabricators who have ever been involved in their space program. I also know how they form, weld and rivet metal. I know what kind of fasteners they use to—"

"Let me stop you here," Brognola broke in.

"You're asking if the craft was something that the Russians, shall we say for sake of argument, collected rather than built for themselves, right?"

That was precisely the question. "More or less," Waters said carefully.

"All I can say at this point is that we don't have an answer to that question. And I'm instructed to tell you that you are not to ask that question again until the President allows you to. Is that understood?"

Waters paused. Now what in the hell was going on? His job was to ask those kinds of questions. What was he going to say to his boss at DARPA?

"Mr. Waters?" Brognola prompted him.

"Yes, sir. I understand."

"Good."

"Now," Brognola continued, "I'm sure your next question is what you're going to be doing next."

Waters nodded.

"After a personal debriefing here by my staff, you'll be transported back to the States, where you will be again debriefed in depth by POTUS."

"POTUS?" Waters asked.

"The President Of The United States."

Before he could wimp out, Waters asked his last question. "Is there any chance of my going along with these men to Russia?"

Brognola studied him for a long time.

Waters tried again. "I think I'll be useful to them. My extensive expertise in this area will be valuable in the data-recovery process, as well as the evaluation of any physical evidence they might come across.

"Also," he added, "I speak and read Russian fluently."

In the silence that followed, Brognola shifted his gaze to McCarter, who nodded slightly.

"I can buddy jump him," Hawkins spoke up.

"On a HALO drop?"

Hawkins shrugged. "It's been done."

Waters didn't know a HALO from a crowbar, but the more he thought about it, the more he wanted to take this all the way. He'd never learn what that thing had been if he didn't track it back to its source. And not knowing would haunt him for the rest of his life.

"Mr. Waters," Brognola said, "you understand that you will be risking your life if I decide to include you? And if you're killed on the mission, we'll have to leave your body behind."

Waters swallowed hard. "I understand. I'm not married, so I won't be leaving a family."

Brognola thought for a moment. "I'll clear this and get back to you."

"Thank you, sir," Waters said before he could change his mind. Something told him that this new mission was going to make Afghanistan look like a walk in the sun.

CHAPTER FOURTEEN

Diego Garcia

Getting permission for DARPA man Craig Waters to join the Stony Man team in Russia took a little less than an hour. During that wait, Gadgets Schwarz and Rosario Blancanales joined their Phoenix Force buddies for a long coffee break and swapped lies and war stories. Since they were teamed up again, they needed to get back into their operational mode. A big part of that was renewing the personal contact and getting into one another's minds again. A successful small team had to be closer than brothers.

While the others were going through the getting-to-know-you-again routine, Hawkins took Waters aside to start briefing him on what he could expect from his second parachute jump. Any kind of buddy jump, to say nothing of one from twenty-eight thousand feet, was dangerous to both the jumper and the buddy. Hawkins wanted to give him enough information to give him a chance to rethink his decision.

Instead, Waters seemed to get amped up at the prospect. Just what the world needed, Hawkins thought, was another jumping junkie.

When Brognola came back in and nodded, Katzenelenbogen walked over to Hawkins and Waters. "You're in, Craig," he said.

The DARPA man didn't know whether to laugh or cry.

"Okay, guys," Katz continued. "We're going to transfer to a C-141 here for the flight to an air base in Japan, where we will refit and go into our mission prep. Once we get the green light from the Puzzle Palace, you'll transfer into another stealth bomber for the insertion."

"Ah, shit," James mumbled to himself. "Another damned PPP ride."

"Jammed in like sardines," Manning added. "Don't forget that we'll have Ironman and his guys with us on this one."

"And don't forget our rocket scientist."

Manning glanced over at Waters. "Since they're buddy jumping, he can sit in Hawkins's lap."

James grinned.

Hawkins flashed a one-fingered salute.

Siberia

ONE OF THE THINGS that Artyom Chazov liked most about working with General Komarov was that the man didn't hesitate once his mind had been made up. He was a man of action, not talk, which was what the new revolution needed if it was to be successful. Four hours after their conversation, Forestry Station 105's radar operator picked up an inbound flight that was squawking the coded IFF required to land at the facility. When radio contact was made with the plane, the pilot had the proper codes to show that he had came from Komarov and he was allowed to land.

When the An-12 assault transport turned on final approach, it was wearing civilian markings instead of military camouflage paint and red stars, more proof that the general didn't miss a beat. After touching down, it taxied to a tie-down point in front of one of the hangars and shut off its four turboprops. As Chazov went to greet the flight, he had his facilities manager get a couple of their trucks over to the rear of the plane to off-load the cargo he knew it would be carrying.

The men who disembarked from the Antonov were wearing plain coveralls and jackets devoid of military insignia as if they were replacements for the regular ''forestry station'' crew. Again, that was a good touch. Chazov still wasn't convinced that he had been spotted on anyone's radar, but professional paranoia was a requirement, not a mental disorder, for any Russian in General Komarov's delicate position. And since paranoia was a well-established Russian cultural trait already, Chazov had it in spades, as well, and trusted the general's instincts.

"Comrade Director," one of the deplaning men said as he approached him. "I am Major Yuri Polinski, commanding Eighth Missile Security Company."

The director extended his hand. "Artyom Chazov. Pleased to meet you, Major."

"And I you, Director," Polinski replied. "The general has spoken highly of you and of the importance of your work to our cause."

"He is too kind," Chazov said. "We all do what we can in accordance with our abilities."

Hearing the catch phrase of their underground movement, Polinski almost stiffened to attention, but caught himself. "Where do you want my men to be billeted?" he asked. "If it is not too inconvenient, it would be best if we can all be put in the same place."

"I understand fully," Chazov said. "I have reserved one of our buildings for your use. It even had communications hookups you can use for a command center."

"Very good, Comrade Director."

"If you will follow me, I'll take you there."

Polinski paused to speak into a small radio, and two other men broke off to follow them. The other troops fell right to work unloading their plane. Though the cargo was crated and palletized, it could only be the weapons and military equipment they would need to secure the station.

AS ISOLATED as he had been in his secret career, Chazov had had little exposure to the military and none at all to the new breed of Russian warriors, the specialist security units. He, of course, had heard of their legendary exploits in the media, as well as from the general. They were his nation's best trained, most dedicated soldiers and had earned the honor of being the shock troops of the new revolution when it was launched.

He had been immediately impressed with Major Yuri Polinski. Young, clear-eyed, fit and eager—the first impression was right out of an old Soviet newsreel from the desperate years of the Great Patriotic War. It did his soul good to see that men like Polinski still existed and hadn't been corrupted by the drugs and easy money of the federation's new society. It was men like him who would spearhead the cleansing of the corruption that had overtaken Mother Russia, and it couldn't come a day too soon for him.

He was also impressed with the men of Polinski's security company. They had calmly but efficiently gone to work establishing their control over his facility. One officer had taken Chazov's own security chief aside to review the facility's physical layout and the minimal defensive measures that were already in place. His extensive recommendations for security changes had been respectful as well as practical and professional. After going over them in detail with Major Polinski and his own man, Chazov approved each and every one of the improvements and the troops started working on them before the day was out.

Chazov realized that installing some of the heavy weaponry that Polinski requested would disrupt his station's well-established routines, but he had relied upon the remoteness of his location to protect him from prying eyes—both foreign and domestic—for far too long and he now recognized the fallacy of that thinking.

The loss of the first prototype had made it essential that the second machine didn't fail. And to insure that, his base had to remain inviolate. Polinski's men would free his mind to concentrate on the tests, and if the Yankees did actually come as Komarov feared, he had no concerns that they would be able to deal with them. The Russian military had a long tradition of holding on to what was theirs.

THE FLIGHT from Diego Garcia to Japan was a chance for the Phoenix Force commandos to rest up after the rigors of the Afghanistan mission. The RC-135 flying commando post they were traveling in was fitted with showers, a well-stocked galley and a bunk area for their normal relief crew. Since the plane had a single crew on board this time, the facilities were available.

"Damn," Hawkins said when he saw their accommodations. "Maybe we should take this thing to Russia instead of that dinky old stealth bomber. We could sleep on the way in."

"Better than that," James commented, "we could just fly it in, land at the forestry station and tell them to hand over the goodies before anyone gets hurt."

"Great idea, Cal." Hawkins fluffed the pillow of the bunk he had picked out as his for the duration. "The New Age Stony Man solution."

James laughed. "In your dreams, homeboy."

"Will you guys take that bullshit somewhere else," Manning called out from his bunk. "People are trying to sleep around here."

"Good luck."

THE RC-135 HAD a secure communications suite that allowed Katzenelenbogen to link up with the Farm and for Brognola to keep the White House updated as the information flowed in. The Oval Office was getting it all from the primary sources, but the Man always liked to have the Stony Man assessment on intel, as well. That way he could check it against the usual sources and pick the one he liked best.

"This sure as hell had better work," Brognola muttered when he raised the privacy hood that had kept his conversation with the President unheard even by Katz.

"What do you mean?" Katz swiveled in his chair.

Brognola shook his head. "He's got a cruise-missile attack locked and loaded if we can't pull this off."

Katz was stunned. Russia might be a semitoothless

bear right now, but she wasn't some Third World pesthole that couldn't defend herself. "What's he thinking?"

Brognola automatically thumbed two antacid tablets off the roll in his pocket, rubbed off the lint, popped them and reached for his cup of coffee to wash them down.

"Damn." He grimaced as he swallowed. "This coffee's worse than Kurtzman's."

"Impossible," Katz automatically answered. The Farm's Computer Room's coffee was so vile that a statement like that couldn't be allowed to stand unchallenged. "But back to the President."

Brognola took another shot from his cup before answering. "Well, Space Command's really fired up about this thing. They went into overdrive and laid a multimedia dog-and-pony show on the Man that showed the total destruction of the land of the free and the home of the brave if we don't kill that thing's nest. They think that where there's one of them, there's likely to be more. They breed, you know?"

"They're probably right. But does it call for a surgical strike against the Russians? I thought we were long past using that kind of brinkmanship diplomacy. That's Cuban Missile Crisis thinking."

"That's basically what I asked him, and he said that he thinks this situation calls for it. He's got a lot more than just several tons of taxpayers' dollars wrapped up in that space station. He's concerned about that thing's weapons systems. Whatever it is, we can't defend against it.''

''Damn,'' Katz muttered.

He'd been in on the Stony Man experiment right from the start, and he'd gone through more of these scenarios than he liked to remember. But there hadn't been a single situation, no matter how dramatic, that had been made easier by having the President looking over their shoulders and making unhelpful hints.

''He's thinking with his prestige again, and you know how that usually works out.''

''Unfortunately, I do,'' Brognola said. '''Mine's bigger than yours' is never a good reason to go to war. But it looks like he's reaching for his zipper again.''

Katzenelenbogen's earphone that linked him to the Farm clicked in and Aaron Kurtzman was on the line. ''We have an update,'' he said.

Katz switched the call to the speaker. ''Send it.''

''Well,'' Kurtzman said, ''Space Command, the NRO, the DIA and all their alphabet spook cousins have been focused in on Forestry Station 105 ever since it was IDed as the most likely spot for the flying saucer's home base. And you know what happens when that many—''

''Bottom line, please,'' Brognola cut in.

''The station just received an An-12 flight originating from a Strategic Rocket Forces base in Mother Russia. The plane was in civilian markings and the men who got out, two platoons or so of them, didn't appear to be wearing military uniforms. But they off-loaded a lot of crates that looked like standard-issue weapons transport crates. There's also a lot of work going on in the area, and it's continued on into the night.''

''What kind of work?'' Katz asked.

''The usual defensive preparations,'' Kurtzman replied. ''They're laying mines, stringing barbed wire, digging firing positions, the whole drill to harden the place. But the kicker is that a second flight brought in a couple of batteries of mobile SA-11 Gadfly SAM launchers that they're setting up on the perimeter.''

''Any armor or choppers?'' Katz asked.

''Not yet, but another plane just landed, another An-12, and it's off-loading now.''

''It can't carry armor or Hinds,'' Katz said, ''so we're still okay.''

''What do you mean?'' Brognola asked.

Battles, both large and small, were not just clashes of men, or contests between equipment, but battles of intelligence. The outcome usually went to the side that had the best information about its opponents, not necessarily just the bigger numbers on the ground. ''Well, before I get into that, we have to ask the real question.''

''And that is?''

''Just who the hell are we dealing with here?'' Katz asked. ''If the guy in charge is a rogue as you said, that's one thing, but if he's got the backing of the Russian military, that's a different story. But what we've seen so far today says that he doesn't have official sanction.''

''Why's that?''

''He might have a backer in the military—every scientist of note over there has. But if Moscow was behind his work, they'd be sending him a parachute division with armor and tac air support, not a couple planeloads of infantry. A couple of SAM launchers could be sent without anyone noticing, but when they start moving in armor, choppers or airborne troops, the orders came from on high.

''Therefore—'' he clicked up the image of the target site on his screen ''—my feeling is that our guys still have a chance of pulling this off.''

He turned to Brognola. ''However, the minute one of those giant An-22s shows up and starts off-loading tanks and Hinds, all bets are off. An-12s are all over the place, but the heavy-lift aircraft are still under central control.''

Brognola had been leading the SOG long enough to put the situation together for himself, but it was always nice to get it from an unimpeachable source like Katz. Once more, the Israeli's Mossad operational experience was coming in handy. The main reason his home country had won as often as it had in its stormy history was its timely intelligence. They'd had it and the Arabs hadn't. It was as simple as that.

"Aaron," Brognola said, "keep on top of the intelligence feeds and keep downloading the latest arrivals at the target as they come in. I'm going to talk to the President, but I can tell you that he's going to want to go ahead with it unless something drastic occurs."

"That's what we figured," Kurtzman said. "I'll send you anything we get as soon as we get it."

When Brognola turned back, he saw that Katz was already working to include the newest developments into his battle plan. "You want me to top off your coffee?" he asked.

Katz shook his head without replying, and Brognola took the hint. Never mess with the master when he was hard at work. He crossed the aisle of the command suite to the duty officer's bunk and lay down. Katz would call him if the President wanted another update.

The steady drone of the plane's four jet engines quickly put him to sleep, leaving Katzenelenbogen the sole Stony Man warrior awake.

BY THE TIME the RC-135 landed in Atsugi Air Base, Japan, the situation in Siberia had been scanned, reconned and analyzed down to the blades of grass. Backtracking the flight paths of the An-12s that had gone into the forestry station allowed their cargo and passengers to be examined in detail. Full, multispectra scans of the site itself had allowed detailed maps of the area and its defenses to be charted, building floor plans to be made and a personnel tracking system initiated to show where every Russian was at any time. About the only thing that hadn't been developed was the specifics of their daily menu. The feeding times, though, were being charted.

Katzenelenbogen had received much of this in bits and pieces throughout their flight, but the entire package with even newer material was waiting for him upon his arrival in Atsugi. After reading it over, he closeted himself with Brognola to work out a plan of action based on the new information.

Brognola took their conclusions to the President over a secure line, but didn't look happy when the conversation ended. "He still wants us to try it," he stated, rubbing an ache in the back of his neck. "The Joint Chiefs have gotten on Space Command's bandwagon and we're at Defcon Two now."

Defense Condition One was peace; Defcon Four was all-out war. The other levels in between were alert levels that required certain steps be taken by the military forces. Defcon Two wasn't that bad. The measures required weren't that hard to hide from the potential enemy. But no one wanted to see the temperature rise to Defcon Three.

Katz gathered his scattered intelligence materials in a neat pile. "We'd better give this to the guys and see what they want to do."

This was the point in all too many of these missions

that Brognola always feared. The Stony Man action teams had done the impossible for so long that it was now expected of them as a matter of routine. The fact that they were all volunteers, not drafted grunts, often escaped the notice of the man who sent them into action.

He feared that the day would come when they would be asked to do too much and would tell the President to send someone else to die trying to do the impossible.

CHAPTER FIFTEEN

Atsugi, Japan

Disembarking in Japan after the RC-135's flight from Diego Garcia, the Phoenix Force warriors were showered, well fed, well rested and ready to go to work. On the other hand, Katzenelenbogen and Hal Brognola felt, and looked, like last week's dirty laundry—stinky and wrinkled.

Their arrival had been expected, and armed APs again escorted them into another secure briefing room where Able Team was waiting for them, having arrived on a different flight. After the greetings, they grabbed coffee and took their seats to continue the mission briefing.

"Okay," Katz started out. "I have all the intel updates and the situation at the target has changed in the last twenty-four hours. There's now an eighty-man Strategic Rocket Forces Security Company providing security at the site along with a brace of mobile

SA-11 Gadfly SAM launchers. On the plus side, though, there's no armor or tac air yet.''

McCarter slowly shook his head. ''Beautiful. There are ten of them, more or less, to each one of us, but they don't have tanks. No sweat, as you Yanks are fond of saying. We'll just nip in while they all have their thumbs up their fundaments, take a little look-see and duck back out.''

''David,'' Hal Brognola spoke up, ''I can still call this thing off if you don't think it's doable. No one, including the President, is asking your men to commit suicide. The problem, though, is that the Man has a cruise-missile strike ready to go if you don't.''

Every one of the Phoenix Force and Able Team warriors had faced this call many times before. With the world the way that it was, often a handful of men in the right place at the right time could prevent a localized problem from becoming a worldwide crisis. If someone had had the guts to send someone in to take care of Hitler, Stalin, Mao or a hundred other disasters in the making, the world would bear fewer scars. Untold millions of deaths could be credited to otherwise good men in power who hadn't had the guts to do something useful when they'd the chance. It was the oldest story in the history of the human race.

For the past several years, though, the United States had had the courage to take these necessary preventive measures. And very often the men who had been on the sharp end of the stick had been from Stony

Man Farm. Sometimes, the President had sent in the military instead, but flexing America's military might always had political drawbacks. So Stony Man was given a chance to try to solve the problem before the cruise missiles or the Airborne was given the job.

McCarter took a silent survey of his commandos before turning back to the podium. "Let's hear the rest of it," he said.

"You will have some assistance," Katz said, "in the form of UAV ECM, decoy and strike aircraft. We feel that if we can suck some of their assets away with diversionary measures, we can open a window for you."

"Keep going," McCarter said.

"We will have an RC-135 at our disposal, where Jack Grimaldi and I will direct the UAVs that have been programmed to confuse the enemy by simulating attacking forces, as well as give you fresh recon data."

"Isn't that going to tweak the Russian Air Defense Command?" McCarter asked.

"These are all stealth unmanned vehicles, the new Tier III UAVs. They were field-tested over Kosovo, where they proved to be immune to missile radars. Since the target has only air-traffic-control radar and the two SAM launchers, we think they'll be okay in that level of air defense. And, of course, we're going to take the SAMs out as our opening number."

Katz shrugged. "Even if we lose one or two, it

won't be that big a deal. Just another couple of mil off of next year's Defense Department's budget.''

"I'd rather have an armored division," McCarter said. "But I guess we can give this a try."

"Good." Katz had been sure that McCarter would come through in the end. When the day came that he didn't, Stony Man would cease to exist. "After we go over the details of the target update and the UAV attack plan, I'll need you guys to go to the mission-prep area and get your gear sorted out."

He glanced up at the clock on the wall. "You're scheduled to be wheels up in less than four hours."

THE B-2 STEALTH BOMBER crew members were in full combat mode as they approached Russian airspace. They were going up against the air-defense systems of the Russian Federation this time rather than some Third World pesthole that hardly had an air force, much less a working radar network.

This particular crew had been chosen for the flight because it had been live-fire battle tested during the short Kosovo bombing campaign. The crew members had tested their radar-evading skills while delivering two-thousand-pound, GPS-guided smart bombs to their targets and had them down cold. But again, while the Serbs weren't as technologically disadvantaged as the Afghans, they had been equipped with obsolete Soviet radars that had been easy to confuse.

That might not be the case this time, but the crew was ready for it.

At the worst, they would be going up against the very same radar systems that their aircraft had been designed to defeat. At the best, the federation's National Air Defense Forces would be in the same sorry state of readiness that the rest of the Russian army and navy was. Whatever came, though, they had to be ready for it. Their lives were on the line, as well as those of the men riding in the Pressurized Personnel Pod in the bomber's bomb bay.

In the B-2's right-hand seat, the command pilot, LTC Jake Evers, flexed the fingers of his Nomex flying gloves, a nervous habit left over from his low-level B-52 days. He was getting too old for this.

"Feet dry," Major Fred Wilks, the copilot, announced as the B-2 entered Russian airspace. Originally "feet dry" had been a Vietnam War naval aviator's code word used to tell the aircraft carrier's combat information center that an aircraft had passed over a coastline. Since then, it had migrated into the Air Force lexicon to mean arrival over enemy territory, water or not.

For this Sneaky Pete mission, the B-2 was carrying an additional crew member, an EWO, or Electronics Warfare Officer. His job was to run the electronic countermeasures suite to confuse and befuddle the enemy by every electronic means possible. That was a much easier job on a B-2 than it had been on the old

B-52s the EWO had served on before. The difference in the plane's radar signature alone almost made his job redundant.

Nose on to a probing radar set, the lumbering old B-52s had a radar cross section of seventy meters squared. That was like trying to sneak something the radar size of a football field through the sky. The stealth bomber, however, had an RCS of one-tenth of a meter squared. That was 3.9 inches squared, less than two packs of smokes lying side by side. A sparrow in flight had a larger RCS than a B-2.

Even so, a low RCS wasn't the total solution to hiding a 172-foot-wide plane in the sky. The ECM suite included radar jammers that operated in a number of modes depending on what the enemy was using. However, on a mission like this, it was better not to use the jammers unless it was absolutely necessary. Activating the jammer was like trying to hide in a dark room while at the same time loudly announcing that you were in the room. You were hard to see, but there was no doubt that you were there.

To help the B-2 stay hidden, it was also infrared radiation masked. With the Russians using a mix of radar-guided and heat-seeking missiles on their interceptors, the bomber's IR signature also had to be reduced. Most heat seekers homed in on a jet's high-temperature exhaust plume, but sneaking a peek at a hot engine intake worked almost as well. A great deal of thought had gone into the design of the B-2's engine nacelles to keep down the IR signature. In addition, outside air was injected into the exhaust stream to cool it before it exited. As a last resort to defeat an enemy missile that achieved an IR lock on, the B-2 mounted a Blackhole IR jammer in the tail that pulsed high-energy infrared flashes to confuse the idiot brains of the missiles.

Even with all this *Star Wars* gear on board an airplane Buck Rogers would have been proud of, there was still that moment of truth when the bomb bay doors had to be opened to let their passengers exit the aircraft. Hanging the huge doors in the wind below the plane played merry hell with their radar signature. In fact, it was kind of like jumping up and down in front of an enraged bull while waving a red flag.

The door's exposed edges were notched with sixty-degree sawtooth shapes to help bounce the radar waves away, but that wasn't much protection. That was why the Pressurized Personnel Pod had been designed to spit the passengers out like a crazed watermelon eater in turbo mode. Even so, a mere thirty-second exposure to an up-to-date Russian radar set manned by a sober operator could spell disaster.

Once spotted, the B-2 would have to do some fancy dancing to break the lock and fade back into the night sky again.

That was why the EWO was sweating bullets.

"Full ECM mode," he reported to the pilot. "Everything nominal."

"Keep it that way, EWO," Evers growled.

"Roger that, sir." The EWO didn't even look up as he answered.

AT THE FEET DRY report, McCarter was on the intercom with the copilot, who would be activating their drop. He, too, was fully aware that jumping into Mother Russia wasn't the same gig as dropping over the barren wastelands of Afghanistan. He was content, though, to leave the details of the trip to the DZ to the blue suiters. He was paid to jump; they were paid to get him there.

This time, McCarter would lead the drop and Hawkins would take the trail position to make sure that Waters got out safely. In fact, they *were* going to buddy jump. Even though Hawkins himself had suggested that they do it this way, the situation wasn't thrilling him. The habit of jumping out of perfectly good airplanes provided a man with several of the world's more interesting scenarios for disaster. Of those, buddy jumping was well at the top of the list.

To help reduce the danger of two men landing on one man's legs and ruining him, Hawkins was going to cut his jumping buddy loose at fifteen hundred feet, deploy his chute for him and let him land all by himself. He had come through one parachute landing intact in Afghanistan and he just might luck out yet again. If he didn't? Well, there was always the shallow-grave option.

But now that the DARPA man had proved himself, it would be a real shame to have to shoot him like a horse just because he'd broken his leg.

"Remember," Hawkins told Waters again over the com link. "When I cut you loose, you're going to lose the com link until we reach the ground. So make sure that you know what you have to do before we separate."

"I think I've got it," Waters answered like a schoolboy reciting his multiplication tables. "You'll cut me loose at fifteen hundred feet and I'll watch the altimeter. The chute will automatically deploy at one thousand. But if it doesn't, I have two seconds to hit the manual release."

"That's about it," Hawkins said. "After we deploy, I'll be right in front of you, and you need to guide on the red light I'll be showing on the back of my helmet. Remember what I said about steering with the toggles. And when you see the ground come up, pull hard on both of them equally to cushion the landing shock. It'll be a lot less than what you felt the first time on that static-line jump."

Waters's heart was pounding so hard that the thought of a little thump when he hit the ground didn't scare him at all. This time he was worried about his chances of surviving to be able to do that at all. The trip down riding on another man's back was much more of a concern. If something went wrong, they'd both die.

"And—" Hawkins couldn't keep himself from re-minding him again "—be sure to keep your body stiff with your arms at your sides and your legs together all the way down. I'll do all the skydiving part to keep us on track. You just hang there and enjoy the ride."

Waters wasn't too sure how enjoyable this was go-ing to be, but it was too late for him to back out now.

When the copilot gave them the five-minute warn-ing, James and Encizo helped Waters climb up on Hawkins's back and hook up to the buddy-jump rig. When every hook-up had been triple-checked, all he could do was wait.

A second after the PPP pod doors opened, Mc-Carter led the drop. He was followed in short order by the rest of Phoenix Force minus Hawkins. The Able Team trio, Carl Lyons, Rosario Blancanales and Gadgets Schwarz, dropped after them. Giving Schwarz a couple of seconds to fully clear the aircraft, Hawkins took a deep breath and launched himself and Waters out into the cold night sky.

Above him, the batlike B-2 banked away for its flight back to Japan.

THE GPS SYSTEM SLAVED to McCarter's helmet dis-play allowed him to keep to their flight plan on the way down with no problem. The drop zone was a natural clearing in the woods and it showed up well on his HUD. All he had to do was keep it centered in his face plate.

At the end of the spread-out file of sky divers, Hawkins was finding that having Waters strapped to his back was messing with his aerodynamics, big-time. His effective weight had doubled, but his frontal area that created his drag to slow him down hadn't. The end result was that he was falling faster than usual.

To keep from running into Gadgets Schwarz in front of him, he tucked in his right arm so he would sideslip in that direction. When he flew out too far, he corrected a bit to come back in. The DZ was small, and he didn't want to be too far off of it when he cut Waters loose.

Even though McCarter was leading the drop, Hawkins had been keeping his own watch on his GPS locator and altimeter. As he passed through the three-thousand-foot mark, he clicked the com link. "Get ready," he told Waters. "I'm going to cut you loose in four seconds."

"I'm ready," Waters called back. His answer was proof of the victory of confidence over everything his imagination was telling him. And he had a vivid imagination.

When the release came, Hawkins slipped to the side to get out of Waters's way while his chute popped. Turning his head, he made sure that Waters's chute had deployed fully. That was the signal for him to deploy.

Grabbing his own toggles at the last minute, he braked as hard as he could, but still hit hard. This time he did a full PLF to soak up the shock.

"WHERE'S WATERS?" Hawkins looked around the drop zone as he punched his harness release.

McCarter checked his tac display. "In the trees. Over to the left."

Hawkins clicked his NVGs up and went to IR. A quick scan showed him a man-size heat source halfway up one of the tall trees. The branches obscured his features, but he could only be their missing rocket scientist.

"Craig, old buddy," Hawkins sent over the com link, "is that you hiding up there in that tree like a little old possum?"

"T.J.," Waters replied, trying to keep his panic out of his voice, "I'm caught up here. I can't get down."

Hawkins refrained from laughing. "Hang in there, Craig, we'll retrieve you."

"Let's get him," James told Hawkins.

"I just hope he didn't break anything." Hawkins sounded concerned.

James laughed. "For a complete cherry, he's been lucky so far."

The IR feature on their NVGs made it easy for the two commandos to reach the particular pine tree on the edge of the clearing that had abruptly snagged Waters out of the air. Being a pine tree with upswept limbs, his canopy was fully trapped. Worse yet, he was a good twenty feet above the ground. Were he to punch the harness release, he'd break something for sure on the way down.

"Waters," Hawkins said over the com link, "you okay?"

"I'm fine, but I can't get loose."

"Don't even try," Hawkins cautioned him. "We're right below you. Just relax up there while I climb up with a rope."

The upswept limbs of the pine made it easy for Hawkins to climb up to where Waters was trapped. When he reached the trapped man, he grabbed a handful of the risers and pulled him close enough to grab his harness.

"Get hold of the limb," Hawkins said, "and hang on. I'm going to release your harness."

Waters did as he had been told and felt the tug of the risers break away.

"Okay," Hawkins said. "Now we get to climb down."

Once he had both feet firmly on the ground, the DARPA man swore that this was the absolute last time he was ever going to jump out of a plane that wasn't on fire.

CHAPTER SIXTEEN

Stony Man Farm, Virginia

Barbara Price paced the floor in front of the big-screen monitors in the Annex as if she were in a cage. One unintended but welcome consequence of the new facility was that it gave her more than enough room to burn off her nervous energy. She hadn't had that luxury in the old farmhouse Computer Room and had had to take it outside on the grounds when she felt the urge to unstress.

Even though she had room enough to stretch her legs, Hal Brognola wasn't here for her to snarl at this time. She knew that she sometimes took her frustration out on him unjustly. But that was only because he was the closest she could get to the man whose ass she really wanted to bite. Brognola always did his level best to protect the men of Stony Man; she had no doubts about that. But he was also always the bearer of bad news that all too often originated from the Man in the Oval Office, and she couldn't rage at him.

Of the Computer Room staff, only Aaron Kurtzman paid any attention to Price's pacing. The amount of energy she was expending told him volumes. Even so, he knew well enough to let her alone until he had some good news to pass on. Brognola wasn't the only one who bore scars from the sharp side of her tongue. She'd taken a strip off him on more than one occasion, but he wouldn't trade places with her for anything.

He didn't have the sheer strength of heart that it took to send men out to die day after day as she did.

"They're down," he called out, "and everyone made it intact, even the rocket scientist."

Price stopped in midstride. "Show me the DZ," she told Hunt Wethers.

Wethers clicked to one of the big monitors, which flashed on to display a scene of the top view of a dark forest clearing in the mountains. The titled icons flashed on to show the positions of the individual men on the ground. The ALOCS suits had personal locators built into their circuitry that could be read from an orbiting satellite or a spy plane.

All of the locators were showing green, which meant that the commandos were alive. If their hearts stopped beating, they would flash red.

"Everyone's confirmed down and alive," he said, counting the icons.

The relief that washed over Price's face was immediately replaced by a new look of concern. Now they had to get into that damned place without being seen, and there were eighty men dug in around it and on the lookout for them.

"Give me the target area," she ordered.

The monitor changed to show an overview of Forestry Station 105.

"The enemy troop positions?" she asked.

Kurtzman's fingers tapped in the icons for the positions and defenses of the Eighth Missile Security Company. Although eighty men weren't that many to find on a modern battlefield, the odds the Stony Man warriors were facing weren't even close to being equal. If Katzenelenbogen's UAV deception plan didn't work, to say that they would be in extreme danger would be an understatement.

With Katzenelenbogen in the air with the UAVs and Brognola staying on in Japan, Price would be directly controlling the mission from the Farm this time. On a job with this much political scrutiny, however, she probably wouldn't be able to call the shots as quickly as she would like. Too many of the decisions would have to be bounced off of Brognola, who might have to take them to the Oval Office before she could make the call.

She was able, though, to command the surveillance of the mission area herself, and she had it saturated. Thanks to Kurtzman's cyber begging, borrowing and flat-out stealing, they had a stellar lineup watching the remote site in Siberia. This sky spying was made much easier this time because of the unique properties of the ALOCS suits the Stony Men were wearing. From the outset, they had been designed to interface with satellites to enhance a number of their functions.

Not only did the ALOCS locator beacons help her keep track of the men, but she could also log into the men's HUD displays and see what they were actually seeing. It wasn't instantaneous, though; no one had yet been able to twist the laws of physics to defeat Einstein. But the signal lag from the ground to the satellite and then back down to the Farm wasn't that bad, just a few seconds.

It was so "real time" that she had to keep remembering that she was only to be an observer and adviser, not a combat commander.

"When's first light over there?" she asked.

"Another four and a half hours," Kurtzman said. "Zero five thirty local time."

"I'm going to get a nap. Wake me then."

"Will do."

Siberia

AFTER DESTROYING all traces of their jump gear and scattering the ashes in the bare rocks, McCarter put the men into a defensive perimeter while he checked in with the Farm. Breaking into this target wasn't something they could just charge ahead and do. To pull this off, they needed all the information they could get about it and every change in status as it occurred.

Keying his satcom link, he connected with Aaron Kurtzman. "Bear," he said, "how does it look?"

"Quiet," Kurtzman replied. "There have been no changes in their positions since the last update."

"Good," McCarter said. "We'll hold here as planned until first light before moving out."

"Sleep tight."

"Right."

"Okay, lads," McCarter said, "no changes, so go into your rotations and let's get all the rest we can."

IT WAS well after midnight when Major Yuri Polinski walked into his makeshift command post in the barracks at the forestry station after making an unannounced inspection of his unit's positions. He stopped and glanced up at the map overlay showing the positions he had just inspected.

"How is the sensor board?" he asked the young lieutenant on duty.

"Everything is in the green, Comrade Major," the officer replied. "None of the sensors have been activated, and the patrols report nothing out of the ordinary."

Rather than spread out his men too thinly, Polinski had chosen to have a tight inner perimeter and let the sensors provide him with early warning. Nonetheless, he had put three walking patrols in front of his positions during the hours of darkness.

"Did the technical sergeant get all of the sensors dialed in to match the movement of the wild animals?" he asked.

As always, as soon as the sensors had been set in place, the local wildlife started setting them off. The devices were useful, but there were more animals here in Siberia than they were used to working with.

"Yes, Comrade Major," the duty officer replied. "We shouldn't get any more false readings."

"Good." Polinski took one last look at the situation board. "I will be in my quarters. Wake me at first light."

The young lieutenant stiffened to attention. "Yes, Comrade Major."

The duty officer remained standing until Polinski departed. He was relatively new to the unit and was anxious to make a good impression on his new commanding officer. He still didn't have a firm grasp on exactly what the unit was doing in this remote location, but as a junior lieutenant, he didn't need to. He wasn't paid to think. The major would do that for him.

WHEN YURI POLINSKI reached his quarters, he didn't drop off to sleep right away. Even though he had checked each and every element of his company's deployment, this mission was too important for him to be complacent. Too much was riding on the ability of his unit to secure this area from any and all enemies of the state.

The young major was a throwback to the glory days of the undefeated Red Army. He had missed participating in the Afghan debacle that had exposed to the world the reality, warts and all, of the cumbersome Soviet military system. Part of him wished that he had been given a chance to face his trial by fire as had so many of his military academy classmates. But enough of them had come home in pine boxes, missing limbs or badly burned that he had learned secondhand what they had faced in that barren land.

He learned that in all too many cases, these valiant young officers were sacrificed by a military riddled with corruption all the way to the top: incompetent officers who were willing to sacrifice their troops to hold on to their jobs or just to be awarded medals; weapons systems that had been totally unsuited to the task at hand; drug use among the troops, commanders selling supplies to the enemy; drunkenness on duty. The list was endless. And it had all contributed to the first major defeat of the Red Army.

This lesson had been burned into him, and he would do everything he could to see that he never did anything to shame Mother Russia. It also gave him the reason he lived for now, rebuilding the invincible

Red Army, and was why he had thrown his fate at the feet of General Fedor Komarov.

The new Red Army that General Komarov envisioned wouldn't be a throwback to the army of the Afghan war. It would instead be a revival of the Red Army that had crushed the fascists in the Great Patriotic War before the cold war rot had set in. This new army would promote and award only those who had proved themselves in the caldron of battle. It would punish all those, regardless of rank, who defamed the military.

As routine as this mission had seemed so far, it was his chance to prove that he was up to the task. It was also his first independent command and a good command it was. His troops of the Eighth Missile Security Company were among the most well trained in the entire army today. In his mind, even members of the vaunted Spetsnaz weren't up to the standards of his men. The Spetsnaz were good—he knew that because he had often trained against them—but they had sold out completely to the new regime. Their officers were totally committed to propping up the federation even at the cost of their honor. He would never betray his officer's oath for any politician.

He had to admit that this wasn't the kind of mission he had envisioned his first major operation would be. But he knew that the general's eye was on him, and how he performed here would determine his fitness for higher command. And perform he would. He wasn't sure of the general's assessment that an American strike force would dare attack a site inside Mother Russia and risk going to war. It was difficult to know what the oft-changing American political climate would cause them to do. In many ways, they were more corrupt than the Moscow criminals who called themselves the federation government.

Nonetheless, as long as he was under the general's eye, he would act as if the attack were a foregone conclusion, and his men would see it that way, as well.

MAJOR POLINSKI WASN'T the only one who was working late at Forestry Station 105. Artyom Chazov was in Hangar 3 going over the day's problems with his chief engineer, Boris Binova. The preflight ground testing of Aerial Vehicle 2 wasn't going as quickly as either one of them would have liked, and the pressure was on them to speed things up.

"I'm still having trouble synchronizing the pulse phasing switching of the main power generator," Binova grumbled. "It's the same damned thing that delayed the flight of the first machine."

Something as radical and complicated as the Ch-101, as Chazov had dubbed the craft in the Russian fashion with the initials of his last name and the project number, took time to be perfected. Its pulse-phased, magnetic-drive unit alone was unique in the history of aviation. Using the gravitational fields of

Earth to propel a machine had long been a dream of engineers, but it was a dream that no one had seriously thought would ever become a reality.

He had to admit, however, that the drive wasn't completely of his own design. He had found it in the systems of an earlier machine he had been given to work with. As a good Russian, he had never asked who had worked on the earlier craft. If his superiors had wanted him to know, they would have told him. Whoever it had been, though, he had been a genius. That this unknown engineer had lost his project merely indicated that he hadn't been politically correct. It wasn't a judgment of his engineering skills.

When he had been given the system, though, it hadn't performed properly, and he was the man who had made it work first in the lab and had then taken it to its fullest potential as a power plant. The craft's defensive shield was an offshoot of the generator's electromagnetic characteristics, and there were indications that it had been the original purpose of the magnetic generator.

The laser weapon that made the craft so valuable for what Komarov had in mind hadn't originated with him, either. The laser had been developed by another design team as a deep-space weapon, and it had been discarded when the Soviet Union collapsed and its funding dried up. Unlike most of the experimental Soviet space technology, this system had been salvaged from the dump and spirited away.

Even though the craft parked in the hangar wasn't one hundred percent his, Chazov felt that it was more his child than any human could ever be. He had built it to put his mark on aviation history and soon on the history of Mother Russia herself. When those thoughts passed through his mind, the fact that the craft wasn't really his vanished.

The director glanced at his watch. "It is late, Boris. Get some sleep and we will get back to this in the morning. We cannot afford to make mistakes, and tired men do not think straight."

Binova stood. "In the morning, then."

Chazov stayed seated and went back to the diagram of the phase pulse unit.

AT FIRST LIGHT, the Phoenix Force commandos had a cold breakfast before moving out. While they were masters of the quick night attack, this was one time that they were going to make a daylight ground recon before they launched.

Before they moved out, McCarter linked to the Farm for the updates. "Give it to me, Bear," he said.

"Same as last time," Aaron Kurtzman replied. "They stood to at first light and started feeding by sections. They haven't started work yet, but I'll let you know when they do and where they're working."

"We're moving out now to test the defenses."

"Take care."

Moving through the forests of Siberia was much

more to the liking of the Stony Man commandos than crossing the rocky deserts of Afghanistan had been. The early-morning mist would have impeded regular troops, but the ALOCS vision devices burned right through it and didn't slow them. Their DZ had been in a mountain clearing, but when they reached the valley below, the land was flat and the trees weren't so thick that they blocked movement. They did, though, provide good cover and concealment.

It was perfect terrain for an infiltration route.

Since McCarter had Carl Lyons's men, as well as Craig Waters with them this time, he'd gone to a diamond formation for the initial movement phase. The Phoenix Force commandos were on the outer edges of the formation, with Able Team in the center as the reserve force and the DARPA man's keepers.

AN HOUR'S MARCH saw Phoenix Force at the edge of what Kurtzman's satellite recon had told him was the boundary of the forestry station's defensive perimeter. McCarter called a halt and keyed his com link. "Gadgets," he said, "it's time for you to do your thing."

While the others went into a defensive semicircle, Schwarz opened his bag of professional tricks and took out several detection devices. Leaving the others behind, he moved from tree to tree, testing the entire EM spectra as he went.

A hundred yards farther on, he took cover behind

a large tree and keyed his com link. "David, I'm getting a lot of ground-sensor readings," he reported. "They've got the whole tamale out there."

"Can we defeat them?" McCarter asked.

"The ALOCS should handle most of them, the IR and MAD detectors. But I'm getting a Doppler radar reading I'm not so sure about."

"Won't that give them false readings when the deer walk through the area?" McCarter asked. Doppler radars had been used a long time ago by NATO forces, but had proved not to be very reliable in actual battlefield use. One of the biggest causes of false readings was wildlife.

"They can set the threshold high enough to filter out the local animals," Schwarz replied, "but I'm not sure that we can pretend to be deer and walk on through it. Our weapons are going to give too solid of a return."

"How about doing that low-crawl number we used to sneak up on that flying saucer?" Hawkins asked.

"That's going to be a long crawl," Schwarz pointed out. "And if they've got seismic sensors, too, they'd pick us up in a minute."

"Let's try another section," McCarter suggested.

"Let me back out of here before you move out," Schwarz replied.

He had a nasty feeling that no matter where they went, they were going to run into this kind of defense.

Someone didn't want unexpected visitors dropping in. They had all day, though, so they would keep looking for the window someone had left open. There was always a window.

CHAPTER SEVENTEEN

Siberia

After probing almost all of the perimeter, Schwarz discovered that the side of the complex facing the mountain wasn't as heavily guarded by sensors as were the approaches from the plain. Since the terrain was so rugged and thickly forested, the Russians had to have thought that it was impassable. The Stony Man commandos would be happy to dissuade them of that idea come nightfall.

Now that they had their weak point, the commandos pulled far enough back into the woods to be completely out of the range of any security patrols. After radioing their findings to both Katzenelenbogen and the Farm, they prepared for the night's activities.

Because the probe had been such a slow process, Craig Waters had been able to keep up with the commandos. He was a little concerned, though, about the upcoming night movement. At the Japanese stopover, he had been outfitted with the full ALOCS equipment, and Hawkins had given him a quick tutorial on its use. That would let him see in the dark and stay in communication, but he was concerned about keeping up with them. As slow as it had been, the day's walk in the woods had about beat him into the ground. Particularly the withdrawal to their current position. If they moved out that fast tonight, he'd be hard-pressed to keep up.

Since he had nothing to check over, Waters ate and rested. When one of the men approached him, he stood.

"We really didn't get a chance to talk in Japan," Schwarz said, extending his hand. "Everyone calls me Gadgets."

"Craig Waters."

Schwarz looked him up and down. "The word around here is that you're a rocket scientist."

Waters grinned. As long as he was with these guys, they weren't going to let the joke go. "Yup. I work for DARPA and do all that rocket scientist kind of stuff."

Schwarz grinned back. "I thought you guys were too smart to get sucked into something like this."

Waters leaned closer. "Don't believe everything you see on TV. I've known some real dumb-ass rocket scientists in my day. And, when I get back, I'm going to put my name on the top of the list."

Schwarz laughed. "You're okay, Craig."

THE END OF ANOTHER DAY saw the last of Major Yuri Polinski's Eighth Missile Security Company's defenses completed. The last position to be finished was the command bunker that would coordinate the defense if they were attacked. The only thing he wasn't pleased with was a shortage of sensors in one of the sectors.

The Stony Man commandos weren't the only ones who had seen the back side of Forestry Station 105 as being the best avenue of approach. Polinski had also spotted it as a weak point and had assigned one of his foot patrols to cover it until he could get more sensors planted there. He had gambled in using his sensors to cover the more likely approaches first, but he had covered his bet with men on the ground.

He assigned standard three-man walking patrols to work the flat land approaches, but the mountain patrol was a heavily armed, ten-man combat squad. If they ran into trouble, he wanted them to be able to hold on until he could get reinforcements to them.

As HE HAD DONE the evening before, Director Chazov met with his chief engineer to go over the day's work and plan for the next. The phase pulse controller was acting up now, and it was as complicated as the generator itself.

"You know how it is with that damned thing," Boris Binova grumbled. "If the harmonics aren't exactly right, we run the risk of burning out one of the cells and getting a dangerous surge."

The miniature nuclear power cells that powered the craft were standard Russian spacecraft issue. The original power source for the main drive had not only been unidentifiable, but also unrepairable. While powerful, these replacement power cells didn't like voltage spikes.

"Just keep working on it, Boris," Chazov said. "The general wants the machine to fly as soon as possible. But don't rush. We can't afford a mistake."

"It was better before he wanted to use it as a weapon," Binova grumbled. "We didn't have all this pressure on us and we could take our time."

"I know," Chazov replied. "But we have to work with what we've been given. We've been through worse before, old comrade."

"That's what I'm afraid of."

As soon as dark fell, the Stony Man team moved out to its launch point. They had to go halfway up the mountain to work their way around to the route they had chosen for the probe. But their ALOCS equipment should make it as easy as it had been when they'd done it during the day.

An hour and a half later, they were in position to start their approach.

McCarter went to Craig Waters. "Look," he said as he took him aside, "I decided to leave you here until we penetrate the sensor ring. When we're inside, I'll send someone back for you."

Waters was eager to get inside the base, find the machine and do his thing, but he also had learned to trust these professionals when they said he needed to keep out of the way while they worked.

"I'll be here."

WATERS WAS WATCHING the team's progress on his HUD when he heard Russian voices that sounded alarmingly close. With the way that sound carried in the trees, he wasn't sure how far away they actually were. But if he could hear them, they were too damned close.

"Oh, shit," he muttered as he keyed his com link. "David, this is Waters. I've got a Russian patrol coming up on me, and I don't think I can dodge them."

"Hang tight," McCarter radioed back. "We'll come back and get you."

"I don't think you're going to have time." Waters reassessed his situation as he clearly heard footsteps coming towards him. "They're almost on top of me."

"Waters," McCarter almost shouted. "Hang on."

"It's too late."

Not wanting to be shot by pure reaction, Waters took a deep breath and called out in Russian, "Over here!"

As if by magic, half a dozen Russian soldiers popped out of cover, their weapons leveled at him. Raising his hands slowly, he said, "I'm not armed."

"On the ground!" one of the Russians commanded. "Now!"

Being careful not to make any sudden moves, Waters obeyed. On the way down, he hit the kill switch on the wrist pad of his ALOCS suit.

MAJOR POLINSKI WAS walking his perimeter when he got the call from his operations center reporting that one of the patrols had captured an intruder and was returning with him. "Send my vehicle," he ordered, "and two men. Tell the patrol that I'm on the way."

To say that Polinski was surprised by this development would have been a gross understatement. Regardless of the efforts he had made to secure the sprawling base, he had never really expected to have to fend off intruders. This incident had suddenly made the general's concerns very real for him and he was angry. What right did the United States have to invade Russian territory?

Racing out of the command post, he slid into the passenger seat of his GAZ. "Get moving," he snapped at his driver.

The driver cranked up and hit the gas.

BY THE TIME the Stony Man commandos got back to the area where they had left Waters, the place was swarming with Russians. There was no way that they were going to be able to intervene and free him. If they got in a firefight now, the mission would be out the window. Their only chance was to pull back unseen and reevaluate this mess.

Flashing his orders to the others, McCarter and the Stony Man commandos silently withdrew into the woods. Once they were clear, McCarter halted long enough to make a call to Katzenelenbogen.

"Katz," he said, "we have a problem."

"We saw his ALOCS beacon go out," Katz replied. "What happened?"

McCarter quickly recounted what had happened ending by saying, "We're canceling and pulling back. I don't want to risk walking into a hornet's nest. They're going to have their blood up tonight."

"That's probably wise," Katz replied. "Give me a call once you're safe for the night."

"Will do."

Stony Man Farm, Virginia

AARON KURTZMAN wheeled his chair around to face Barbara Price. "He was alive when he was captured," he stated flatly. "His locator beacon was still showing green when it suddenly cut off."

"What would happen if his circuitry was damaged in the process of killing him?" she asked.

"Then it would go dark, yes," Kurtzman agreed. "But since we heard Russian voices over his com link as he was surrendering, I don't think they killed him outright. It could be that he punched the autodestruct button and fried the circuits himself.''

One feature of the ALOCS equipment was that it had a kill switch to destroy the electronics so they couldn't be captured and used by an enemy. Doing that would give the same locator result as the wearer dying.

Price had to admit that it had taken a lot of guts on Waters's part to key his com link to send a warning to the Stony Man commandos. For a lab scientist with no military field experience, he was showing great courage, as well as the expected smarts. Maybe that was what it took to become a rocket scientist, guts and intelligence. His profession took a lot of ribbing in the common culture, but he had single-handedly rebutted all those jokes with his bravery. It would be a shame to lose him.

''Hook me up with Katz,'' she told Kurtzman.

Atsugi, Japan

HAL BROGNOLA LOOKED as if his favorite dog had just died as he turned away from the radio. He had to pass this on to the Oval Office, and the response he knew he was going to get would make him wish that he had died instead. Even though the President had agreed to have Craig Waters join the Stony Man mission, the Man had a bad habit of forgetting minor details like that. Particularly when they had resulted in a major screwup. It was a well-known D.C. maxim that defecation rolled downhill. And this time it was going to roll down on him and it wasn't going to stop anytime soon.

Yakov Katzenelenbogen was no more happy about this development than was his boss. To make a silk purse out of this pig's ear, he was going to have to pull a tactical rabbit out of a Siberian hat ASAP. The problem was that when the bad guys had snatched one of your men, you had few options to remedy the situation. In fact, only two. Leave the poor bastard behind or shoot your way in to try to get him out. He didn't have to poll the President's views to know that neither would be an acceptable option to him.

In fact, if past history meant anything, once the Man heard of the situation, he would start loading up his third option. But while it might calm the President's fears to obliterate the evidence of an American incursion with a nuclear fireball, it wasn't acceptable to Stony Man. Incinerating Phoenix Force and Able Team simply wasn't on.

Going into mental high gear, Katz decided to open his game by tossing a grenade into the discussion.

"Hal," he said, "when you talk to the President, you might want to make sure that he's fully aware there's a Russian army missile security company guarding that place now. I don't think that nuking them is going to go over too well with the Russian general staff. Their boys and all that.'' He shrugged. ''They aren't going to like it if we blow them to atoms.''

Brognola instantly knew where the wily Katz was heading with this. ''What's your solution?''

''Well,'' Katz said, ''the Man is worried about the space station, and rightfully so I might add. But as long as that thing, whatever it is, remains on the ground in Siberia, it's no danger to us. And we haven't yet established that there actually is a second machine. If it turns out that there isn't another one, the problem is solved.''

Not exactly, but Brognola didn't say a word. He was, however, listening intently. The old master was at the top of his game again.

''Then,'' Katz said, ''we've been working under the assumption that this is a 'rogue' operation, but now we have Russian army troops guarding the site. This tells me that one of two things is going on there, and neither of them is very good. One is that this 'rogue' site has clandestine backing from a larger group. For sake of argument, let's just say that they're someone who's trying to overthrow the federation. You know, the old boys who think their pensions aren't big enough. And for further sake of argument, let's say that they think zapping our space station will help their cause.''

Brognola didn't like to hear that, but he knew that it was true. The transition from the Soviet Union to the Russian Federation hadn't gone smoothly. In fact, it could hardly have gone much worse. Would-be coup leaders ranging from the far, far right to the totally whacked-out left popped up almost monthly. Then, of course, there was the constant threat from the Russian Mafia. And of all the threats, the Russian Mob was the most troubling.

"Or," Katz concluded, "it could be that the attack against us was sanctioned by Moscow as a black operation, and that's even worse."

"How do we deal with it?"

"Well," Katz said, "first we try to convince the President to let us do the work he keeps us around for. Try to get him to hold off on the nukes unless it look like there actually is a second or even third machine and they are preparing to launch for another shot at the space station."

"The Space Command brass isn't going to like that," Brognola predicted.

"Tell them to cool their jets and let us grunts do our job. They still have a couple of Guardians left, and they did a number on the bogey before. We can keep a constant overwatch on the Siberian site and catch a new launch when, and if, it happens. That would give the astronauts time to evacuate the station if need be and let the Guardians engage at a longer range than before."

"You're leaving out a few details."

"Quite a few, actually, but first things first. I'll get

with David and see what we can come up with to try to get Waters out of there. I know the President isn't comfortable having a high-level DARPA guy hanging in the wind. He knows too much. Then, of course, there's that damned flying saucer. If there's actually another one hiding around there somewhere, one way or the other we have to take it out. The Man's right that it's too dangerous to be allowed to exist outside of our control.

"But first we have to put the cruise missiles back in the barn and shut the door."

"I'm on it," Brognola said. "And while I'm arguing with him, get with Barbara and David and see what we can realistically put together. And make sure David knows that I don't want them to put it all on the line for this one. If the Man has to make a glowing hole in Siberia to deal with it, that's better than wasting our people."

Katz had no problem suggesting a nuclear solution when it looked like nothing else would work. But any time that Russia was involved, he liked to swing way over to the cautious side of the road. Nonetheless, no matter how this worked out, Hal's heart was in the right place.

"And while you're selling him on a nuclear stand-down for the moment, how about asking him if we can get some help from certain air assets."

"Like?"

"I want to upgrade the deception plan. I'd like to

get my hands on a Global Hawk and a few of her nastier relatives. I happen to know that there's a detachment in South Korea that should have what we need.''

''Good idea. I'll try it.''

''Make it work,'' Katz said seriously. ''Short of pulling them out right now, it's the best chance they have.''

CHAPTER EIGHTEEN

Siberia

The Stony Man commandos pulled back from the forestry station's perimeter and headed deep into the forested flank of the mountain. Once they were a safe distance away, they found a good defensive position and dug in. They would wait there until Katz and Brognola could hash this out with the President and decide where they would go from here.

While they waited for the word to come down from on high, though, they examined their options on their own. Orders from the Oval Office were fine, but they owned their own fates, not the President.

"I'm for going in there after him," Hawkins said flatly. "I've never lost a rocket scientist on a mission yet, and I'm not going to start with this one."

"You've got to watch that buddy-jumping stuff," James said, "but I won't ask if you don't tell."

"Look," Hawkins replied, "he's not one of us, but he's got more guts that I'd have in his position, that's for damned sure. How many jumps did you have under your belt before you did your first HALO?"

"At least it wasn't a buddy jump." James grinned.

"I'm with T.J.," Carl Lyons spoke for Able Team. "For the duration of this rat screw, as far as I'm concerned, Waters is one of us. Plus, we still have to see if we can pull this damned thing off. I didn't come all this way just to freeze my butt off in Siberia while Hal and Katz play pass-the-political-football with the Man. We have work to do."

"You go, Ironman," Hawkins said.

McCarter looked around at the rest of his team and saw nods. "When we go in, we're going to change our mission profile to a straight snatch and destroy. There's no way that those people down there are going to sit on their thumbs while we rifle through their filing cabinets and computers to get data for Space Command. Since they have Waters, there's a good chance they know we're out here somewhere and they'll be expecting us."

"That's if he talked," Encizo pointed out. "There hasn't been an increase in foot patrolling, so they might not have broken him yet. I don't see him as the kind of guy to start shooting off his mouth from the get-go. Like T.J. says, he's got guts."

"Good point," McCarter conceded.

"Carl," he said, turning to Lyons, "I'd like you and your guys to go in there and do what you do so well. Blow the damned place up. I'll give you Gary to lend a hand.''

Lyons didn't change expression. ''Can do.''

''While you're doing that, the rest of us will get Waters out and give you covering fire. Your first priority is that damned flying saucer, if it's there. Second priority is everything else in sight. Our only chance is to cause as much damage as we can to distract them.''

''How about that diversionary plan Katz mentioned?'' Rosario Blancanales asked.

''As far as I know, it's still laid on,'' McCarter replied. ''We'll have to wait to confirm the details. But, UAVs or not, we're going in.''

THE STONY MAN WARRIORS had already made their minds up when a call from Katzenelenbogen came in. ''Before you even get started,'' McCarter told him, ''you need to know that we're going to have a go at freeing Waters. We're not in the habit of leaving people behind.''

''I thought that you might feel that way, David.'' Katz chuckled. ''If you'll remember, we did work together for some time.''

''Rather.''

''Anyway,'' Katz began, launching into his spiel, ''I've got Hal working on getting the Man to back off and let you do your job. But I can tell you that if they have a second flying saucer down there and if it launches, everything's out the window. You're all going up in a mushroom cloud.''

''And?'' McCarter said.

''Just wanted to let you know.''

''We know.''

''With that out of the way,'' Katz said, ''the good news is that Hal's going to try to rustle up a little fire support for you.''

''I thought they were trying to keep this low-key?''

''This will be a little less than low-key, but I'm working on cutting the odds down a little.''

''I'm listening.''

''Along with the deception birds,'' Katz explained, ''I'm asking for a Global Hawk to be allocated to you along with a few loaded Strike Stars. I'm thinking that if I can get the Russians to believe that they're under a full-scale attack, they'll be too busy to notice you guys coming in the back door.''

''It beats us going in with our Johnsons leading, as you Yanks say,'' McCarter replied. ''When are you thinking of setting up this reverse Trojan horse?''

''I don't have all the edges nailed down, but I'm looking at tomorrow night.''

''That leaves our asses in the wind for twenty-four hours.''

''We'll have everything at our disposal watching over you, and if we see a threat, we'll get you out.''

''Since we have to wait,'' Schwarz cut in, ''how about we order out then. These MREs aren't cutting it. I'm up for a Big Mac, large fries and medium drink. Do they deliver in Siberia?''

"Only by cruise missile," Katz replied.

"Bummer."

WHEN MAJOR POLINSKI saw the captured American intruder, his first inclination was to shoot him on the spot as a spy. How dare a Yankee so brazenly invade Mother Russia? But a radio call to the general changed that. He forbade him to even question the man until he could interrogate him himself. Faced with specific orders, Polinski put his inclination on hold, but hoped to be given a chance to carry out the execution later. He took his duties very seriously.

To get the American out of his sight as much as to confine him, the major had him locked into the smallest bare room he could find in the main building. Until the general arrived the next morning, he didn't see any need to provide the spy with any amenities including food or water. If Komarov wanted him to eat, he would be fed then.

CRAIG WATERS HAD never been in jail before, but he'd seen enough James Bond movies to know how to act when he was locked up. The first thing he did was examine every inch of the small cell to see if there was anything he could use or any way to get out. He checked twice, but found nothing.

He didn't know if that was because he was a rocket

scientist, as T.J. had good-naturedly dubbed him, and didn't know what to look for or simply because it was absolutely bare and there was nothing to find.

And he was almost bare, as well. The first thing the Russians had done after he'd been driven to the base was to strip him of his ALOCS suit and give him a thin pair of Russian fatigues to wear. Without a jacket or a blanket, he was facing a cold Siberian night. Since his room was also bare of sleeping accommodations, he'd probably stay awake so he could keep moving to stay warm.

He wished that T.J. or his tough British leader were with him right now. They'd know how to get out of this mess. That was a skill they didn't teach at rocket scientist school.

Atsugi, Japan

BROGNOLA WASN'T UNAWARE that he was the bearer of bad news more often than he liked. It was a dirty job, but someone had to do it, and it went with being the leader of the Sensitive Operations Group. During his long career as a federal officer, he had always tried to faithfully and professionally carry out his orders as they were given to him. As long as he was taking Uncle Sam's money, that was part of the deal.

That didn't mean, though, that he always agreed with the orders he was given or who had given them to him. Orders were orders, but that didn't mean that he wouldn't try to bend them when he thought it was necessary and this was one of those times.

The President had reluctantly agreed to hold off on the nuke strike as long as the Russians didn't launch another flying saucer. He had also agreed to Katz's plan for the additional air assets. That should get the commandos in the back door and maybe give them the cover they would need while they were on-site. But that still left the withdrawal and extraction phase. To pull that off, McCarter would need all the help he could get, and Brognola knew where he could go to get it.

Katzenelenbogen wasn't the only sly weasel working for Stony Man. Brognola knew that he wasn't in Katz's class when it came to finding clever new ways to untie the old Gordian knot. He was, however, almost as well connected as the ex-Mossad agent. And he'd been in the connecting business for a long time.

It just so happened that he had the phone number of Vladimir Nefyodov, the Russian Federation's chief of the RSV. Nefyodov was a truly rational man, and they'd exchanged sensitive information before that their respective bosses hadn't known about. They had also worked together on several joint operations that had benefited both nations. It was time for more of this under-the-table cooperation.

Reaching for his secure phone, he dialed a number. "Vladimir," he said, "this is Hal Brognola."

"How fortunate that you have called, my imperialist spymaster friend.'' Nefyodov chuckled. ''I was just clearing my office so I could give you a call.''

Brognola didn't have to see it in black-and-white to know that the Russian had been making sure that there were no active listening or recording devices that might cause him problems later on. Of all of the millions of gadgets produced by modern technology, tape recorders had brought down more men of power than armored divisions. And nowhere on Earth was that more true than in Russia.

''What's on your mind?'' Brognola decided to let the Russian lead off.

''Well, as you know,'' Nefyodov started out, ''we Russians have always had a very strong interest in space travel. The first rockets in orbit, the first man in space, all that. Even after the competition with your NASA ended, some of the more interesting ventures our two nations have conducted since the end of that madness you called the cold war have been in space.''

''Interesting that you should mention that,'' Brognola said, trying to cut through the bazaar-bargaining routine that was so much a part of dealing with the Russians on anything, no matter how trivial. ''I wanted to talk to you about a recent incident we encountered in space.''

''I swear we had nothing to do with that.'' Nefyodov also got right to the point. ''On my brother's grave, I swear it. That was not one of our space vehicles.''

With that out of the way, Brognola got to the meat of the matter. "We know that the attacker wasn't a craft of the Russian Federation, Vladimir."

"I hear what you have not said, old friend."

"As always, your ears are as sharp as a fox's."

"I'm waiting," Nefyodov prodded him. Once the Russian spymaster smelled a clue, he was eager to drop the BS and get right at it.

"By any chance," Brognola said, "is the federation missing a small aerospace research project? Maybe something involving a radical new kind of technology that kind of fell out of the sky? Something that was put in a tightly secured agency for further examination?"

Nefyodov was silent for the longest time.

"Vladimir?" Brognola prompted him.

"When I was a young KGB officer, I was once given an assignment to take a convoy of Ministry of Interior troops to a remote location in the Ural Mountains to recover some aircraft wreckage. The assignment was unusual enough for the KGB, but I was really surprised when my superiors ordered me take a camera crew to document the recovery operation. But, as you remember, in those days one did not question one's orders."

"I do remember," Brognola said.

"Anyway, I followed my orders and a film was made of what we did. In case you might have seen it when it was shown on your television, I was the officer in the lead GAZ. I made sure, though, the cameraman did not take a full face shot of me. I was very careful back then.''

Brognola knew of the film, but he hadn't seen it when it had aired on a late-night cable channel several years ago. The CIA intel summary on the film, though, was that it had been faked. But intel summaries were known to be wrong more often than not.

''We recovered the crashed machine, and it was turned over to a small facility that we called the Copper Research Organization, and it was soon forgotten. That was all too common back then. Once you make something not exist, it is difficult to keep track of it.''

''Where is this thing now?'' Brognola asked.

''Well, that seems to be the problem,'' Nefyodov admitted. ''In the aftermath of the great events of 1989, it seems to have been misplaced. As have all the records and files that go along with it, except for that film. It was somehow misplaced and ended up on your television. We've been so busy with other matters that finding it was given a low priority, but we'll find it.''

''Would you like me to give you a hint?'' Brognola asked.

''It wasn't the craft that your people investigated in Afghanistan,'' Nefyodov stated, anticipating Brognola's information. ''The one I recovered was much smaller.''

"You watched that operation?" Brognola asked to confirm his hunch.

"Oh yes," the Russian said offhandedly. "Don't forget, old friend, that we have spy satellites too. They may not be quite as sophisticated as yours, but they do well enough for our purposes. Remember, we learned about your secret F-117 stealth fighter long before your press did. We keep a close watch on your Area 51."

"I know," Brognola said. "One of my people has that aerial photo poster of Dreamland your people sell."

Nefyodov laughed. "I don't have to tell you how wonderful capitalism is, do I, Hal? You can't imagine how many of them we sell every year to pay for little extras around the office here."

Brognola could imagine very well. He knew what a shock it had been for the Air Force to learn that this photo of the most tightly guarded location in the history of the United States was available on the open market. Dreamland and the surrounding area hadn't been on any map or air navigation chart available in the States until then. UFO freaks now used the Russian photo poster to plot new ways to try get in to watch the supersecret base. In response, the Dreamland security force had been doubled and the perimeter enlarged to keep unauthorized personnel far enough away.

"New topic," Brognola said. "How close an eye

are your people keeping on your retired generals and marshals? You know, the troublemakers, the leftover Bolsheviks and old Red Army heros?''

''We have a file on each one of them,'' Nefyodov said cautiously. ''Why?''

''Can you share the names and files of, let's say, the top five candidates for the position of the next would-be coup leader? Particularly any of them who have experience in the space program.''

Brognola paused. ''Or were in command of the Strategic Rocket Forces.''

There was another long pause. ''You ask a great deal, my friend,'' Nefyodov said. ''But you have told me much, too. I will see what I can do.''

''Thanks, Vladimir, I appreciate it.''

''What are friends for?'' the Russian replied. ''And speaking of friends, Hal, when are you going to tell me who you really work for? I want to update your file.''

Brognola chuckled. ''Vladimir, you remember that old KGB saying? 'If I told you, I'd have to kill you'?''

''I've heard it.''

''We have the same saying here.''

When Brognola put the phone down, he had a big grin on his face. He'd told the Russian nothing of substance. But since Russians were paranoid, particularly their spymasters, he had planted a seed. And he expected the seed to turn out to be a ''Jack and the Beanstalk'' variety; the Russian way of doing business would ensure that. Within hours, several elderly Russian generals would be sitting in dank cells in the basement of the Moscow RSV headquarters being talked to by men who didn't smile very much.

In other circumstances, he would have felt sorry for the retired soldiers. But not this time. One of them was bad, and it was better that a few men feel pain than a nuclear weapon be detonated in Russia, even in remotest Siberia.

That done, he glanced up at the clock showing East Coast U.S. time before dialing the video phone number to Barbara Price's office. He was smiling as the signal shot up to the satellite and back down to Earth.

CHAPTER NINETEEN

Stony Man Farm, Virginia

"You look like the proverbial cat after a gourmet canary dinner," Barbara Price said when Hal Brognola's grinning face appeared on the monitor above her desk. Since it was night in Siberia, she was in her office working on her routine chores instead of watching an unchanging scene of a dark Siberian forest in the Annex. "What have you done now?"

"I just had a little chat with my old friend Vladimir Nefyodov," he replied. "You remember Vladimir. He runs the RSV now."

"I see you're planning to retire early, Hal." She sighed. "Maybe to one of those country club federal prisons we keep hearing so much about on the news. I understand the food's a cut above what they serve in maximum security."

"Oh no, Barbara," he said, playing innocent. "I know better than to give our Russian friends and allies any advance notice of an American nuclear strike on their territory. Doing that would be considered treason.''

Price shook her head. ''Maybe the court will take pity on you.''

''Barbara,'' he protested, ''it's nothing like that at all, really. We just talked about technology falling out of the sky back in the sixties and how hard it is to keep track of things like that in a country as big as Russia. We even talked about the mental status of a group of restless, retired generals. You know how troublesome they can be, particularly with Strategic Rocket Forces generals. It was just a friendly chat between professionals without giving anything away.''

''So it is a UFO,'' Price said. ''I'll be damned.''

''Actually, it's not. But I think its mother was a UFO, or its father was. I don't know how those things go with machines.''

''A Deep Dreamer project?'' She mentioned the hyperclassified operation hidden inside Area 51 that not even Stony Man could get access to. The persistent rumor was that a team of engineers and scientists was trying to reverse engineer a captured UFO.

''It looks like it,'' he agreed.

''In one way, that's even worse.''

''I agree.''

''Now what?'' she asked.

''Now we go back to trying to get our people out

of there while we still can, and that includes Craig Waters.''

''I hear that.''

''Katz and I have come up with a plan that should give them a better chance of survival and we've jacked the mission profile around a little.''

''And you ran all this through the Puzzle Palace?'' she asked.

''Most of it.'' He grinned. ''I got the Man to hold off on the cruise missiles unless the Russians launch again, and I got permission to bring a Global Hawk and a few Strike Stars online to give Phoenix and Able a hand. The Space Cadets at Cheyenne Mountain aren't going to get the data sweep they wanted and they won't be pleased with that. But if this works, we'll get Waters back. The Man's really worried about him being in their hands. And if they actually have another one of those damned flying saucers there, we'll destroy it.''

''I like it so far,'' she said. ''But what are you not telling me?''

''I'm also trying to get a little Russian involvement as part of the deception screen.''

''Hal, Hal, Hal...'' She wanted to bang her head on the desk. ''You're playing with a live grenade. What in the hell are you trying to do?''

''I'm trying to stop the President from launching a nuclear strike on Russia,'' he explained. ''That's what I'm trying to do. Having a big bunch of Russians in the area, friendly Russians this time, is the best way I can think of to ensure that our guys will be able to do their job and not go up in a mushroom cloud. NASA's gotten together with Space Command, and they're lobbying for an immediate hard strike.''

"What's wrong with those people?"

"They're scared—it's as simple as that," Brognola said. "If the space station and one of the shuttles gets zapped with a great loss of life, the public will go ballistic, and they'll likely all be out of a job. It's turf-protection time, and they're fighting for their existence.''

"That's real shortsighted," she said. "If the Russians take exception to our nuking their turf, we'll all be out of a job.''

"That's what I told him.''

"What did he say?''

"He gave me what I asked for.''

"Let's pray that it works.''

Siberia

WHEN GENERAL FEDOR KOMAROV flew into Forestry Station 105 the next morning, his second in command, Colonel Nikoli Romodin, and a small detachment of bodyguards accompanied him. Yuri Polinski had always felt uncomfortable around the scar-faced veteran colonel of the Afghan campaign. The crash of a helicopter during the war had burned Romodin, which had deeply scared his soul, as well as his body.

Seeing him almost made Polinski feel sorry for the Yankee spy.

After leading the party into the briefing room in the main building, Polinski recounted the capture of the American by his foot patrol. Without asking questions, Romodin took over the interrogation.

"Bring your prisoner in," he ordered.

"As you command, Comrade Colonel."

CRAIG WATERS KNEW he'd hit the big time when he was led into the interrogation room. He wasn't up to date on Russian military organization, but he knew the uniform of a Russian general when he saw one. He couldn't read the rank of the scar-faced officer with the general, but he didn't need to know. His gut told him that the guy was Major Bad News. The last time he'd seen anyone as scary as that had been Freddy Krueger in *A Nightmare on Elm Street.*

The scar-faced man stepped into the light, and Waters tried not to stare at him. He had been horribly burned, and the extensive skin grafting hadn't done him much good. Keloid scars and imbedded carbon stains mottled his entire face, stretching his features into a grotesque mask. His dark eyes stared out from half-burned lids, and his mouth was only a slash across his face.

When the general stepped up to him, Waters had a

reason to move his head. "I am General Fedor Komarov," the man said in barely accented English, "of the Strategic Rocket Forces and the commander of this installation. Who are you?"

Waters didn't even try to extend his hand. This wasn't a social occasion.

"Craig Waters, sir," he answered in perfect Moscow-accented Russian. "I work for the Defense Advanced Research Projects Agency."

"You are American," the scar-faced officer stated in Russian.

"Yes, sir," Waters confirmed. He stood stock-still as the man stared at him again with an intensity he had never seen before. It was almost as if he were the one with the scars, not the other way around.

"This is my second in command, Colonel Nikoli Romodin," the general stated, "and he will conduct the interrogation today. He does not speak English very well, but since your Russian is so good, we will not need to use a translator."

The general turned to the third man in his party, a bushy haired, older man wearing a white lab coat, a tie and glasses. "This is Artyom Chazov, director of research here."

Waters nodded.

"What are you doing here?" the colonel fired the opening shot.

"I came to see if I could get a look at your facility," Waters answered honestly. "The attack by your machine on our space station has raised serious concerns in Washington. I'm sure you can understand that. I was sent to evaluate the threat of future attacks.''

"Then you admit that you work for the CIA?" Colonel Romodin snapped.

"As I told you before," Waters repeated, "I am from DARPA, where I am an expert in foreign aerospace technology, particularly Russian. It is my job to keep up to date on breakthrough space developments like your vehicle."

"In our country, that work is done by the KGB."

The colonel's use of the Communist term KGB—instead of the modern RSV—for the Russian intelligence agency gave Waters pause. It could mean that this secret program was being run by a dissident hardline element. It that were the case, it would explain everything.

"DARPA is a government agency," Waters explained, "but I am a civilian."

"Are you the man who examined the crash site in Afghanistan?" The colonel changed topics.

"I am." Waters nodded. He had known that there had been a good chance that the Russians had also been keeping a close eye on that incident.

"What happened to the two pilots who were in Aerial Vehicle 1?"

"I do not know, sir." Waters shrugged. "They were dead when I got into the machine. There were no marks on them that I could see, but I did not examine them closely. I was more concerned with examining the propulsion system.''

He turned to Chazov. ''Comrade Director, I am very impressed with what you have accomplished here. I didn't have much time to examine your machine before the self-destruct mechanism went off, but I saw enough that it was obvious that you have solved the problem of magnetic propulsion. That is a great accomplishment.''

Chazov wasn't immune to praise, even from a Yankee spy, and nodded his thanks.

General Komarov had been silent throughout the interrogation so far. He was inclined to take the American at face value. Engineers had their own way of speaking, and Waters knew the language. Also, he had shown none of the evasiveness he would have expected of a traditional spy. In fact, the man seemed to be completely unaware that he was marked for death. He was far more interested in the machine in the hangar than he was about saving his skin. That was typical of a man who was an engineer.

''And you say that you were brought here by a stealth bomber?'' The colonel continued the questioning.

''That's correct,'' Waters admitted. ''I made a HALO jump from twenty-eight thousand feet and landed in the forest. From there, I made my way here to see what I could see.''

"How were you to make your escape after you had spied on us?" Romodin asked.

"I was only told that I would be given instructions over my radio when I was ready to leave."

"Why doesn't your radio work now?"

"I don't know," Waters said. "It worked right up to the time I was captured."

"What message did you last send?" Romodin pounced on Waters's admission.

"Only one telling my headquarters that I was about to be captured."

"What did they say?"

Waters shook his head. "Nothing. They cut off."

"Speaking of the advanced developments you say you work on," Komarov asked, "what do you know about the camouflage suit you were wearing? It is unfamiliar to us, and we cannot get its electronics to work."

"Very little actually." Waters again stuck to the truth. "I'd never even heard of anything like it until they gave it to me and showed me how it worked. I work in aerospace technology only, not ground combat systems."

"Why were you not armed?" Romodin asked.

Waters shrugged. "As I said, sir, I'm not a soldier. I'm not trained in firearms. I'm a civilian scientist."

COLONEL ROMODIN GLARED at the Yankee. Of course, this spy wasn't a soldier. A soldier was an honorable man, a man who put his life on the line in defense of his people. There was honor in being a soldier, but it was obvious that this man didn't know the meaning of the word. He was a scientist, a man who had never risked his life for anything more than his paycheck. He could escape being a man of honor who used weapons and laid his life on the line to defend his nation by hiding behind his test tubes and his mathematics.

It was an American rocket scientist like him who was responsible for the scars he bore. That man had invented the Stinger ground-to-air missile that had shot down his command helicopter and had almost cost him his life. It was true that the politicians and the CIA had put the weapons into the hands of the Afghan barbarians, but had it not been for men like the scientist turned spy standing in front of him, there would have been no Stinger missiles and hundreds of Red Army airmen would be alive today as they deserved to be.

When this Waters was of no use to him, Romodin vowed to soak him in jet fuel and set it alight. Let him see what it felt like to be burned alive. It was too bad that he didn't have a Stinger missile to shoot at him so he could watch the smoke plume and see his death coming.

When the Soviet marshall in charge of the Afghan war had admitted that the American Stingers were the major reason for the Soviet defeat, Romodin had wanted to skin the man alive. How dare he reveal their vulnerabilities to their enemies in the West? That statement, as well as those from others who had tried to put the blame of the Soviet defeat on someone other than themselves, was what had driven Romodin to Komarov's movement. The general was weak and he was a fool, but he was a good figurehead.

Romodin wasn't unaware of how his appearance affected people. He had been reminded of it each and every day, and he was immune to the looks of shock that came over the faces of those who were meeting him for the first time. Most of the time, this amused him and he had learned how to use the scars as a weapon. Nonetheless, he was fully aware that there was no way he would ever be able to lead a movement to return power in Mother Russia to its rightful owners, the Red Army. To do that, he needed to work with a man like the general.

Komarov could meet with the important men they needed to support them, and they wouldn't be distracted by his face. They would look instead at the medals on his chest and know that he spoke from the heart of a hero of the Soviet Union. They would also see him with his younger mistress and know that he was a real man. Romodin no longer had any use for women as did other men—his burns had scarred more than just his face—but he still used them for his amusement. When the time came that Komarov was no longer of use to him, his mistress would still be.

Pushing that thought into the back of his mind, he turned his attention back to the Yankee spy.

"IF YOU ARE NOT a soldier," he asked, "how is it that you know how to use a parachute?"

"I was put through a one-day training course," Waters said honestly. "It was quite easy because all of the equipment was automatic. All I had to do was fall out of the plane and it opened by itself."

"Where is this marvel of a parachute?"

Waters shrugged. "I burned it and scattered the ashes like they told me to."

"You say you want to see Director Chazov's machine," Komarov asked.

"That is why I came," Waters replied.

He had no idea why he was being offered this opportunity. If these people were renegades, the last thing they would want him to do was see their big secret. That could only mean that he wouldn't be returning to the United States.

He had figured that part out already, which was why he hadn't mentioned the men still in the woods. As long as the Russians didn't know about them, he still had a chance of being rescued.

Komarov studied him for a long moment. "Come," he said as he turned for the door.

Waters followed him.

FLANKED ON BOTH SIDES by half a dozen hard-faced, armed troops, Waters, Komarov, the colonel and the director walked across the base to the largest hangar. More armed men guarded the building and they brought their rifles up to a salute when they spotted the general.

Komarov returned their salutes, opened the smaller personnel door in the large sliding door that was the end of the hangar and walked inside. Waters followed, but stopped when he saw what was sitting in the middle of the hangar. This really was what he had come all this way for.

Unlike the machine he had seen in Afghanistan, this second version was half again larger. It was sitting on conventional aircraft-style landing gear, and it had a more pronounced pilot's canopy. Twin bulges in its upper surfaces could only be weapons housings, maybe lasers like the first craft had been armed with. If this thing took into space for a second attack, space station *Freedom* was doomed.

Almost in a trance, Waters walked forward, stopping right in front of the craft. Under the muzzles of half a dozen AKs, he didn't want to touch it without permission.

"It's magnificent," he said.

Chazov positively beamed. He knew his machine was an unsurpassed marvel, but it never hurt to hear another aerospace professional's praise. "Would you like to see the inside?" Chazov reached for the handle in a hatch.

"No!" Colonel Romodin barked. "I don't want him inside of it."

"It will hurt nothing, Nikoli," Komarov said.

"It is not good security," Romodin replied. "If he is exchanged, it could damage our cause."

Komarov had learned to trust his scar-faced second in command on security matters. His organization had remained completely hidden all these years while other patriots had been betrayed. "A walk around only, then."

Waters was naturally disappointed, but this was better than not seeing it at all.

CHAPTER TWENTY

Siberia

General Fedor Komarov hadn't yet made up his mind about the American spy's ultimate fate. He could never be allowed to return to the United States under any conditions, not even after the new revolution was successful. But there were sound reasons to keep him alive a little longer, at least for now. First and foremost was the technical encyclopedia he had in his head. His position at his research agency gave him access to a wealth of information about not only American technology, but also European technical systems.

As a rocket forces officer, Komarov didn't have to be convinced of the vital need for continuing technical intelligence as a condition of survival. His own branch of the Red Army had been developed on foreign technology, first German and later American. Even after the federation was gone, the restored Red Army would need techintel to stay ahead of both the

Americans and NATO forces to protect the sacred soil of Mother Russia.

Komarov took his second in command aside. "Nikoli," he said, "I have to return to Moscow this morning for an important meeting. I want you to stay here and continue to find out what our prisoner knows, but I do not want him harmed in any way. I want him well cared for, too. I will send you a chemical-interrogation team, so the information you get will be what he really knows, not just something he says because he's in pain."

Romodin trusted his own methods more than he trusted any chemical, but this wasn't the time to argue the point with Komarov. Waiting a few days to finish questioning the Yankee spy in his own way wouldn't make any difference to his immediate plans.

"As you command, General," he replied. "But while we wait, I want more of my special unit troops flown in. Now that the Yankees know what we have here, I fear that they will send another man, or even a strike team, when they do not hear back from their spy. Major Polinski's men are good, but you know that I like to work with my own people."

From the first, Komarov had known that bringing the new revolution to life would require brutal measures. Lenin himself had said that change was impossible without violent revolution. While he had been a soldier all of his life, he had never been comfortable with brutality for brutality's sake. Instead, when it had been required, he had picked hard men to be brutal for him. That was why he had recruited Romodin and his handpicked butchers to his cause.

Komarov knew that he had to walk a fine line with the Afghan veteran. Romodin been a hard man even before he was burned, but that incident had added brutality to it. At this point in the new revolution, Romodin was a useful tool. But Komarov was acutely aware that at some point in time, he would have to be purged.

"As you want, Nikoli," Komarov promised. "I will order them flown out to you today."

"Very good, sir."

"Now—" Komarov signaled to his aide to ready his plane "—I have to leave."

ROMODIN'S HATRED of scientists did not only apply to the American scientists who had developed the Stinger missile. He loathed all scientists, including the director of the research going on there in Siberia. As soon as General Fedor Komarov's Yak-40 VIP jet lifted off the runway, he turned to Artyom Chazov.

"Comrade Director," Romodin snapped, "until further notice, all activities at this facility will come under my direct command."

Chazov had absolutely no interest in the workings of the military as long as they didn't keep him from his work. Who wanted to take the credit for it was also no concern of his. "As you will, Comrade Colonel."

"Does that include the security duties?" Major Yuri Polinski asked. The general had said nothing to him about this before he left.

Romodin spun on him. "It particularly includes the security of this base, Major," he snapped. "Your people failed in that the Yankee spy was able to make radio calls back to his handlers before he was captured. That was inexcusable and it will not happen again. Do you understand?"

Polinski was stunned as he stood unblinking in the barrage of rage directed against him. He started to rebut the colonel's charges, but the look on Romodin's face froze him. He didn't have to be told that if he opened his mouth, the V-68 Skorpion holstered at the colonel's waist would be used on him.

Komarov needed to be informed immediately of what was taking place here in his name, and he would do exactly that at the first opportunity. Until then, if he wanted to live the day out, he could only exactly do as he was told, when he was told to do it.

"As you command, Colonel," Polinski said, then saluted.

WHEN POLINSKI RETURNED to his command post, he was shocked to see two of Romodin's men armed with AK-74 submachine guns standing guard over his radio operator and duty officer. "What is the meaning of this?" he snapped.

The sergeant guarding the young lieutenant turned slightly so that the muzzle of his submachine gun was aimed directly at Polinski's belt buckle. "The colonel has commanded that this facility be secured against intruders and traitors."

"That is absurd, Sergeant," Polinski snapped. "There are no traitors here. Those are my men, and I can vouch for the loyalty of each and every one of them."

"Tell that to Colonel Romodin. He is in command here now."

Polinski stopped himself from saying anything more. This situation had gotten completely out of control, and he feared to cross Romodin. No man with any sense wanted to go up against that maniac. Polinski's plan to take this matter to Komarov had just been made null and void. The base's only long-range radio was in this command center. Maybe he could risk a landline telephone call.

He walked out without saying another word, but he was aware of the sergeant's eyes on him.

WHILE MAJOR POLINSKI was learning the extent of Romodin's control, the engineering staff, including Director Artyom Chazov, was learning it, as well. Romodin had called a meeting of the staff in the mess hall. They all sprang to their feet when the colonel walked in, but he ignored them and walked up to their leader.

"How long will it take you to get that machine of yours in operational condition?" the colonel snapped.

"Well…" Chazov thought for a moment. "That all depends upon—"

"Give me a time!" Romodin's hand went for the grip of his weapon.

Chazov hadn't survived as long as he had by being stupid, but he was also no pushover. He had faced worse than this scar-faced maniac in his days. Why the general had put this man in charge, he had no idea. Since he had, though, he knew that he had to play the game or die on the spot.

"General Komarov and I—"

"Komarov is no longer in charge of this operation," Romodin cut him off abruptly. "I am, Nikoli Romodin! I conceived this operation, and I am going to see that it is carried out properly. Every day that you sit here and play with your toy is another day that the Yankee scientists are closer to having their missiles hanging over all of our heads."

Chazov was surprised to hear that the colonel believed the Americans planned to move missiles onto the space station. Since half the crew would be Russian astronauts, that made no sense at all. But this conversation wasn't about reason and logic. Romodin was clearly insane.

The colonel's face twisted into an even grimmer

mask. "As long as I am alive," he shouted, "I will not live in a world dominated by the imperialists and their cowardly inventions. You will have that machine ready to destroy that space station in no more than two days."

Romodin's eyes bulged in their burned sockets, and spittle flew from what was left of his lips. "Two days! Do you hear me, Chazov? Two days!"

Chazov calmly looked the colonel straight in the eyes. "I hear you, Comrade Colonel. And I will obey."

He would also make sure that he had a seat in Aerial Vehicle 2 when it lifted off. It was obvious that his work here was over; Romodin had made sure of that. That didn't mean, however, that the project couldn't be continued somewhere else. The Chinese had always welcomed Russian scientists, and they also knew the value of commanding space. He would hide the computer disks of the project's master files in the ship before it launched and, after destroying the space station, he would simply land it in China.

Komarov would have his mission completed, and he could continue to work on his spacecraft.

Atsugi, Japan

KATZENELENBOGEN KNEW that parking the Stony Man team in a static position for an entire day wasn't without danger. By its nature, a strike force wasn't designed to sit and wait in a defensive posture very long. The best defense was always a strong offense. In this case, though, going offensive alone against the kind of odds they were up against was tantamount to suicide. But to gather the force multipliers he needed to cut those odds took time, so the commandos had to risk sitting still for a while longer.

The UAVs he planned to use were available at the air base in South Korea, where they were kept in twenty-four-hour-alert storage. That meant that upon receiving an alert, twenty-four hours was required to make the planes ready for launch. They had to be fueled, armed and have a series of diagnostic checks run on their complicated systems to insure that they would function properly. The biggest problems with using UAVs in a close-support role was that they were UAVs. Without a pilot to apply the critical human-judgment factor of conventional aerial combat, a computer glitch could spell disaster for both the machine and the friendly troops on the ground.

As soon as Brognola had received the presidential code word, it was relayed to the headquarters of the Eleventh Reconnaissance Squadron at South Korea. On receiving the alert, the blue-suited technicians sprung into action to prepare their birds for flight. The tentative time on target was 2200 hours local Siberian time. That would give the Stony Man team time to get in, do their thing and pull back far enough to be extracted.

Now that everything was in motion, he and Katz did a final face-to-face. "Jack and I have fine-tuned our end of it," Katz reported. "And our crew is locked and loaded. In case this thing goes south for McCarter, I have a KC-10 laid on, so we can stay on station as long as we need to cover them."

Katz's face broke into a grin. "And I kind of added a second Global Hawk to the mix if we do go into overtime. With it and the extra Strike Stars on hand, I can give them cover for at least two days."

He glanced up at the wall clock. "Got to run."

"Good luck," Brognola said to his retreating back.

THOUGH HAL BROGNOLA was the Lone Ranger in the Atsugi command post now, he hadn't been cut out of the loop. High-tech warfare had its tricks. Streaming satcom feed from both the RC-135 flying UAV command post and the Farm's Computer Room would keep him up to a minute within the speed lag of long-range electronic transmissions. With Price in the Annex and Katzenelenbogen in the RC-135 doing their usual good work, he was just going to sit and watch.

Until, that is, it was time for him to play his Russian trump card. That play was likely to get him early retirement, but he didn't give a damn. If he was responsible for the Stony Man warriors putting their lives on the line, the least he could do was risk his job. In no way was it the same thing, but it was the least he could do to share their risk.

A few hours ago, RSV chief Vladimir Nefyodov had called saying that he was holding a retired general of the Strategic Rocket Forces for questioning.

"I want to thank you for the tip on him," the Russian spymaster had said. "It looks like he is a very bad man indeed, just like you said."

"Glad to help."

"Because of what we learned," Nefyodov added, "I have alerted a reinforced company of Spetsnaz and have them standing by in case we uncover a nest of vipers somewhere that should be under our control, shall we say in Siberia. In fact, they are now landing at a small airfield in Siberia itself."

Brognola smiled. The wily Russian had just let him know that he was waiting to be invited to support the Stony Man effort. He would have to finesse this to keep the good Russians from firing on his people, but he had wanted the extra military muscle on hand. The trick lay in knowing exactly when to bring them into play.

"That is good news, Vladimir," Brognola said. "But I need to caution you not to deploy them too soon. I hate to ask this of you, but to protect my own people, I would like you to hold your troops until I give you the word."

"I appreciate the tip you gave me and I owe you for it," Nefyodov admitted, "but you are asking something that no Russian can agree to. You know our history."

"Look, Vladimir, here's the deal. Our Space Command was scared shitless when that damned machine attacked the space station. It was only a fluke that they were able to drive the craft off, and they still don't know how they managed to do it. Once we learned that it had taken off from Siberia, our generals went to the White House and demanded that it be eradicated with a nuclear strike."

"A nuclear attack!" The Russian was indignant. "Tell me you are joking."

"I wish I was, but our people are afraid that they can't defend against that craft, whatever it is. Half of them actually think that the machine could be under the control of the federation. That's why our President didn't get on the phone with your President and discuss it. The old fear is back, and they are very afraid. Mostly they're afraid that you have another one of them and will try again."

"I can understand part of it," Nefyodov admitted, "but the rest..."

"I was able to get the President to let me see if I could defuse this threat without the missiles flying. We would have been able to do that easily if the general in your basement hadn't sent in a missile security company with SAM launchers to reinforce the site. When we saw that, even though it is certain suicide for my team, I still asked permission to send them in. The alternative was too terrible to contemplate for both our peoples."

"You are a hard man, Hal Brognola."

"Not really." Brognola sounded tired. "It's just that I believe the good of the many always outweighs the good of the few."

"How do you see this operation taking place?" the Russian asked.

"My people are going to move into the base under the cover of a UAV attack that will take out the SAM launchers and crater the runway so more troops couldn't be flown in. I recommend that your forces wait until the SAM launchers are taken out so they don't get shot down on the way into their DZ. As I'm sure you know, there's a suitable drop zone within a few klicks."

"When will you order them in?"

"After we destroy whatever spacecraft may be there," Brognola said. He didn't need to add the problem of the captured Craig Waters into the mix at this time. If the Russian learned of him later, he'd deal with it then.

"I can see what this plan will do for the United States," Nefyodov said, "but what does it do for Russia? If this works as you have said, we will be out a very advanced spacecraft, a company of trained troops and one forestry station. If your men fail, you will have lost a small commando unit and nothing else."

This was where the rubber met the road, and if he failed to convince the Russian, he'd have to pull his people out and the President would almost certainly issue the launch order.

"If I lose, as you say, old friend," Brognola replied, "I think that we will have lost the peace between our countries, as well as my team. I don't think that I'll be able to stop the missiles."

In the silence from Moscow, Brognola continued. "Whoever is controlling that machine, neither of our nations needs it. It's too powerful and the danger it presents is too great. I don't want to see another arms race get started because of it. Particularly not in space."

"You are asking a lot of me," Nefyodov finally said, "and of my country. Like you, I have to answer to other men, and as you well know, we Russians have never liked having foreigners on our soil."

"Just consider us as technical consultants this time," Brognola said. "We're outsiders brought in to provide you with specialized assistance. The way I see this working out is that once we have destroyed whatever is being built there, the danger will be over and we will pull out immediately. Your men will then go in and arrest a group of criminals who were plotting the end of your Russian federation. We both win, and our nations will remain at peace."

"Will you send flowers when I am put up against a wall and shot?" Nefyodov asked.

"Better than that, Vladimir," Brognola said. "I'll see that you're awarded a NASA medal."

"That will insure that I am liquidated." The Russian laughed bitterly.

"At least it won't be a CIA medal."

"I'll tell you what," the Russian said. "I'll see what I can do to get you a Hero of the Russian People award in return. That will even things up."

Now it was Brognola's turn to laugh. "But I don't have a dacha to retire to."

"You can hide out in mine."

CHAPTER TWENTY-ONE

Siberia

While Katzenelenbogen put his revised UAV strike program together, David McCarter and Carl Lyons refined their attack plans. In the revision, McCarter, T. J. Hawkins, Calvin James and Rafael Encizo would take the snatch part of the job. Lyons, Blancanales and Gadgets Schwarz would be joined by Gary Manning for the demo mission. They were too few to split up like that, but they had no choice.

While those details were worked out, the rest of the Stony Man commandos went into mission prep. Since they hadn't come to Siberia equipped to perform a major demolition mission, they were going to have to work with what were known in the trade as field expedient explosives. In this case, though, that meant that they'd have to use whatever they could find once they got inside the base. Manning and Schwarz both had a few small demo charges in their packs that could be used to initiate other explosive material they came across.

The upside was that an airfield should have a lot of things that could be used to help their program along. Servicing aircraft required lots of things that would burn.

"Remember," Schwarz said as they prepared what few explosives they had with them. "Since we have to take out that damned machine above all, we need to keep an eye out for readily combustible materials in that hangar. You know, fuel drums, propane tanks, oil cans, that kind of thing."

Manning reached over and patted his shoulder. "We know the drill, Gadgets."

Stony Man Farm, Virginia

THE STONY MAN crew kept a close protective watch over the Siberian forestry station while the teams prepped for their night's mission. The priority of the mission had given them residential authority to get all the on-site time they wanted from any of the American spy satellites. With all that horsepower going for them, they kept close watch on any changes in both the security troop's deployments and the physical defenses.

They had also spotted the small Yak-40 VIP jet that had flown in that morning and then took off a few hours later.

"My take on it," Aaron Kurtzman told Hal Brognola over the videophone, "is that was a VIP visit. Some big shot, probably that general we think's behind this, wanted to see what the guards found in the woods."

Brognola had watched the scenes of the plane's arrival from Atsugi, but he didn't have the enhancements of the Computer Room. "Do you think they took Waters back with them?"

Kurtzman's fingers typed out a command that brought up two scenes of the Yak jet, one of the party disembarking and the other one of them loading, and flashed them to Brognola in Japan.

"I checked these closely," he said, "and six fewer people got back on that plane than came in with it. The computer matched the three who made the return flight as being men who got off earlier. My feeling is that he's still there, which would fit with their wanting to keep him on ice while they see what he knows."

"I don't wish him any bad luck," Brognola said, "but I hope he can avoid mentioning Phoenix and Able at least for today."

"We're tracking their security patrols," Kurtzman said, "and they're running the same strength and pattern that they were yesterday. If Waters had mentioned anything, they'd have everyone but the mess cooks beating the brush for them, so we're okay on that issue."

"You're right, of course." Brognola both looked

and sounded dead tired. "This has turned into a world-class rat screw."

"We're on it, though," Kurtzman said, trying to reassure him. "And the fat broad hasn't stepped on-stage yet."

"How about kidnapping her and locking her up."

Kurtzman laughed.

KATZENELENBOGEN WAS in the air in the RC-135 flying command post when he received word from Korea that his UAV strike force was ready to launch. He immediately got on the satcom radio to McCarter in Siberia.

"David," he said, "I'm waiting right now for word that the birds have been launched, but it'll be any minute now and the in-flight time to the AO is under two hours."

"Get them in the air soon," McCarter replied. "We have to go in tonight or forget it. In case you missed it, they got a dozen more reinforcements in right before dark."

"We spotted them, and I've got a package coming in that'll close that airfield to further traffic."

McCarter stopped himself from saying that they had needed that six hours ago, but their success at this depended on their not alerting the Russians that something was going on until the right time. Blasting them earlier would have blown the plan, as well as the runway.

"Just get them on the way."

"Just had the first launch," Katz confirmed.

KATZENELENBOGEN SAT in the command-and-control center on the RC-135 like Darth Vader in the Death Star. With Hal Brognola remaining behind in Atsugi, he was "the man" this time.

In front of him was a bank of video monitors, digital readouts and instruments that allowed him to control the unmanned air force he had launched from South Korea. From his battle station, he had more power at his command than a WWII wing commander. The RC was in a wide orbit over the Pacific, miles from Siberia, but with a satellite parked right over the center of his orbit, he had instant communications with his unmanned aerial forces.

It was a lot for one man to keep track of, and he was glad that he'd been able to get Jack Grimaldi flown to Atsugi before they'd taken off.

"We're go for the attack," Grimaldi reported from the seat to his right. Traditionally, that was the co-pilot's seat, but he didn't mind since he'd be doing all of the actual human flying. The birds all had programmed attack sequences in their microprocessor brains. But a steady hand on the stick and rudder was still going to be needed, and he was the man who could do it.

The aerial armada he was working with was impressive. The matte-black Tier II Plus Global Hawk

UAV looked like a kid's toy on steroids, a lot of them. Its shape—kind of a cross between a boomerang and a flying disk—helped it evade enemy radars. Its carbon-composite structure did the rest to make it the stealthiest aircraft that had ever taken to the skies. Its small, low-burn, Rolls-Royce jet engine was also maximized for its sneaky-pete mission with shielded intakes, muffled fans and diffused exhaust.

This particular Global Hawk had been programmed to be the tactical air controller for the unmanned strike. With a battlefield loiter time of some twenty hours, it could stay on station to cover both the Stony Man team's attack and its withdrawal. With video eyes and sensors covering the battle area, little that went on below it would escape its electronic attention. And anything it did miss would be seen by the spy satellites controlled by the Stony Man Computer Room crew.

Orbiting well out of range of the SAM-11 launchers at the forestry station, a pair of Tier III Strike Star UACVs waited for the "go" signal from him to kick off their part of the assault. Developed from the Dark Star recon birds, the *C* in their designation stood for "combat" indicating that these unmanned planes were equipped with more than recon sensors and cameras. The bellies of these stealth birds were engorged with a mixture of goodies, most of them highly explosive in nature.

Since the most immediate identified threats at the

forestry station were the two SAM-11 Gadfly mobile launchers, they had to be taken down first. Once they were out of the picture, one of the Strike Stars would make a single pass over the runway to deliver a JDAM—a Joint Direct Attack Munition—which was a bomb-shaped carrier that could contain a variety of submunitions. In this case, the submunitions would be shaped-charge, runway-cratering bombs.

When the Strike Star's pass was completed, the tarmac would be cratered deep enough to prevent fixed-wing aircraft from landing until the damage was repaired. To limit the destruction of Russian property, and the resulting political problems, these would be the only two explosive ordnance aerial strikes on the SAMs and the airstrip. What followed them would be a deception attack.

A further trio of Tier IIIs with very special non-lethal weapons loads would swoop down out of the night sky and deliver a cross between a Hollywood special-effects extravaganza and a battle reenactment. When it kicked off, the Stony Man warriors would make their move.

"David," Katzenelenbogen radioed McCarter, "the mother ship is on station with the UACVs and the deception flight is in orbit around it. Are you in position?"

"Roger," McCarter called back. "We're ready to go. Send them in."

"The SAM strike will commence shortly."

Katz turned to Grimaldi. "Maestro," he said, "do your thing."

Grimaldi took his control stick and clicked in Bird One. "One UAV attack coming up."

Stony Man Farm, Virginia

THE STONY MAN Annex was buzzing as the crew waited for Katz's UAV assault in Siberia to kick off. Stony Man often worked with electronic battlefield aids, such as the satellite network that they couldn't live without. But this was the first time they would be conducting a completely remote controlled air strike. In fact, it would be a first for anyone.

The Farm's part in this operation would be to provide the commander-in-the-sky overview through their satellite assets to spot any target opportunities that might appear after the initial strikes. This included keeping a close eye on the enemy's movements to try to keep the Stony Man team out of trouble when they infiltrated.

The ALOCS suit beacons showed in two groups, Carl Lyons's break-it-and-burn-it team on one side of the perimeter, and McCarter's rescue unit on the other. Lyons planned to break through the defenses directly behind the big hangar while McCarter's group would make straight for the large building that had been identified as the headquarters. The satellite recon indicated that if Craig Waters was still alive, he was being held there.

"We're ready for it," Kurtzman announced.

Price was more than ready for this to begin, as well. Like Brognola, the specter of nuclear fire played large in her mind, but her concern for her guys on the ground wasn't diminished. If anything, it was greater than it had ever been, and the old fear was back as it had not been for a long time. Anyone who thought that the Russian bear had been tamed was living in a childish fantasy.

She stopped and stared at the big monitor. "Give Katz our status," she said.

"I already did."

Siberia

McCARTER'S RESCUE TEAM had worked its way right up to the edge of the sensor ring and was keeping low until Katz gave the signal. Encizo had his night-vision glasses focused on the nearest of the SAM-11 mobile launchers on their side of the airfield. The armored tracked vehicle was in standby mode as it had been all day, its engine idling, its missiles in the lowered position and its radar antenna dish slowly rotating.

While Encizo couldn't hear or see anything in the moonless night sky, the SAM launcher suddenly came awake. Its radar dish locked on a target, and he heard the drive motors whine as the missiles snapped up to firing position. They spun to point in the direction of the contact and locked, ready for the launch command. He froze in place, wondering what had gone wrong. Katz had said the UAVs were radar proof.

Encizo had no way of knowing that Katzenelenbogen had ordered one of the stealthy Strike Stars to launch a small unstealthed decoy to draw the attention of the SAM launcher's radar. As soon as the radar locked on the easy-to-see decoy, the Strike Star would launch a HARM—Highspeed Anti-Radiation Missile.

Once launched, the missile would key onto the enemy radar transmission, ride it all the way into the target and blast it out of existence. Even if the radar was turned off, the missile's microchip brain had already made an internal GPS map of its location and would kill it anyway.

A second later, Encizo caught a flash in the night sky right before the track exploded in a boiling ball of flame. The flash had been the submunition releasing to produce a double strike.

An instant later, a second thundering explosion sounded from the other side of the field where the other SAM launcher went up in flames, as well. The flames from the wreckage ignited the missile's launch motors and, since they were still locked down, they detonated, adding to the destruction.

The base's alert sirens started wailing, and the off-duty troops started pouring out of the barracks, racing for the trucks to take them to their alert positions. The first truck that pulled away from the barracks was crossing the runway to the defensive positions on the other side when it was enveloped in an explosion.

Though he hadn't seen it come over, Encizo could imagine the matte-black, batlike plane swooping down and releasing her ordnance on the runway. The special-purpose munitions in the JDAM it carried used a shaped-charge warhead to blast holes three yards wide and two deep in the concrete. It didn't destroy the runway, but no one would be using it for fixed-wing aircraft until the holes were filled.

The second and third blasts finished off the runway job and, with the SAM launchers out of action, as well, it was show time.

"Okay, lads," McCarter said over the com link, "let's do it."

James and Hawkins moved out to take on the first ring of sensors.

JACK GRIMALDI FELT like a whacked-out teenager in a mega video arcade with the world's largest bucket of quarters at his side zapping the evil galactic overlords. With Katz monitoring the feed from the orbiting Global Hawk, he could concentrate on delivering the goodies from his squadron of loitering Strike Stars. Although the President had only okayed armed attacks against the SAM launchers and the runway,

Katz had managed to get another armed UACV added to the mix as his up-the-sleeve cards.

Before either one of them would sit and watch the Stony Man team go down, they'd use the JDAMs packed with antipersonnel cluster bombs in the bellies of the additional attack bird to even up the odds. If it wasn't enough to make the difference, Grimaldi already had a plan worked up to use the UAVs themselves as missiles. Their fuel loads exploding on impact would make a nasty surprise for someone.

Rolling the control stick in his hand as he followed the blip on the monitor, Grimaldi brought the first Strike Star of the diversion flight out of its orbit into action. The first run would be a simulated parachute drop on the opposite side of the site from where the Stony Man team was waiting.

In his command chair, Katz ordered the Global Hawk to go into its radar-and-communications-jamming mode. Blanking the enemy's radios would put the imminent contest on a more equal footing. The commandos would still have the use of their com links and satcom radios, but the Russians would have to shout back and forth to be heard.

Warfare had come a long way since he had first fired a round in anger, but Katz liked the idea of sending machines instead of men into danger. That didn't mean that the Stony Man commandos would have a milk run this time, but they would have some strong, shadowy companions hovering over them on the battlefield like black angels.

COLONEL ROMODIN HAD BEEN out along the perimeter defenses of the Eighth Missile Security Company when the UAV strike came in. Immediately, he raced back for the main building and stormed into the command center, finding Yuri Polinski there ahead of him. The major's uniform blouse was unbuttoned and his shirt wasn't tucked in, indicating that he hadn't been on duty when the attack had hit.

Almost automatically, Romodin's hand snaked down for the Czech 9 mm V-68 Skorpion submachine gun he was never seen without.

The movement caught Polinski's eye and he turned. Seeing the colonel's weapon poised in his hands, he paled and stepped back. His Makarov officer's pistol was in its holster on the belt in his room.

"Colonel," he said, "the Yankees—"

Romodin's finger tightened on the trigger and the subgun spit a long burst of 9 mm rounds. The slugs tore through Polinski's chest, slamming him against the wall of the CP.

The young lieutenant on duty automatically fumbled for the Makarov on his belt, but he was too late. A second long burst flung him from his chair.

Romodin eyed the technical sergeant, who was frozen in his chair, as he calmly dropped the empty magazine from the subgun and snapped a fresh one into place. "Report," he ordered.

"The Americans are attacking, Comrade Colonel…" the sergeant began.

"I can hear that, you idiot." Romodin's hand tightened on the Skorpion's grip.

"Where are they attacking?"

"Apparently—" the sergeant started.

Romodin's finger twitched, and the sergeant was blown out of his chair. He didn't have time for "apparently" this night; he needed hard information.

Picking up the fallen microphone, Romodin glanced at the grease-penciled list of the unit radio call signs before keying the mike. When a series of calls to the strong points in the line gave him conflicting reports, he flung down the microphone in disgust. Had he known the quality of the troops Komarov had sent to this place, he would have insisted that his entire unit be brought in.

Racing out the door, Romodin headed for the GAZ parked out front. Two of his personal guards were already in it waiting for him with the engine running. "To the command bunker," he ordered.

Without answering, the driver snapped into first gear and spun his tires in the dirt as he obeyed.

CHAPTER TWENTY-TWO

Siberia

Lyons and Blancanales led the penetration for the destruction squad. For this to work, they were going to need both guts and microchips, a mixture of old-fashioned caveman courage and the best that twenty-first century technology of the world's most advanced nation had to offer them. If it went as they planned, the ALOCS suits would let them slip close enough to the sensors to disable them.

If their technology failed against the Russian sensors, and they were spotted, they would fight their way through and go for it as men had done since the dawn of time. Even in a battle of technologies, raw guts and willpower were still often the deciding factor.

Manning and Schwarz held back fifty yards while Lyons and Blancanales did their thing. They were packing the demo bags they had been able to make up from the small amount of explosives they had gathered from the other commandos. Quarter-pound blocks of C-4 had been folded over with a flash-bang fuse and detonator in between the halves to create monster grenades. All of Phoenix Force's frags had been added to the pile along with their five thermite grenades.

With a facility as large as the forestry station, it wasn't much. But if they used it properly, it would cause quite a bit of damage. Particularly if they could find fuel drums, oil cans and other flammable material. Being in the middle of a dense forest, all of the buildings of the station were wooden and would burn nicely.

Lyons and Blancanales had their bellies in the dirt as they slowly approached the first ring of sensors. Their suit readouts indicated that these were simple motion detectors. They were counting on the fact that such sensors usually had a blank zone from eighteen to twenty-four inches above the ground so small animals wouldn't set them off.

Lyons inched along, being careful to keep as flat as he could. This wasn't something that could be rushed. Once he had passed it, he stayed low, but turned to see if he could find an off-on switch on the back.

"It's hardwired," he reported to Blancanales.

"Wait one."

When Blancanales joined Lyons, he found that the sensor's wires were dug into the ground to keep animals out of them, but were routed up the support pole. Taking a length of wire with an alligator clip on each end, Blancanales snapped it in place on the wires leading both in and out of the sensor.

After checking to make sure that the power was flowing, he clipped the wires where they went into the sensor head.

"That should do it."

With a hole in the sensor ring, Lyons and Blancanales next moved out individually to the sensors on the flanks of the one they had disabled. Since there was an overlap in their coverage, they had to be disabled, as well. When they were also cut out, Manning and Schwarz moved through the gap.

The next ring of sensors had been tagged by the satellites as MADs, Magnetic Anomaly Detectors. Before approaching them, Blancanales slipped out of his assault harness and left his weapons behind. With very little metal on his person, and what little there was masked by the ALOCS suit, he was able to get past the first MAD sensor. Again, a piece of wire cut it out of the circuit. This time he took out the sensors on each side himself.

When the others joined him, Blancanales, Manning and Schwarz remained behind while Lyons went after the last of the sensor defenses, the Doppler radar ring.

COLONEL ROMODIN HELD on tightly as the GAZ jeep sped to the perimeter command bunker. As it raced across the runway, he noted the three craters that had been blasted in the concrete when his driver swerved around the middle one, dodging the bigger chunks. They only added to his belief that this was a major attack, and he would have to get the holes filled before he could fly in more reinforcements.

First, though, he had to blunt this attack.

He reached for his radio mike to call the perimeter command bunker, but all he got when he keyed it was a burst of stuttering static. Screaming his rage, Romodin tried to throw the microphone out of the vehicle. It reached the end of the cable and rebounded. That enraged him even more, and he jerked the cable out of the radio box.

The two bodyguards sitting in the back of the vehicle didn't even change expression. They knew better. They did, however, check the magazines in their ammo pouches. Before this night was over, they'd need all the ammunition they could get. They had served with the colonel for a long time, and they knew what to expect when he was in this mood. Before this night was over, there would be more than just the bodies of the intruders lying in their blood. The scar-faced man wasn't one to spare anyone who he felt had been deficient in his duties. The rumor about his having crucified some of his own men in Afghanistan wasn't just a rumor.

Atsugi, Japan

HAL BROGNOLA'S MONITOR in the Atsugi command center displaying the tactical situation at the forestry station showed that the Stony Man team had made its penetration without being detected. He could see Lyons's team moving up behind the biggest hangar and McCarter's force closing in on the headquarters building. The IR icons for the enemy forces showed most of them on the other side of the perimeter reacting, as planned, to the sound-and-light show of the diversion.

It was time for his Russian trump card to be played.

It would have to be played with great care and at exactly the right moment. But it was time for it to be laid on the table, albeit facedown.

The RSV number was on his speed dial, and Vladimir Nefyodov picked up his phone on the first ring. "Is it time now, my friend?"

Brognola chuckled. Putting one over on the wily Russian was a full-time job, and even then it didn't always work. "If your men have been given the proper orders, Vladimir," he said, "it is indeed the time for them to make their move."

"And may I ask what those orders would be?"

Brognola didn't have to be sitting across the table from the man to see the look on his face now.

"I need your people on the ground within immediate striking range of Forestry Station 105," he said carefully. "Call it five minutes or so away just as long as they're out of the way of small-arms fire. Which, by the way, will all be coming from the security troops there, General Komarov's people. My people won't be in a position to bring fire on your team.''

Nefyodov didn't waste time asking how Brognola knew the name of the general in their cells. Spymasters had their secrets.

"As I said before," Brognola continued, "for this to work to both of our benefits, Vladimir, your men are going to need to hold there until exactly the right moment.''

"And why is that?" the Russian asked. "You have told me of a nest of traitorous vipers in my country and now you do not want me to move on them immediately. Why is that, Hal?''

Brognola took a deep breath as he mentally flipped his ace face-up. "Vladimir, I know you want to do what is best for the federation and I understand that. But I ask you to trust me this time. My President has no desire to bring back the bad old days, but if you move your people in too fast, both of us will end up facing firing squads and our nations might just go to war.''

There was a long pause on the other end of the line. "It is that serious?''

"I'm afraid it is, old friend." Brognola wished that he had the legendary powers of personal persuasion Rosario Blancanales was so famous for. If he screwed this up, he'd be lucky to just be shot.

"I am sorry to hear that, Hal.''

"So am I, Vladimir, so am I."

"I, too, will take a risk," Nefyodov said. "I will put my life and the lives of my family in your hands and do what you say. I want my grandchildren to have a chance to live."

"As do I."

"My troops are in the air and they will be touching down in five minutes."

"Thank you, Vladimir."

"Just don't make me curse you with my dying breath."

Siberia

As SOON AS the rescue team breached the sensor ring, Hawkins took the point for his group. His instinct was to move as quickly as he could. They were several hundred yards from their target, but speed had to take second place this time to his maintaining a full situational awareness. Even with the stealthing features of the ALOCS suits, this wasn't a time to miss anything, no matter how trivial.

The base was completely blacked out, which made it better for the commandos. With his NGVs switched to plus two, they gave him a clear view out to three hundred yards. But it meant that he would miss out on the peripheral-vision abilities of his bare eyeballs. This would require his Ranger best, and he was giving it.

When he got within fifty yards of the target, Hawkins paused to give it a thorough checking out. The building was a long two-story structure with a ground-floor door on the end facing them. A more formal entryway was situated in the middle of it.

"I'm going to try the front door," he called back to McCarter.

"Go for it."

WHEN ROMODIN DIVED through the door of the perimeter defense command bunker, he didn't have to shoot anyone. The officer on duty was yelling into the radio trying to get reports from the line, and the men were all at their weapons as soldiers should be.

"Report!" he shouted.

The captain stiffened to attention, the dead radio microphone in his hand. "Comrade Colonel," he barked loud enough to be heard, "the radio does not work. Some kind of static is being transmitted on all frequencies."

Earlier that afternoon, Romodin had seen that the late Major Polinski had laid landline phones in to all the perimeter bunkers as the perimeter defense manuals called for and that was good. Had he not, Romodin would have executed him even earlier for dereliction of duty.

"Use the landlines."

"Right away, Comrade Colonel."

The captain turned to the old-fashioned landline

phone system and started calling one bunker at a time. When he was done, he turned back to Romodin. "None of the bunkers report incoming fire yet, Comrade Colonel."

"Tell them to contact us the instant they do."

"As you command."

That report forced Romodin to reconsider his situation. Even with all the storm and thunder taking place right outside his perimeter, he wasn't taking any casualties. There were no explosive shells falling on his positions, and he couldn't even see muzzle-flashes. The thought flashed across his mind that this all might be just a feint designed to draw his forces to this part of the perimeter.

He'd give this a few more minutes, though, before he started moving troops to the other sectors.

"Alert all sectors to be on watch for small infiltration parties," he ordered, "particularly in the rear and on the flanks."

The captain jumped to obey.

LYONS AND BLANCANALES stayed on point for the movement to the big hangar at the end of the runway. Though no one had spotted another flying saucer at this place, if they had one, it would likely be in there. Even if the hangar was empty, they would destroy it to give the snatch team cover before moving on to check the smaller buildings.

As with the rescue team, they moved cautiously,

clearing everything in front of them as they went. They were still a couple of hundred yards away and Lyons decided to pick up the pace.

"Cover me," he told Blancanales, who was back on his slack.

AT THE FIRST thundering explosion, Artyom Chazov and his night staff didn't wait for the alert siren to sound, but did as they had been drilled to do. They immediately stopped work and sought shelter in their air-raid bunker between the hangars. Racing for the blast door, Chazov saw the first blazing SAM launcher and caught the flash of the HARM missile taking out the second one. He had no idea what was going on out here, but it had to be the Americans attacking, and he knew that they had come to destroy his craft.

Chazov wasn't psychotic about the Americans like Colonel Romodin, but he was paranoid about protecting his life's work. That the machine had been dragooned into being used as a warship didn't bother him that much. He had little empathy for the men, some of them Russians, who would die when the space station was destroyed. In fact, he had little concern for anyone other than himself, his design team and his work. Even then, between the three his work came first.

When the sounds of the cratering bombs faded away and he didn't hear more bombs falling around the hangar, he tried to radio to the command post. For some reason, the radio wasn't working. Knowing nothing of ECM warfare, he figured that it was just shoddy ex-Soviet equipment and was glad that the equipment he needed for his work was almost all Western.

With the radio out, Chazov decided to check on things himself. "Remain here," he told his crew. "I'm going out to see what is happening."

Undogging the bunker's blast steel door, he climbed up the ladder to the second hatch at ground level. From the sounds that greeted him when he emerged from the bunker, they were under a full-scale attack. He didn't, though, see any explosions occurring even close to the hangar. Maybe the Yankees had come to steal his craft, not just destroy it. That thought chilled him even more than the thought of the craft being destroyed. He couldn't live if they stole it and called it their own. It was his work, and he would die before he would let anyone else take credit for it.

CHAPTER TWENTY-THREE

Atsugi, Japan

Now that Hal Brognola had put his trump card into play, it was time that he let Katzenelenbogen and Price in on his private game. The satellites were going to start picking up the arriving Spetsnaz any moment now, and he didn't want to panic anyone. It was going to be touchy enough to play them without having any blue-on-blue incidents. All it would take would be one of those, and they'd all be back to the unthinkable. Even though the end of the cold war had brought no peace, it was nice not to constantly have to look over one's shoulder for the devil in a mushroom cloud.

Reaching out, he quickly punched in Price's secure cell phone number.

"Price," she answered moments later.

"Barbara," Brognola said, "if your satellites start picking up some choppers moving in to the east of the target area, don't panic."

By this time Price could see the display Kurtzman had thrown up on the big monitor. "What do you mean 'don't panic'? I've got a two-platoon lift and they're hitting their LZ right now. Who are they?"

"I invited some friendly Russians to act as a backup for our guys and to clean up what's left after we're done with the place."

"Nice of you to have given me an advance warning." Price sounded disgusted.

"I'm going to have Katz call the guys," Brognola said, "but I wanted to wait until I knew that the Russians would actually be coming in. They're Minister Nefyodov's personal Spetsnaz cleanup crew, and they're gunning for the hard-liners who put this thing together."

"For god's sake, Hal, do they know that our guys're operating on the ground over there, too?"

"Yes," Brognola said, "and I've been assured that they won't take our people under fire."

"Right," Price snorted. "It's dark, there's a war going on and you expect the guys who invented the old kill-'em-all-let-God-sort-'em-out style of combat to be on the lookout for our people? Get serious!"

"Barbara," Brognola said patiently, "the main reason I invited them in is to have them on the ground for cover so our own President won't be so willing to pop a nuke to erase his little problem."

"Have you told him what you're doing?"

"That comes next," he said. "Minister Nefyodov

has a general named Fedor Komarov in custody, and I'm going to tell the Man that this site came up during interrogation. Vladimir gave me a courtesy call, and I had to tell him that we were already on the ground working the problem. Barbara, I couldn't let him nuke Russia. I just couldn't.''

Price sighed. ''I know, Hal. But dammit! You could have at least trusted me enough to let me in on what you were doing. You talked about it a little bit, yes, but I thought you were just playing with yourself again.''

''I couldn't risk bringing anyone else on board in case it turned bad and questions were asked.''

''Turned bad? Jesus!''

''Look, I've got to call the President. Keep an eye out over there, will you?''

''Right.''

Siberia

RATHER THAN PARACHUTE his Spetsnaz unit into a forest in the dark, Vladimir Nefyodov had decided to send them in by helicopter. Taking a page from the U.S. Army Vietnam playbook, the Russians had developed sophisticated chopper capabilities and had employed them to good advantage in the Afghan war. Only the massive use of Stinger missiles by the mujahideen had defeated their rotary-winged armada. This time, the only ground-to-air missiles in the area had been taken out by the Americans, so they were home free.

While the spymaster's gut told him to trust the American Hal Brognola on this one, old habits died hard. Even though the Yankees had been Soviet allies during the Great Patriotic War, they had been the enemy far too long for him not to cover his bets. The Spetsnaz would try not to interfere with the Americans, but if the Americans didn't return the favor, they would be eliminated.

While a pair of Mi-24 Hind gunships orbited the LZ, the troop lift ships started touching down. As each chopper landed, eight heavily armed Spetsnaz commandos in black-and-gray night-camouflage uniforms with red berets piled out and took positions in the wood line. As each chopper emptied, it lifted off to let another one take its place. Once on the ground, the forty-four-man commando unit broke into two platoons and gathered around their commander for a last word.

Major Ari Yekatov was young to hold such rank in the Russian army, particularly in an elite unit. In fact, his men called him the Boy Major as an affectionate nickname. But he didn't owe his rank to the old system of knowing the right people in high places. He had earned the stars on his shoulders, every one of them, by being an odd combination. In a unit known for its toughness, he was a bull of a man. Those who wore the red beret were fearless, but he didn't even know how to spell the word and he always led his men from the front. To that, he added one of the finest tactical and political minds Mother Russia had ever produced, and that was tempered with judgment that few of his senior officers could match.

This was why Nefyodov had sent the young major into this very unusual situation. Too much was on the line this time for both Russia and the United States to risk sending anything but the very best. On one of his many trips to the United States, Nefyodov remembered having seen a greeting-card company slogan about caring enough to send the very best, and he had always liked that. He cared a lot and he was sending the very best he had at his disposal.

The Boy Major, however, was having his doubts about the wisdom of this operation as the minister had explained it to him. The sounds of battle he was hearing sounded real to him, and he hoped that the minister hadn't been duped. He also had doubts about being held back, in reserve as it were, while the American commandos went in to destroy the mystery craft of the dissidents.

But his doubts always took second place to the orders he was given to preserve the Russian Federation, and he would spare nothing to carry out those orders.

Even though the Russian Federation was a work in progress that was far from perfection, Yekatov revered the accomplishments of the new government.

He knew that the struggle to bring democracy to a people who had been held in bondage for centuries, first by the czars and then by the Soviets, would be a long, difficult journey. Even so, he was proud that he was in the forefront of the battle against those who would reverse that and those who sought to take advantage of the infant republic for their personal gain.

While he mostly led his troops against black marketers, drug dealers and the Russian Mafia, Yekatov had also been sent against various dissident elements, the so-called Hard-liners, which to him was just another way of saying traitor. Those men had had their chance for over seventy years and they had failed miserably. Now, in bitterness, they would bring slavery back to the Russian people, and the major had vowed to die before he lived to see that happen again.

Nefyodov had warned him that he would be going up against Colonel Nikoli Romodin and his butchers, and that prospect filled him with a fierce joy. Romodin was a stain on the honor of the Russian military tradition and one that he would be proud to remove personally.

Gathering his junior officers, Major Yekatov nodded toward the sounds of battle.

"That's where we're needed, men," he said simply. "Just remember not to shoot at the Yankees if we run into them. They're on our side this time."

"How will we know who they are?" one young lieutenant asked.

Yekatov laughed. "That's simple. If they're not shooting at us, they're on our side. Anyone who points a weapon at us is dog meat as usual."

That got a laugh from the commandos close enough to hear it, and Yekatov smiled. He liked it when his men could laugh.

"Yes, Major." The young officer stiffened to attention.

"Okay—" Yekatov used the popular English word "—let's move out."

With their Boy Major leading from the front as always, the Spetsnaz force started running through the forest toward the forestry station. As they cleared the LZ, except for a single Hind gunship flying top cover, the lift choppers landed in the clearing and shut down their turbines.

They would wait there until this was decided.

Atsugi, Japan

As SOON AS Barbara Price clicked off, Hal Brognola clicked his hand mike and radioed to his team in the RC-135 orbiting over the Pacific.

"Katz," Katzenelenbogen stated.

"You're going to pick up a chopper lift coming in from the north."

"I've got them right now," Katz cut in. "Who the hell are they?"

"They're Russians, but they're on our side."

There was a brief pause while Katz processed this information. "What the hell are you talking about, Hal? Did you pull another end run on me?"

"I couldn't help it, Katz," Brognola explained. "Until a second ago, I didn't know if I could get them to come in. I had to hide this from everyone in case the Oval Office caught wind of it."

"Who are they?"

"It's a company of Spetsnaz working for Nefyodov. They're going to hold back in the woods until I send word that we're finished up in there."

"Do you trust him?"

"We have to," Brognola said. "We don't have a choice."

"You want me to let the guys know?"

"Not yet," the SOG chief replied. "Let them get Waters out first."

"I sure as hell hope you know what you're doing."

"So do I."

Siberia

AFTER KILLING Polinski's original radio crew, Colonel Romodin had put two men from the second shift on to man the radios with one of his own men guarding them. But with nothing coming through but broken static, they had no communication with anyone on the base or with General Komarov's headquarters.

They had run a series of equipment checks, but something, or someone, was blocking their transmissions.

The UAV strikes and the runway job were clearly heard in the radio room, and they spooked Polinski's men. "Shouldn't we get to the bomb shelter?" the senior radio operator asked their hard-faced guard. "We're under attack."

"The colonel wants you at your duty station," the sergeant said emotionlessly. "You will stay."

Since Romodin had taken the radio room crew's weapons, they could only obey the man's orders.

WHEN HAWKINS SLID through the front door of the main building, he found himself in a long corridor as expected. The place was completely blacked out, but that favored him. Hearing voices from his left, he hugged the shadows of the wall and sent an alert to Encizo on his slack.

When McCarter and James slipped in, James took the door-guard position while McCarter and Encizo moved down the hall to seek out the voices Hawkins had heard. With them going left, Hawkins went to the right to look for Waters. The nice thing about searching a building in Siberia was that the permafrost kept it from having a basement.

Hawkins went from door to door and found most of them open. Usually a quick look was all it took to clear it. The few locked doors he marked to save for later. At the far end of the hall, he saw an open door leading into a hallway. Peeking around the corner, he spotted another door inside the room with light showing under it.

In the dim light, he saw a pair of legs in combat fatigues and boots sticking out from behind a big storage closet. Bingo!

"I think I've found him," he whispered over his com link. "I've found a guard by a door."

"Need help?" McCarter sent back.

"I can handle it."

Hawkins could see the guard's lower legs and combat boots, but his head was hidden. To maximize their low profile in the building, he needed a silent head shot.

Drawing his silenced Beretta 92 from his shoulder rig, Hawkins scraped the sole of his boot lightly against the floor twice. As expected, the guard moved out from behind the cabinet to see what had made the noise, clearing him for a shot.

The red dot of the laser sight appeared on the man's forehead, and Hawkins fired.

The guard's head snapped back from the impact of the slug and then automatically jerked forward as his nerves reacted for the last time. He was dead before he hit the floor. Fortunately, his AK fell on top of him and didn't make any noise.

"Guard's down," he sent to the others.

Stepping over the guard's body, Hawkins tried the door. It was locked. Dim light showed around the edges of the door, so something interesting was in there.

"Waters?" He moved close to the door and whispered. "You in there?"

"T.J.?"

"Wait one."

"I've got him," Hawkins sent over the com link. "Take out the radio room."

"Going in now," McCarter replied.

McCarter and Encizo made their move on the radio room. A dim light was showing from the threshold as they silently made their way down the darkened hall. It would be best if they could keep this silent, as well, but with Waters in hand, it wasn't critical.

McCarter signaled that he would make the entry, and Encizo slid over to back him up. On a silent count of three, the ex-SAS man stepped out. His eyes sped past the two men seated at the radios and fixed on the single man standing with an AK across his chest.

Never one to give a sucker a break, McCarter stitched him across the chest with a burst of silenced 9 mm slugs. The Russian fell back against the wall and slumped to the floor.

The two men at the radios threw their hands up and started speaking in Russian.

"Shut up!" McCarter snapped at them in English.

Apparently, the Russians had enough English to understand, because they shut their mouths.

Catching a whiff of stale blood over the cordite, he noticed three bodies in Russian army uniforms rolled over against the wall, one of them an officer. It looked as if he had stumbled into some kind of internal dispute. And if that was the case, all the better for him. Nothing screwed up a military operation like infighting, particularly when the other guys were doing it to themselves.

"What do you want to do with them?" Encizo asked.

If McCarter had read the scene correctly, these two poor bastards were being held under guard and weren't, in the finest sense of the word, combatants. He could afford to be a nice guy and give them a break.

"Tape them up," he said. "We'll stash them somewhere."

Encizo produced plastic riot restraints and motioned for the two to turn. The Russians meekly submitted to being cuffed and taped. When they were secured, the two commandos led their prisoners out and looked for the nearest unlocked door to leave them behind. Finding an office, the two Russians were led in and had their legs shackled, as well.

Once they were on the floor, Encizo leaned down

and put his fingers to his lips. "Shhh," he said and patted his SAW. Eyes wide, the Russians nodded.

"Let's get the hell out of here," McCarter growled.

"STAND BACK," Hawkins told Waters. "I'm going to boot the door."

Snap kicking, the ex-Ranger put the heel of his boot flat against the lock plate. The door slammed open, and Waters was standing in the dim light of the single bulb with a big grin on his face. "Man, am I glad to see you."

"You're my favorite rocket scientist. I couldn't leave you behind."

Waters shook his head. "It's a good thing I wasn't too much of a butthead."

"You got that right."

In the hall, Hawkins reached down and retrieved the dead guard's AK subgun and pulled two magazines from his ammo pouch. "You know how to shoot?"

"A little." Waters shrugged. "But I've never fired a full-auto."

"Nothing to it." Hawkins handed the submachine gun to him. "Just remember to back off the trigger every now and then. And, of course, you may want to reload occasionally, as well, but that's pretty easy."

He worked the magazine release and popped the full mag out of the AK. "It goes in like this," he explained as he snapped it back in the magazine well. "It ain't rocket science."

"I think I got it," Waters said.

"Good. I left the safety off so you won't have to mess with that. Follow me and keep quiet."

Hawkins keyed his com link as he moved back into the hall. "We're coming out."

"Get a move on it," Encizo responded. "It looks like it's heating up outside."

CHAPTER TWENTY-FOUR

Siberia

When Hawkins and Waters reached the door leading out of the building, McCarter was on the radio to Katzenelenbogen in the flying command post over the Pacific, making his report.

"The diversion seems to be keeping them occupied," he said. "We're going to try to link up with Lyons at the hangar now."

"He's still short of the hangar." Katz read the icons off of his screen.

"I'll let him know we're coming."

AFTER TAKING McCarter's report, Katzenelenbogen linked up a three-way conference call with Barbara Price at the Farm and Hal Brognola in Japan.

"David has Waters in hand now," he said, "and they're going to move to cover Carl's attack on the hangar. If we can keep the Russians on the perimeter busy for a little while longer, they should be able to pull it off.''

''Have you told them about Hal's 'good' Russians?'' Price asked.

''Not yet,'' Katz came back. ''We want them to get in position to do the hangar job first.''

''Isn't that cutting it a bit close?''

''I'm keeping a close watch on everyone's positions,'' Katz promised her. ''And if the Spetsnaz start moving out of the woods, I'll alert them.''

This three-way, long-distance, high-tech way of doing business was driving her crazy, but she held her tongue. If ever the Stony Man team needed to trust one another's abilities and instincts, it was now. Even so, this was nerve-racking to say the least.

WHEN KATZ HUNG UP, Brognola felt that he had the loneliest job of all on this mission. He sorely missed the personal electricity and close camaraderie of working together in the Farm Annex. It produced a synergy he needed. He had the same data feed showing up on his screens that they did, but it was just not the same.

High-tech dispersed command and control might be the future of warfare, but he missed having the players in the same room with him.

AFTER A SECOND CANVASS of all of his perimeter positions, Colonel Nikoli Romodin was even more convinced that what seemed to be probing attacks were not. He wasn't sure what they were, but he had seen that the troops weren't taking casualties. Remembering that he had a landline connection with his radio room, he wanted to talk to the senior radioman on duty and see if the channels to Komarov were working yet. The line rang and rang, but no one picked it up.

"Damn them!" he spit. "They do not answer."

He turned to one of his personal guards. "Radchetski, go back to the radio room and kill everyone there."

"As you command, Comrade Colonel."

"When that is done, try to reach our home base on the long-range radio. If you can get through, tell the major that I want the rest of my men up here as soon as he can get them here. When that is done, contact General Komarov and tell him that we are being attacked."

"As you command, Comrade Colonel."

"Do not fail me," Romodin said. "I do not want to have to order you to kill yourself."

"Yes, sir." Radchetski didn't change his expression.

"Go now."

As soon as the sergeant cleared the bunker, Romodin turned to his other bodyguard. "Come with me."

The bodyguard didn't ask where the colonel

wanted to go. He had already followed the scar-faced man to hell a number of times and would do it again.

NOW THAT WATERS had been sprung, phase two of the Siberian operation, the destruction of the flying saucer, could commence. First, though, McCarter wanted to check in with the demo squad.

"Ironman," he sent over the com link, "we have Waters with us and we're moving in your direction to go into a supporting position."

"Roger," Lyons called back. "We're still trying to get past a few of these guys so we can get in the hangar."

"We can help when we get there."

"Take your time," Lyons said. "We'll leave a few of them for you."

With Hawkins baby-sitting the rocket scientist, Encizo went up on point when they moved out. James took his slack with the OICW. Since this was their only long-range, heavy firepower, it would be up to him to sort out the bigger pieces that showed up. He was packing a double basic load of 20 mm, and each of the other men was carrying a couple of extra magazines for him. That should be enough to keep him going long enough to pull this off.

Fortunately, there were no armored vehicles on-site, at least none that had been seen from space, so his 20 mm would have no trouble chewing up the trucks and light vehicles they had seen. If a little distraction was needed to cover their withdrawal, he could easily blow holes in the wooden buildings and set them ablaze.

Encizo was a quarter of the way to the hangar when he caught the sound of a racing engine. When he spotted it crossing the runway, he keyed his com link.

"Got a vehicle coming right at us," he said to McCarter. "Looks like a GAZ."

"Take it out, Cal," McCarter ordered.

Flicking his HUD display over to the OICW's 20 mm AP sight grid, James acquired the charging vehicle, locked it in and triggered a single round. The 20 mm hit the center of the GAZ's radiator, punched through it and hammered a hole through the engine that cracked the block.

The sudden stop of the engine's rotating mass sent the GAZ crashing to a halt.

Even before the vehicle came to rest, Encizo stitched it from bumper to bumper with a long burst of 5.56 mm from his M-249 SAW, and it immediately burst into flame.

"Damn," he muttered.

They didn't need to be backlighted by the fire, but the color-shifting ALOCS suits took the change in illumination in stride.

Now that they had exposed themselves, the commandos picked up the pace. Hopefully, no one would spot them against the background of growing chaos, but the hangar suddenly looked farther away.

HIGH IN THE NIGHT SKY of the Pacific, Jack Grimaldi sat at his UAV command-and-control station in the

RC-135 and watched the screen displaying the sensor feed from the Global Hawk circling over the forestry station at thirty-five thousand feet. His data stream showed the locations of the Stony Man commandos, the forest station's defenders and the new players, the Russian Spetsnaz. Since the men of each group had their own distinctive icons, he could keep track of the ground action as it took place. Another screen gave him the positions and status of his UAV fleet.

"Katz," he said as he turned to his partner in the chair next to him, "it's starting to look like they're ignoring us down there. I'm seeing some of the defenders pulling back. I'm going in for another diversion attack. A low-level sweep across their heads this time."

"Go for it."

Reaching for his controller, Grimaldi clicked onto one of the Dark Star UAVs and directed it to make a low-level pass across the enemy's front-line trace. On that run, it would drop submunitions that would simulate assault fire on their bunkers. These would be fairly substantial charges and could kill if they landed too close to the defenders. They were supposed to leave the bad Russians alive for the good Russians to deal with themselves, but tough toenails. Accidents happened in war.

Once the UAV was on its programmed way, Grimaldi took his hand off the controller. This was no time for a human hand to upset hours of careful cyberwonk programming. He was having fun with his radio-controlled planes, but he'd much rather have had his gloved hands wrapped around the control stick of a Strike Eagle with her wings loaded down with 750-pounder Snake Eye bombs and a little nape. That would solve a lot of problems this night.

ROMODIN WAS in the perimeter command bunker taking reports from the man on the field telephone when one of his men guarding the entrance shouted. "Colonel! Someone shot at Radchetski's GAZ and blew it up!"

"Where?"

"Over by the main building," the soldier answered.

Romodin should have followed his initial gut instinct. Whatever was going on in front of his position, it was a feint. He looked for his radioman before he remembered that the radios were out. Damn those Yankees anyway!

"Call the bunkers in sector three," he ordered the telephone man. "Tell them that the Yankees are behind us! Tell them to send half their men to the hangar and surround it."

"As you command, Colonel."

AS THE RUSSIAN TROOPS started forming into assault teams, Grimaldi's UAV passed two thousand feet overhead. On its way out of orbit, the microchip brain in the matte-black Dark Star had ingested its new orders from the Global Hawk and went to work immediately. Its bomb bay doors opened and started disgorging a variety of submunitions.

Whistling as they fell, they sounded like an artillery barrage coming in. The detonations when they hit the ground also simulated artillery or bombs. The Russians scattered like chickens caught in a hailstorm.

MAJOR ARI YEKATOV studied the forestry station's perimeter from a sheltered position inside the edge of the wood line two hundred meters away. His men had taken cover and were fairly safe from the sporadic fire. They could hide there safely until daybreak, when they would have to either assault the station or withdraw. He didn't, though, plan on withdrawing, not when he had the enemy in his sights.

He was shocked when he heard the falling simulators and watched them explode. "Who the hell's got air power coming in here?" he asked himself.

Suddenly, the bunker line responded to the air attack by exploding with a blaze of fire into the wood line. Since there were no real targets to shoot at, most of the fire was high and wildly inaccurate. But enough was getting through to start causing casualties among his people.

Yekatov was never one to cower when someone

was shooting at him. Worse than that, these were traitors who were firing at him, and that decided it for him. To hell with Minister Nefyodov. If the desk-bound bureaucrat wanted to be a field commander and make the tactical decisions, he could put his scrawny ass into uniform and get into the woods. Since he wasn't here, Yekatov called it himself.

"Okay, men!" the Boy Major shouted as he got to his feet. "For Mother Russia!"

None of the Spetsnaz commandos wanted to be on their bellies when their leader was on his feet and charging their nation's enemies. Shouting their war cries, the red berets followed him into the face of the fire of the Eighth Missile Security Company's bunker line.

COLONEL ROMODIN HAD BEEN through enough ground attacks to know the sound of a real assault. Over the gunfire, he thought he heard shouts in Russian, but ignored them as coming from his own bunkers. Even though his outbursts has killed a dozen of the defenders, he still had more than enough troops to take on this new attack, as well as chase down those damned Americans inside the perimeter.

"Call all the bunkers," he told the man on the landline network. "Tell them action front."

"How about the earlier order to sector three?"

"Tell them to continue."

"As you command, Colonel."

AS A LIGHT airborne strike force, the Spetsnaz unit had few fire-support weapons. There would be no rolling thunder of artillery fire falling to keep their enemies' heads down and no steel rain from the battalion mortar platoons. But their RPG gunners fired their rocket launchers and the grenadiers their semiautomatic 37 mm grenade launchers as they advanced.

The unit's snipers and their SVD Dragunov rifles were in action beside the RPG gunners, aiming for the firing slits of the machine gun bunkers, too. It took several shots for many of them, but one by one, the automatic weapons ceased firing.

That still left the riflemen with their AKs, but using an RPG to hunt down individual infantrymen wasn't a good use of limited ammunition. They were, however, good targets for the snipers, and they continued taking their aimed shots.

The first of Yekatov's troops had gotten close enough to lay down a barrage of hand grenades against the key holdout bunkers. That was an old Russian light-infantry assault technique. It was costly but effective, and he knew he would be adding names to the unit's honor roll before the night was out.

AFTER THE GRENADE BARRAGE, it would be time for hand-to-hand combat, and that would add to his casualty list. But there were few troops, even Russians, who could stand up to his men when they had their blood up.

"Get them, boys," the major yelled.

Screaming their battle cries, the red berets clamored over the bunkers to toss grenades into the rear openings. More of them crawled through the firing apertures in front, their submachine guns blazing.

For every bunker the Spetsnaz took the hard way, though, there were two more that the defenders simply deserted. The troops of the Eighth Missile Security Company had thought themselves tough, but they had never been up against madmen like this. Faced with certain annihilation, they broke and ran.

Seeing the traitors run, the Spetsnaz major called out, "Hold here!"

As the firing died down, the cries in Russian for the medics could be heard. "Treat our people first," the major yelled. The traitors could take their chances, but since they would all be facing firing squads anyway, it would be a waste of precious supplies to patch them up.

THE INSTANT the Spetsnaz commandos jumped off and hit the bunker line, Katzenelenbogen was on the line to Hal Brognola in Atsugi. "I thought you told me that you had those Russian bastards in line," Katz exploded.

"Vladimir said that they would hold in place until his call," was all Brognola could say. "I'll get to him immediately and make sure."

"Get them stopped fast," Katz warned, "or we're going to have a hell of a mess down there. If they punch through that perimeter and fan out inside, our guys are going to be in a world of shit."

Brognola hit his speed dial for the RSV headquarters in Moscow. "Yes, my friend," Vladimir Nefyodov answered on the first ring.

"Your Spetsnaz are on the move, Vladimir, and that puts my people in serious danger."

"I was just talking to young Ari," the minister explained. "He was taking serious fire from the bunker line and had to move to secure it. He promised me that he'll remain there until I call him."

"Make sure that they do," Brognola warned. "I haven't told my people that yours are in there yet."

"But why not?"

"My people work best alone, and I don't want them to be distracted until they take out that flying saucer."

"Do what you think is best."

Regardless of what any Russian, even Nefyodov, thought, Brognola intended to do exactly that.

"It has to be that this time."

ALTHOUGH LYONS HAD TOLD McCarter that his destruction squad was moving out for the hangar, he hadn't counted on the Russians. Romodin's call for the troops from sector three to surround the hangar was effective. The Stony Man bombers hadn't gone more than a dozen yards before the first shots started snapping over their heads.

Finding more Russians between them and the hangar that they wanted to lay into, they had to go to ground in a defensive circle and fight. Manning and Schwarz, the team's two demo men, took off their packs and placed them well behind. They wanted them far enough away so they wouldn't get caught up in the blast if the explosives were hit and detonated.

That done, they lay down three feet apart and got to work killing Russians.

After dumping a magazine of well-aimed fire, Lyons paused long enough to key his com link. "We're up to our asses in Russians over here," he called to McCarter. "We could sure use a little help."

"Hang on to your knickers," McCarter called back. "We're coming."

CHAPTER TWENTY-FIVE

Siberia

The fury of the Spetsnaz assault took Colonel Romodin completely by surprise. Coming as it did in the middle of the air attack, and with his radios out, he was helpless to rally the troops in the face of the onslaught. When the cowards manning the bunkers started to pull out, he had no choice but to withdraw himself.

"To me!" he shouted over the roar of gunfire to gather his dozen personal troops. Forming them into a small unit, he directed a fighting retreat, pulling back a hundred meters before finding a dip in the ground out of the line of fire. Seeking the cover of darkness, Romodin halted and his men took up positions in the dip.

One of his men, a veteran follower of many years, stumbled into their group. He was wounded, but carried a red beret in his off hand.

"Colonel," the man gasped as he held out the

blood-soaked headgear, "it's the damned Spetsnaz. They've turned on us again."

That didn't surprise the colonel. The federation had used the red berets more than once to strike at the true patriots of Mother Russia. He was surprised, though, to see them teamed up with the Yankees. Had they forgotten what the Americans had done to the Red Army in Afghanistan? This was a filthy betrayal, and he vowed to survive this so he could take his vengeance on them. In fact, it was time that he took over the new revolution and General Komarov was retired again. This time, though, with a bullet in his head.

First, he had to survive this. Knowing what he did of Spetsnaz tactics, Romodin was surprised when the paracommandos seemed to halt after taking the bunker line. They should have paused only momentarily to straighten their line before moving out again.

But if they were going to stay where they were, he might have time to finish the hunt for the Yankees.

"On your feet," he ordered. "Take control of all our troops you find and sweep this place from one side to the other."

Encizo's superior ALOCS night-vision gear let him spot the Russian skirmish line running toward the hanger long before they could spot him. He keyed his com link. "We got a lot of customers coming up on our left,'' he told McCarter, ''and they're moving fast.''

''Ironman,'' McCarter sent to Lyons, ''we're 150 meters east of you, but we've got to stop and play for a while. Since we've got more firepower than you do, maybe we can give these bastards some major grief and pull your playmates over here to join the party. If they leave you alone, try to link up with us.''

''Roger,'' Lyons answered as he checked their location on his HUD screen. ''If you draw them off us, we'll come up on your right flank. Keep an eye out for us.''

Rather than moving into the contact, McCarter decided to go to ground where they were and fight. ''Okay, lads, let's do it to them here. There's not much cover around here, so this is as good a place as any.''

The four commandos lay down in an arc and waited. Hawkins motioned Waters to his side. ''Stay behind me out of the line of fire. If someone slips past me, try to shoot at him for me, okay.''

Waters laid down, his subgun ready. Without night-vision goggles, he couldn't see what was stopping them, but maybe it was better that he couldn't. He honestly didn't think he could hit a barn door with his gun, but it was better than having empty hands.

Encizo sincerely regretted not having his old favorite over-and-under M-16/M-203 combo and a bucket full of grenades with him this time. Reaching out with the Thumper worked wonders to bust up attacks. But the SAW had served him well so far on this gig, and it would have to do again. Snapping down the bipod legs, he laid a spare 200-round assault magazine within close reach and got ready to go to work.

On the far left of their pitifully small line, James laid his 20 mm magazines on the ground by his side. This was the time for him to put his OICW's airburst-fire mode to the test. One of the futuristic features of his comboweapon was its ability to deliver timed detonation 20 mm HE airburst fire like artillery. The ranging sight was able to set the time fuse in each round as it was fired over the heads of attacking troops to rain shrapnel on them.

The 20 mm rounds weren't big enough to produce much frag themselves, but they had notched, hardened wire springs inside to give the same frag effect as a 40 mm grenade. They had a five-meter killing, fifteen-meter wounding radius.

"Okay," McCarter said laconically, "Rafe, Cal, if you will be so kind, start the party."

Sighting low, Encizo cut loose with a long sweeping burst of 5.56 mm rounds. Grazing fire it was called, and the Russian point element took it right at the belt line.

On his teammate's lead, James triggered the first of his airburst 20 mm rounds. He was rewarded with a sharp crack a few yards above the mass of Russians, and his NVGs showed several of them going down. Shifting targets, he fired again, and yet again, sending the deadly razor-sharp frag raining to the ground. Most of it wasn't killing them, but wounded men had other concerns than attacking.

The Russians quickly went to ground and, as McCarter had predicted, whoever was directing the Russian attack made it a priority to take out the SAW and OICW first. As they moved to surround the commandos, the pressure on Lyons's group moved away to help.

"They broke contact," Lyons radioed. "We're moving."

"Come on over," McCarter sent back. "There's lots to do here."

KATZENELENBOGEN STARED at his screen in the command-and-control center in silent frustration. The gods of war were a fickle bunch of bastards, and they weren't smiling on their favorite sons this night. So far, though, none of the Stony Man commandos had been hit. But with those odds, it was just a matter of time.

"What do you have left in the bag?" he asked Grimaldi.

"Not a hell of a lot," the pilot answered. "One more diversion run and a Strike Star full of HE."

"Make a diversion drop at minimum altitude and ready the Strike Star."

Grimaldi's fingers flew. "What target?"

"Those goddamned Russians."

Grimaldi didn't have to ask which Russians. He coded in the number of the diversion bird and sent its orders.

WATERS COULDN'T believe that he had come all this way, jumped into the night sky from a stealth bomber, been captured and rescued only to be stuck in the middle of a firefight unable to finish the job. Of all of the people involved, and that included the President, he knew the fullest extent of the danger that the craft represented to the world. If that thing got turned loose, no matter who controlled it, nothing on Earth would be safe.

So far, he had been nothing more than an observer in this expedition. He had become the pet rocket scientist of a group of gutsy men who were putting their lives and the fate of the world on the line. But they were the ones who were doing all the fighting while he was still observing and trying to keep out of their way. That wasn't how he wanted his life to end, so that had to change.

Since he was wearing a Russian uniform, he figured that he could make his way into the hangar without anyone shooting at him. He had no idea what he would do once he got inside, but it beat being anyone's pet anything. Hawkins was too busy right now trying to stay alive to notice if his charge slipped away. He hoped that the Southerner wouldn't get too angry at him for this, but someone had to try to kill that damned ship, and he was the only one available to do it.

Suddenly, he heard a whoosh in the sky as an unseen aircraft swooped over the Russians and the ground lit up with diversion explosions.

Using the diversion attack as it had been intended, a diversion, Waters cradled his weapon across his arms and started crawling away from the Stony Man commandos as he'd been taught. They'd called it the low crawl in Afghanistan, but with people firing across him from both directions, he didn't think it was low enough.

He raised his head for a quick peek at his destination, the open door in the side of the hangar. He had a long way to go. He ducked back down and picked up the pace. Every minute he spent playing soldier made him realize more and more what a hard life it really was. Killing and dying wasn't the worst part of it at all. As Hawkins had said, it was going to the work site that really got to you.

THE NEXT TIME Waters raised his head, he saw that he had left the fighting far behind him and the hangar door was just a short sprint away. Getting to his feet, he cradled the submachine gun across his chest and went for it. A Russian ran out of the door and skidded to a halt when he saw Waters in his Russian uniform.

"Get to the shelter, you idiot!" the man called out.

"Is everyone else gone?" Waters yelled back in Russian.

"Yes." The Russian motioned for him to hurry up. "Get moving, dammit!"

Taking a deep breath, Waters brought up his AK and triggered off a quick burst. His shots went wild, but the Russian took off running into the dark.

Keeping his finger ready on the trigger, Waters raced for the hangar door.

Holding at the door frame, he looked around the corner and saw that the hangar was empty. Slipping inside, he held his subgun out in front of him like a guy in an action flick. The ship sat in the middle of the hangar like a prop for a science-fiction movie, resting in some sort of a transport dolly so it could be towed by a tractor. This craft was bigger than the one he had visited in Afghanistan, but they were basically the same design. Spotting the air lock on the crew enclosure on top, he decided to take his efforts inside.

Turning, he saw a workbench against the wall and raced over to see what he could find. Laying his subgun aside, he grabbed a double handful of tools and ran to the ladder leading up to the ship.

UNDER THE COVERING FIRE of the OICW, Lyons led his demo team to Phoenix Force's small defensive circle.

"Damn," he said as he slid in beside McCarter. "Couldn't you guys find a better place to do this? You really got your asses hanging out here."

"This has been screwed from the get-go," McCarter said, using one of Hawkins's favorite phrases. "Why should we try to get it right at the end?"

"Whatever."

With Able Team and Phoenix Force linked up again, they went into their well-practiced battle drill. If they were going to die in Siberia, at least they could do it together. No man liked to die far from his home and friends. What home they had was far away, but their friends were close at hand and that would have to be enough.

Schwarz and Manning had brought their demo bags and, since reaching the hangar wasn't an option right now, they decided to put their handiwork to good use. Pulling the pin on one of the monster grenades he had made from C-4 blocks, Schwarz lobbed the bomb as far as he could in the direction of the Russians. It wouldn't have any frag effect, but it might raise the pucker factor.

"Give me one of those," James called out.

When Manning passed over a monster, James grabbed it like a football, pulled the pin, reared back and lobbed the grenade into the end zone. The demo block landed in a cluster of Russians attempting to flank them and did fearsome damage.

Grabbing up his 20 mm again, James added a couple of airbursts for good measure.

CHAZOV STEPPED OUT of the dressing room in a cosmonaut space suit, the helmet in one hand and a Makarov pistol in the other. When he saw that the hangar was empty, he raced up the ladder into the spacecraft and through the open air lock. He didn't stop to close it behind him because he didn't want to take the time now. The nuclear power cell that drove the craft's engines wasn't an instant-on power supply. It took a few minutes to come up to full operating capacity, and any delay could be fatal.

Sliding into the pilot's seat, the Russian hit the switches and buttons to bring the power cell on line. He anxiously watched his instruments, and as soon as the nuke was powered up, he snapped on the protective shield. Only then did he activate the automatic controls for closing the air lock.

WATERS HAD ONLY started looking for something critical to sabotage when he heard someone come into the machine behind him. Holding his biggest wrench as a weapon, he pressed himself into the shadows between two banks of gauges and equipment. He had a small field of vision and wasn't surprised to see Artyom Chazov rush up the passageway to the cockpit. The gun in his hand kept him from doing anything rash.

As soon as Chazov was out of sight, he turned back to his work, but the whine of motors and the sound of pumps told him that the Russian was going to try to fly the craft. He was fascinated by the machine, but the last thing he wanted to do was to be trapped in it when it took off.

Hearing the whine of electric motors from close by his head, he looked and saw the inner hatch of the air lock start to swing closed. Without thinking, he broke from his hiding place and dived through it. The closing hatch caught the cuff of his jacket and the sleeve pulled off when he tried to jerk it loose.

He made it through the outer hatch, but his feet skidded on the smooth slope of the disk and he rolled over the side onto the concrete. The fall stunned him for a moment and when he rose, he realized that he had broken his arm. That's what he got for trying to play commando. Hawkins was going to kill him for this stunt.

The whine of the ship's drive motors told him that Chazov was going to try to take off. Holding his injured arm, he scrambled to get out of the way.

WHEN THE INDICATOR LIGHTS showed that the air lock was closed and locked, Chazov released the brakes and brought the power of the magnetic-lift engine up to full. He wasn't a trained pilot, but he had personally designed the control system for his spacecraft. Only the chief test pilot, now dead in the Afghanistan crash of Aerial Vehicle 1, knew more about it than he did. He might not be as smooth on the controls as one of the regular pilots, but he could at least fly his craft to a place of safety. And with the bubble shield to protect him against all weapons, no one could shoot him down.

It was obvious that the new revolution had failed. But he would still go down as the father of practical space travel. It just wouldn't be as a Russian achievement, but he didn't care as long as his name was on it.

MAJOR YEKATOV'S Spetsnaz commandos were waiting at the bunker line for the call from the RSV minister to take out the rest of this nest of vipers. They had gotten a good start, but too many of them had fled into the cluster of buildings that made up the station. That didn't really matter, though. His red berets all had night-vision goggles and would dig them out like cats hunting rats in the Moscow sewers.

He could hear sporadic fighting going on inside the perimeter and wished that he had communication with the Americans to know what was going on. From the fighting, though, it was obvious that they weren't making good progress. It was too bad that he and his men hadn't been brought in on this operation from the very beginning.

From the way the minister had spoken, it was obvious that this operation was mired in politics again.

As a soldier, he liked his battles kept pure and clean, not muddied by old men who fought with telephones and secret deals, not rifles. But, as a soldier, he was glad to have any chance at all to kill his nation's enemies.

EVEN OVER THE ROAR of battle, the opening of the hangar doors caught the attention of the Stony Man commandos. In the struggle to stay alive for the moment, the reason they had come to Siberia in the first place had been forced into the backs of their minds.

"That damned flying saucer's getting loose!" Lyons called over the com link.

James was stunned. The flickering lights of the battle made the shimmer of the protective shield around it even more visible. They all knew what that shimmer meant, but he automatically snapped the OICW to his shoulder and started firing anyway, dumping a magazine of 20 mm AP at the machine as it crossed his front.

To his complete dismay, he saw the rounds detonate without penetrating. Each time, the 20 mm round bounced off of the bubble surrounding the ship.

Even so, James snapped a fresh mag in place and kept firing at it until it was out of range. He felt defeated when he brought down his weapon.

"Katz," McCarter called over his satcom radio to the RC-135 flying command post, "that damned saucer got away from us. You probably saw it, but we took it under fire and couldn't get any good hits.''

"Roger, we saw," Katzenelenbogen said.

"What do you want us to do now?"

"Damned if I know," he replied. "Just try to keep out of the way as you pull back."

"We're gone as soon as we can disengage from these bastards."

"Call if we can help."

"How about a B-52 strike?"

"I've got a Strike Star left and we can use it."

"Anything will help."

CHAPTER TWENTY-SIX

Siberia

The distant stutter of the OICW 20 mm drew Spetsnaz Major Yekatov's attention, and he saw the spaceship, or whatever it was, rising off the ground. It was different than the photos he'd seen of the one that had crashed in Afghanistan—for one it was much bigger. But it had the same shimmering bubble surrounding it. It had to be the mystery craft the Americans had come to destroy, and that's what the minister got for leaving that part of this job to the overrated Yankees. They'd blown it, and it was his turn now.

"Boris," Yekatov yelled to his best RPG gunner, "take a shot at it."

The Russian commando raised his RPG-9 antitank rocket launcher to his shoulder and locked the craft in his optical ranging sights before firing. It would be at the maximum range for his rocket, but he knew how to compensate for the extreme range.

The 85 mm warhead left the launcher with the

characteristic whoosh of the prop charge burning out in the launcher before the main motor ignited meters out. Riding the rocket's plume, the antitank missile sped skyward. It struck the bottom of the craft and detonated.

When the flash faded from his retinas, Yekatov was shocked to see the craft fly away apparently completely undamaged. He had seen RPG-9 rockets blast holes in three meters of solid concrete, but it hadn't even dented that thing. The commando wasn't a Christian, but he felt suddenly like crossing himself as if he had just seen the devil.

Snapping back, he made his decision. That half of this affair was obviously a failure, but he would make damned sure that he would successfully complete the rest of the mission. The traitors would die.

"Spetsnaz!" he called out. "Follow me!"

In a skirmish line, the surviving red berets moved out of their positions on the forestry station's perimeter. As always, the Boy Major was a meter ahead of everyone else, his AK submachine gun at the ready.

HAL BROGNOLA HAD SEEN the mystery craft escape from its base, as well. He had gambled big on his plan and had lost the whole ranch, including the outhouse. With the machine going God only knew where now, it would become an angel of death visiting destruction anywhere in the world. And, like an angel, it would be immune to the weapons of men.

This insured that the next time it was spotted on the ground without its bubble protecting it, no matter where that might be, the President would have no choice but to launch a nuclear attack to take it out. Downtown Moscow or downtown L.A., it wouldn't matter. It would have to be killed.

What would happen after that would be anyone's guess, but he didn't want to be around to see it.

Walking across the room, he reached for the handset of the bloodred phone.

CHAZOV WAS FINISHING his post-takeoff checklist before sending his craft up to the edge of space when he saw a red warning light blinking. Peering closer, he saw that it was indicating a problem with the air lock pressure. This wasn't the first time that there had been a malfunction in the automatic locking system, and he couldn't spare the time to recycle it. He would just watch his altitude and stay below three thousand meters instead of going suborbital.

He had wanted to take his machine into space and see the stars against the velvet black himself. But he would have all the time in the world for that later.

JACK GRIMALDI HAD watched in horror as the flying saucer flew through the barrage of ground fire as if it were made of solid steel. He had seen the tapes the Farm had made of how the bubble shield had made the other craft impervious to even tank gunfire and hadn't quite believed them. But he had now seen it himself and had to believe what he had seen.

Even so, he decided to have a go at it anyway. He had one UACV left in the line-up with her belly full of fuel and HE, and it would make a dandy air-to-air missile if he could get it on target. It was a little larger than most missiles, to be sure, and it wasn't self-guided. But the principle was the same as he hoped the result would be.

Clicking over to the channel for that individual bird, he flashed its video camera feed up onto his monitor. That gave him a bird's-eye view, as it were, of the escaping saucer and it was time for his hawk to strike.

He ran the UACV's turbine to 110 percent emergency power before tipping it over into a steep dive. The laws of kinetic energy always favored the fastest-moving projectile and the fastest speed his Strike Star had been designed for was just sub-Mach. His digital readout soon clicked up to show 0.92 Mach, as fast as the machine could safely fly.

Piloting the Strike Star with his right hand, he backed off the turbine RPM so as not to exceed the airframe's mach number. This was no time for an airframe or control surface failure.

Guiding by the radar plots, he quickly acquired the enemy machine in the UACV's video eye. Though it was a small speck in the middle of the screen, it quickly grew in size as the Strike Star dived on it.

Whoever was flying that damned saucer thing wasn't doing a good job of it, which made his own job that much easier. The craft was flying straight and level as if it were hauling pigs or a load of fat-assed tourists gawking at the Grand Canyon.

He no idea why the pilot wasn't taking it into space where it would be safe from anything anyone on the ground could do, but that was okay with him.

As the diving UACV got closer, its camera started picking up the shimmer of the craft's protective shield. It had stood up to an RPG rocket and a 125 mm tank gun shell, but he was hoping that it had its limits. Maybe the god of physics would prove stronger than whatever that shield was. He didn't know and didn't even dare hope.

He could only try it and see what happened.

The view through the UACV's video didn't have crosshairs superimposed on it, but the bulges on the top of the craft could serve as Grimaldi's aiming point. He was acutely aware of the built-in electronic time lag on the controls and knew that he wouldn't have a second chance to make this work. If he missed, by the time he could get the UACV turned, the saucer would have vanished.

Using the width of the screen as his targeting grid, he raised his line of sight a bit ahead of dead center to compensate for the relative speed of the two objects. A deflection shot, as the fighter jocks called it. He'd made enough of them in his time, but he'd always had a computing gun sight doing most of the work for him.

Almost too fast for his eyes to follow, the saucer jinked to the left at the last moment. Slamming the control stick over with his right hand, he ran the turbine back up to emergency RPM. He got the craft centered on the screen again right as the monitor went black.

"You got it, Jack!" he heard Katz shout. "You killed the damned thing! The satellite radar is showing a falling debris cloud."

Grimaldi released his hand from the UAV control stick and flexed his fingers to work the cramp out. Damn, that was some good flying!

The Global Hawk had caught the intercept on video and he ran the tape. It showed the saucer making its sharp turn and the UACV banking over to impact to the right of the cockpit canopy.

For an instant, the shield held and the UACV seemed to morph into a bizarre mechanical construct as it smashed against it, but didn't penetrate. Then the bombs detonated and overcame the shield.

For an instant, the craft staggered in the night sky intact but for the hole blown in its upper surface. An instant later it, too, exploded in a ball of fire, completely destroying itself.

THE DISTANT FIREBALL in the sky flickered across the faces of the Stony Man commandos.

"Sweet Jesus!" Hawkins said softly.

"Did you see that down there, David?" Katz's voice cut in on the com link.

"We saw it," McCarter replied. "What happened?"

"Old Flying Jack scored again."

"Do you want us to light this whole place up on our way out?"

"Better not," Katz said. "I haven't had a chance to mention it yet, but there's a Spetsnaz unit waiting in the wings to clean up after you guys. I don't want you to blaze them by mistake."

"Thanks for letting us know in a timely manner." McCarter sounded completely disgusted.

"That was Hal's call," Katz said, "but, I agreed to let you guys concentrate on what you were doing before I told you. Now that we're done, they'll be coming in."

"If you don't mind, could you inform them that we're still on the playing field? And you might want to let them know that we still have a couple dozen bad guys cornered over here."

"No problem."

"Thanks awfully, old chap."

COLONEL NIKOLI ROMODIN saw the ball of fire form in the sky, and his face drew itself up into a mask of rage. The Yankees had destroyed the spacecraft, and

Russia would continue to be threatened by their damned space station and its nuclear missiles.

Without even thinking about it, he seized the Skorpion and his finger went to the trigger. The first short burst slammed into the chest of the late Major Polinski's second in command. Two more long bursts killed the surviving enlisted man from the Eighth Missile Security Company in the group with him.

When the subgun's bolt locked back on an empty magazine, only the colonel's dozen troops remained on their feet. "Find the Yankees and kill them," he ordered.

THE BRIEF RESPITE that had been offered by the destruction of the flying saucer gave the Stony Man commandos time to get reloaded and ready. When Romodin's Russians charged, they met a hail of gunfire, exploding 20 mm rounds and the last of Schwarz's monster grenades.

It was a slaughter, and it was over in seconds.

"That looks like the last of them," McCarter said as he dropped the empty magazine from his weapon.

"I'll go take a look," Lyons volunteered.

"I'll go with you," Schwarz said.

One of the dead Russians in the center of the group was obviously an officer; the uniform tunic, epaulets and knee-length boots were distinctive. Reaching down, Lyons rolled him over and saw that his face was badly scarred. He had just noticed that the man wasn't wearing any bullet holes when his eyes fluttered open and fixed on him.

Lyons stepped back to cover him and keyed his com link. "I've got a live officer over here," he sent to McCarter. "You might want to check this guy out."

"On the way."

"Okay," Lyons said as he made a motion with his off hand. "On your feet buddy."

When Romodin's hand patted the ground for his Skorpion, Lyons kicked the weapon away. "Try that again, asshole, and you die. Now get on your feet."

Romodin didn't speak English, but there was no mistaking the taunting tone in the hated Yankee's voice. His sneer only reinforced it. It was the same sneer he had seen on the faces of those who had dared take a full look at his face. He would make sure this Yankee lost that look before he died.

Lyons stepped back again when the Russian got to his feet, his scarred face snarling.

"I've got you covered, Carl," Schwarz called over the com link and Lyons smiled. It was nice to have friends.

Romodin seem to snap out of his fury long enough to notice that he was surrounded by the hated Yankees in their strange camouflage suits. They would ensure that he died here, but he had stopped fearing death a long time ago. Bathing in burning jet fuel could do that to a person.

"Okay, Yankee," he said, exhausting his English vocabulary. His hand snaked down to his belt and came up with a long curved Arabic dagger he had taken from one of his personal kills.

If the Russian wanted to play, Lyons was in the game. But he had no intentions of making this a fair fight. He had a hot date lined up when he got back to the States, and he wasn't going to miss it.

Slinging his H&K across his back, Lyons went for his own fighting knife. "Come and get it, you scar-faced bastard," he said softly.

The Russian came on, his body turned to the side as he lashed out.

"Look out, Ironman!" Schwarz said as he triggered a single shot.

The round punched Romodin right in the forehead, snapping him back. In the flickering light, Lyons saw that he'd palmed a small pistol in his off hand.

"He was trying to cheat," Schwarz stated as he walked up. "And Mom always told me to play fair."

Schwarz peered down at his victim. "Ugly bastard, isn't he?"

"Dead ugly bastard," Lyons corrected him.

In the distance, they could see the Spetsnaz commandos approach. Their NVGs were good enough to pick up the berets instead of helmets on their heads and their camo uniforms. The scattered Russians they came across carefully laid their weapons down and put up their hands. No one wanted to mess with the red berets.

"The cavalry's here," McCarter said.

"About fucking time."

"I'LL CALL the Farm and tell them it's really over now," McCarter said.

"No, it isn't," Hawkins spoke up. "We've misplaced our rocket scientist."

"Where the hell is he?" McCarter snapped.

"When we were pinned down," Hawkins explained, "he got up and ran."

"Did he get killed?"

Hawkins shrugged. "I didn't see it if he did. Remember he was wearing a Russian uniform, and they might have taken him for one of theirs."

"Dammit," McCarter muttered.

"Let's try the hangar," Hawkins suggested. "I don't think he bugged out on us, and I don't want to leave him behind."

"I don't, either," Manning said. "The guy's got guts."

"Okay." McCarter sighed. "Let go look for him."

"I'll stay here with my guys to talk to the good Russians," Lyons said.

"Keep your finger on the trigger, Ironman," McCarter warned, "until we can get this rat screw sorted out."

Lyons dropped a half-full magazine and snapped a fresh one into place. "You got that right."

WATERS WAS SITTING on the floor nursing a broken arm when the Stony Man commandos found him.

"What in the hell did you run off for?" Hawkins exploded. "You could have gotten yourself killed."

"I wanted to try to sabotage the ship," he explained, "but I didn't have much to work with. I found some wrenches on one of the benches and went inside to see if I could take something apart. But before I could do anything, a pilot showed up. I think it was the designer Chazov."

"Why didn't you shoot him?" Hawkins asked.

Waters looked sheepish. "When I picked out the tools, I kind of forgot and left the gun you gave me on the bench."

"Oh, Jesus."

"Anyway, I got out of the machine when he came on board, but I slipped off the slope of the disk when he fired up the magnetic field. I think I broke my arm."

Hawkins shook his head. "You know, for a rocket scientist, you can be a real dumb bastard sometimes. I think I'm going to break your other arm to match it."

"Hal, Katz," McCarter called over the satcom radio, "we have Waters back. Can we go home now?"

"I'll have Hal clear it with the good Russians," Katz said.

Atsugi, Japan

"Your plan worked, my friend." Vladimir Nefyodov sounded relieved when he called Brognola in Japan. "The threat to all of us is gone."

"Make sure your people clean that place out and burn everything they find," Brognola cautioned. "Every last bit and the computers, too."

"They will," the Russian stated firmly. "That machine was too dangerous for anyone to have."

"I also need your help in evacuating my team. I'd like to do it open and aboveboard so no one gets hurt."

"No problem. I'll have my choppers fly them back to the Spetsnaz base."

"Thank you."

"What happens now?" Nefyodov abruptly changed topics.

"I have been recalled to Washington to brief the President on how I conducted this operation," Brognola said. "It doesn't look good, but at least the missiles weren't launched."

"For that, my friend, I thank you," the Russian replied. "As for your President, would it help you any if I have our President call him?"

Brognola laughed. "Thanks for the offer, Vladimir.

But at this point in time, that'll just put my neck in a noose. Let me save that as a last resort.''

''I would not like to play cards with you, my friend.''

''You're not such a bad player yourself.''

CHAPTER TWENTY-SEVEN

Atsugi, Japan

When the Russian rang off, Hal Brognola called for the commander of the Air Force security team that had been guarding his operations room. The Air Police captain appeared in the briefing room like magic. When you had POTUS command authority working for you, things like that happened.

"What can I do for you, sir?" he asked.

"I need the fastest immediate transport to Andrews Air Force Base," Brognola said. "Comfort is not a consideration, only speed."

"Yes, sir," the captain said as he reached for his radio.

TEN MINUTES LATER, Brognola was wearing a G suit and being strapped into the back seat of a two-seat F-15 Eagle. It would give him a Mach 2.2 flight to Elmendorf Air Force Base in Alaska, and the pilot would only come out of afterburner to meet up with an aerial tanker halfway there for a drink.

As soon as they touched down in Alaska, Brognola would transfer to an SR-71 for a Mach 6 flight to Andrews. He'd be on the ground in DC before the RC-135 even got back to Atsugi, and that was good. He wanted to have this out with the Man before anyone else could get caught up in it. If anyone was going to hang for this fiasco, it would be him and he would hang alone.

Plugging his helmet intercom cord into the jack, he keyed his mike. "Okay, partner, light the fire."

"Yes, sir."

Stony Man Farm, Virginia

IMMEDIATELY AFTER Hal Brognola had ended his conversation with Barbara Price, she made the decision to put Oplan Jericho into effect. As with all federal agencies, SOG also had a double-locked file drawer full of contingency plans to be put into effect if things went bad. She hadn't discussed doing this with Brognola, but went ahead anyway.

She was only the second in command of SOG, but if it went the way in Washington that it looked it was going to, she wanted to have a good start on the shit storm that would surely follow. Not wanting to wait even another minute, she called a phone conference instead of a War Room meeting.

"Okay, people," she said when she had everyone on the line, "I want you to start preparing to implement Oplan Jericho immediately. Buck, first I want you to go to fullest alert. When that's done, get the burn bags ready and have your people get the shredders in place and on-line. Aaron, you and Hunt prepare to wipe your hard drives and all electronic data storage units right down to the bare plastic."

She paused for a moment. "And that includes the mainframes, Aaron."

"Got it," Kurtzman said.

"Comm center," she continued, "I want you to be prepared to drop all your satcom links, burn your code books and crash your encryption programs."

She paused to let this sink in. "Any questions? Any questions at all?"

A chorus of "nos" answered her.

"Get to it, then. But," she cautioned, "this is prep only. Wait for my word to implement."

That said, Price holstered her phone and walked over to Hunt Wethers's workstation to see how the recovery of the field teams was going.

THE PASSING of the next twenty-four hours saw both Able Team and Phoenix Force on the way home from Moscow and Katz with Grimaldi from Japan. The cleanup of Forestry Station 105 was in the hands of Brognola's "friendly" Russians. Stony Man Farm was prepared to self-destruct on command and was waiting for the order.

While she waited to hear from Brognola, Price haunted the Annex, drank too much coffee and burned off her excess energy pacing back and forth.

"Hal's inbound," Kurtzman called out. "Echo Tango Alpha five mikes."

The cyber ace had never served in the military, but when the stuff really started flying from the ventilation, he always reverted to sounding like a lifer. Being around so much testosterone would do that to you.

"I'm gone," Price said. "But hold on the shredders until I call in."

PRICE HURRIED to the chopper pad to await Hal Brognola's arrival. It had become a tradition with them that she would be waiting with the blacksuit security team when he came in. This time, though, Buck Greene, the Farm's security chief, was on hand, as was Kurtzman. Greene had put him in the passenger side of his Jeep so he, too, could hear the news as soon as Brognola stepped off his chopper.

The black JetRanger flew in and flared out over the landing pad. Brognola looked like a train wreck when he opened the chopper's door and stepped down to the ground. His suit looked as if it had been through a tag-team match with him wearing it, and he had on his game face.

"What's with the reception committee?" he asked. "You guys look like you're on a death watch."

"What'd he say?" Price asked.

"Well, he actually had a lot to say...."

"Dammit, Hal," Price exploded.

Brognola's face broke out in a big grin. "Gotcha."

"You bastard."

Her com link chirped and she jumped. "Hold the burn," she answered. "We're still in business."

"For as long as we want to be," Brognola promised. "And while I know it doesn't mean diddly squat, as T.J. would say, the Man is putting another commendation in all of our files."

Price took a deep breath. "The next time you see that individual, Hal," she said evenly, "tell him for me to take that scrap of paper, roll it into a thin tube and shove it—"

"Barbara—" Brognola grinned as he interrupted her "—just a minute, please. Since I outrank you in federal service, your scrap of paper will have to follow mine up there."

She grinned back. "That's a deal."

James Axler
Outlanders

EQUINOX
ZERO

As magistrate-turned-rebel Kane, fellow warrior Grant and archivist Brigid Baptiste face uncertainty in their own ranks, an ancient foe resurfaces in the company of Viking warriors—harnessing ancient prophecies of Ragnarok, the final conflict of fire and ice, to bring his own mad vision of a new apocalypse. To save what's left of the future, Kane's new battlefield is the kingdom of Antarctica, where legend and lore have taken on mythic and deadly proportions.

In the Outlands, the shocking truth is humanity's last hope.

James Axler
Outlanders

TALON AND FANG

Kane finds himself thrown twenty-five years into a parallel future, a world where the mysterious Imperator has seemingly restored civilization to America. In this alternate reality, only Kane and Grant have survived, and the spilled blood has left them estranged. Yet Kane is certain that somewhere in time lies a different path to tomorrow's reality—and his obsession may give humanity their last chance to battle past and future as a sinister madman controls the secret heart of the world.

In the Outlands, the shocking truth is humanity's last hope.

THE

Destroyer ®

UNNATURAL SELECTION

Sexy scientist Dr. Judith White, who first attempted to repopulate the earth with mutant, man-eating tiger people, is back with a new plan for world domination. She's putting her formula into a brand of bottled water that's become all the rage in Manhattan's boardrooms and cocktail parties. Remo and Chiun hit the Big Apple and find that it literally is a jungle—even the cops have gone carnivorous! And when one of CURE's own falls prey to Dr. White's diabolical scheme, his top secrets may give the insane doctor the extra bite she needs to eat The Destroyer for lunch!

Available in April 2003 at your favorite retail outlet.

DEATH LANDS®

Skydark Spawn

Available in March 2003 at your favorite retail outlet.

JAMES AXLER

Skydark Spawn

In the relatively untouched area of what was once Niagara Falls, Ryan and his fellow wayfarers find the pastoral farmland under the despotic control of a twisted baron and his slave-breeding farm. Ryan, Mildred and Krysty are captured by the baron's sec men and pawned into the cruel frenzy of their leader's grotesque desires. JB, Jak and Doc enlist the aid of outlanders to organize a counterstrike—but rescue may come too late for them all.